THE COLONEL'S DAUGHTER

Cynthia Harrod-Eagles titles available from Severn House Large Print Books

The Horsemasters
Julia
The Longest Dance

THE COLONEL'S DAUGHTER

Cynthia Harrod-Eagles

Severn House Large Print
London & New York

This first large print edition published in Great Britain 2006 by
SEVERN HOUSE LARGE PRINT BOOKS LTD of
9-15 High Street, Sutton, Surrey, SM1 1DF.
First world regular print edition published 2005 by
Severn House Publishers, London and New York.
This first large print edition published in the USA 2006 by
SEVERN HOUSE PUBLISHERS INC., of
595 Madison Avenue, New York, NY 10022.

British Library Cataloguing in Publication Data

Harrod-Eagles, Cynthia
    The colonel's daughter. - Large print ed.
    1. Love stories
    2. Large type books
    I. Title
    823.9'14[F]

    ISBN-13: 9780727875372
    ISBN-10: 072787537X

Printed and bound in Great Britain by
MPG Books Ltd, Bodmin, Cornwall.

For Hannah, with love and thanks

Chapter One: 1954

I remember so clearly the first time I saw her. I had not long been stationed at Bovingdon, and was spending one of my free days exploring the country. I had a car then – a dilapidated but reliable old girl who made me almost embarrassingly popular with my companions in that back-of-beyond region. I kept it in a shed in a farmyard about five minutes from the camp gates, for which privilege I paid the farmer a shilling out of my meagre weekly wages. However, I didn't have much else to spend it on, and petrol was once more freely available. So I drove myself out to Maiden Castle, which I had seen marked on a map.

It was a lovely day, with all the force of that much-abused adjective: early May, and softly summer, a day that held its breath as if astonished at itself, like Narcissus taking his first look into the pool. Memory enhances, but I felt it even then. Having looked at, and been awed by, that ancient place, I retired to a small, thatched pub and in its cool and polished parlour lunched on what nowadays would be called a 'Ploughman's dinner': cheese, pickled onions and crusty bread, washed down with a pint of ale from the wood.

Then I got back into my car, put away the map, and let my fancy direct me. After driving pleasantly and aimlessly for an hour or so, I stopped in a narrow lane, pulled old Betsy off the road in front of a five-barred gate, climbed over and just walked. In that part of the country you are always within a minute's walk of a hill, and I found myself among a particularly fine crop of them. I strode out across the chalkland turf and lost all sense of time.

I saw her first on the crest of the next hill, separated from me by a shallow dip. She was trotting the horse, and their movements were gracefully in tune with each other; but then she saw me and turned the animal's head towards me. This was apparently the direction away from home, for co-operation instantly fled away. I saw it swing back and forth for a moment, and then come cantering towards me fighting for its head, moving in unwilling fits and starts. The pair disappeared for an instant in the dip, but the gallop must have settled the horse, for when they reappeared it was going smoothly, bounding up the slope, lifting its forelegs high as if it were trying to climb the air. She rode the animal right up to me and then snatched it to a halt, and it stamped and fretted a moment almost on top of me.

Close to, it was huge, and I felt its heat and smelled its sweat. It seemed to fill my sky, shaking its head and snorting, beating its forefeet in a tattoo of anxiety to be off. She, above, was small and cool and quiet. She seemed very young – I took her for a girl of no more than fifteen – but there was a surprising strength to her. Her narrow wrists and forearms made a spring which, connected to the corners of the horse's mouth, controlled its whole weight. She was so slight, yet she could gather up this great sweating brute in her hands and hold it with a touch as delicate as it was ruthless.

She looked down at me with an air of suppressed laughter, and I guessed that the riding-on-top-of-me had been meant to make me flinch, but I stood my ground sturdily and waited for her to speak. Outlined against the sky, she had a clear-cut look. Her eyes were grey and steady, her skin the colour of pale, clear honey; her hair, so fair it was almost white, was drawn back into a short, thick plait which lay just then across her shoulder. You would not have called her pretty, but she had the still beauty of an animal in its own element.

It seemed a long while before she spoke. She regarded me with a curious, bright gaze while the horse moved restlessly under her.

The afternoon was growing cooler, the sunlight more golden, and the summer-mad larks were the only sound carried to us by the breeze. The moment held us, as in a crystal drop. Is it hindsight, or did I feel a shiver of fear mixed in with my admiration? No, I think there was something. Perhaps not fear, only a sense of impending fate. Does the fieldmouse feel something like it when the shadow of the owl passes across the grass? She seemed a child, yet her hands were brown and strong, her face clearly carved. I had no sense of what might happen next.

'I saw you watching me,' she said at last. 'Do you like horses?'

'Yes,' I said.

'Do you ride?' Her voice was as cool and bright as her gaze.

'I used to,' I said, mentally conflating a few lessons at a riding school and a few beach-pony rides. Did I want to impress her?

'Everyone always says that,' she said, with a hint of impatience. 'Why can't someone for once simply say yes? As if riding is just something for children.'

'It mostly is, isn't it? But I would love to ride, if I had time.'

'You can always find the time, if that's what you want to do with it,' she countered.

How marvellously black-and-white everything is to her, I remember thinking. She's so

10

young – she'll learn as she gets older. I was twenty-two, then; I knew the world.

The horse, thinking perhaps she was inattentive, snatched his head away, and she checked him with a slight but decisive movement.

'You've been having trouble with him?'

'He's fresh. He hasn't had much exercise recently. He's out of condition – that's why he sweats and blows so much.' She stroked a hand kindly down the damp bay neck.

'Is he yours?' I asked.

'My father's. We have two. If you want to ride, you can come with me to the stable, and ride the other one.'

'That's very trusting of you. I wonder what your father might think about it.'

'He'd like it. They don't get enough exercise.'

'But you know nothing about me.'

'It doesn't matter. Even out of condition, Mistral is the fastest horse in the county. I'd soon catch you if you made off with Tambour.'

That wasn't what I had meant, of course, but I left it, and for conversation's sake, I said, 'Is that his name – Mistral?' I put out a hand to stroke the horse, but he jerked away from it, making me feel foolish.

'He's half brother to Sirocco,' she said. 'You know – Sirocco who won the National last year.'

'Even I have heard of Sirocco,' I said.

'He jumps, too. He's what my father calls a "lepper".' She grinned suddenly. 'In Sunday school, when I was little, I used to get very confused when they kept talking about lepers.'

I laughed for her; but I felt she was growing bored with me, that any minute she might say goodbye, quite abruptly, and canter away out of my life. I realised that I didn't want this to happen, so I asked, 'Do you ride here every day?' At least then I might know where to find her again.

'Not every day, but I ride here often. I ride as often as I can, now. I'm enjoying the last of my freedom.'

She waited for me to ask what she meant.

'I'm going to university in September.'

I looked my surprise. 'I didn't realise – I took you for younger.'

She shrugged. 'I'm seventeen. Nearly eighteen.'

'And why does university mean the end of freedom?'

'I'll have to work hard to get my degree, and then I'll have to get a job, and then I'll never be free again. Working every day, and only two miserable weeks' holiday a year. I shall hate it! So I'm making the most of it while I can.'

It was still odd, in those days, to hear a girl talking about getting a job for life. I thought she would soon marry and was likely to have a job only for a year or two; but I had the sense not to say it aloud. Instead I said, 'Then I'm glad the weather's so nice for you.'

She smiled then, properly, a personal smile that was really for me, and something in me quivered. She was definitely seventeen, a different prospect altogether from a child of fifteen.

'Do you live near here?' I asked.

'Not far, as the crow flies. I live in Lulworth.'

'Oh, that's near me,' I said innocently. 'I'm stationed at Bovingdon.'

'I know.'

'How do you?'

'Oh, not that you were at Bovvy, but that you were a soldier. Your hair, your clothes, the way you stand – you look like a soldier.'

'Is that a compliment or an insult?'

'Neither,' she said. 'It's just an observation.'

I had never known a girl to talk like her. She disconcerted me, and I said clumsily, 'You are a very observant young lady.'

She screwed up her nose. 'Pompous. Do try not to be patronising.'

'I'm sorry,' I said, more disconcerted than ever. The next words jumped out of me – perhaps fortunately without my volition, for if I'd thought about it I might not have had the courage. 'Will you come out with me tonight?'

'Yes,' she said. Just like that. No hesitation, false modesty, playing hard-to-get. She had known, I believe, that it would come to this from the moment she saw me on the skyline. In fact, if it had been revealed to me then that she knew everything that was to happen, I should not have been surprised.

But now that we had a 'date', I was in charge again. 'Where shall I meet you?' I asked. 'I have a car,' I added, with just a little importance, 'so I can come and collect you.'

She shook her head, just once in either direction. 'The Castle. Eight o'clock. Don't be late.'

The horse leapt into motion at some invisible signal from her, tramped a sweaty, excited circle so close to me that I could not help stepping back, and then was away in a tight, bounding canter that swallowed the ground.

So I was not to be in charge after all. But I did not think that at the time. I was too excited by the prospect of the evening, too stirred by all that had happened. I watched her out of sight, and then walked back to my car through the warm afternoon light.

I had been lucky with my National Service. First of all, I had been able to defer it while I did my degree in architecture at London

University, and by that happy means managed to miss the whole of the Korean War. Then, when I was called up, although I had been sent to Malaya, I had spent only eight months there before the army mill ground small enough to recognise my particular skills and decide that I would be better employed elsewhere. So I was transferred to Dorset, without ever having contracted either malaria or dysentery – and of course, most importantly, without having been shot by communist bandits. At Bovvy, if you managed to avoid getting run over by a tank, your chances of surviving National Service intact were excellent.

It was, as my mess-mates described it, a 'cushy billet', and I was delighted with the posting. I was a Hampshire man, brought up in Bournemouth, but that was close enough – and the Dorset scenery was familiar enough – for me to feel at home. Above all, I loved the downs. Eight months in Malaya were enough to give me an unassuagable longing for treeless places where you could see the sky; high places where you could see for miles; open places where the air came to you clean and cool and sharp, without human stinks. Those rolling, sheep-bitten, green billows spoke to something deep in me. Whenever I saw them I wanted to climb up to the highest place and lie down, press myself against the turf and feel the life of the earth under my hands.

My mess-mates, of course, thought I was 'barmy'. The pursuit of girls – or 'tarts', as they called them – was their whole *raison d'être*. So my controlled excitement, and the care I took over my appearance that evening, earned me much ribbing. Some of it was due to not-very-well-concealed envy – girls were thin on the ground in those parts.

'So,' said Smart, reclining on his bed and screwing up his eyes against his cigarette smoke, 'who is it, then? Local tart?'

'Local, yes. Tart, no,' I answered. I didn't want to talk about her to them, but I guessed my life would become unliveable if I made too much of a mystery.

Weddell stared porkily at me, baffled. 'Not a tart? It's a bloke, then?'

'It's a girl,' I said patiently.

'Ooh, it's a girl!' Horrocks mimicked, and smirked at his oppo, Smart. 'He must be in *lurve*.'

'Can it, you ass,' I said, without emphasis.

'Well, a tart's a tart, for all that,' Horrocks said mysteriously.

'Has she got a sister?' Weddell asked. Always original, was Weddell.

'Where's she live?' Smart doggedly pursued his original line. 'Not round here?'

'Lulworth,' I said shortly.

'What's her name, then? I might know her,' said Evans, who was a regular. An inoffensive local boy, he had joined the army for love of tanks and guns, and spent most of his time off looking round the tank museum.

'How would you know her?' Smart said derisively. 'If it don't lay tracks, you don't even see it.'

'I might,' Evans said stubbornly. 'I've lived here all my life. What's her name?'

With four of them staring at me, I was forced to answer. 'Well, actually, I don't know.'

'Well, ecktually!' Smart mimicked me, even more inaccurately than Horrocks. 'You soft get! Didn't ask her name. Didn't get her address either? I suppose you *did* find out where you're meeting her? Blimey, you must have come down in the last shower.'

'I said it was *lu-u-urve*!'

'Shut up, Horrocks! Of course I know where I'm meeting her. I just didn't get round to asking her name, that's all. We were talking.'

'Talking?' Smart laid a fatherly hand on my shoulder. 'I gotta tell you, mate, that's not what tarts are for.'

'You don't really think she's gonna turn up, do you?' Horrocks enquired. 'Blimey, with lays as rare as hen's teeth round here, you prac'ly have to stamp and address 'em to make sure they get there.'

'If she didn't want to come, she wouldn't have made the date, would she?' I said reasonably.

'There's one born every minute,' Smart said, rolling his eyes. 'Where've you been up till now?'

'Listen, tarts don't think the way we do,' Horrocks instructed.

'She not a tart,' I said stubbornly.

Horrocks shrugged. 'Bint, then. What's the odds? You don't expect them to be logical. They got minds like corkscrews—'

'If they got minds at all,' Smart took over. 'When they say one thing, they mean the exact opposite. You gotta make allowances for that.'

I started laughing. 'Listen, you characters, when I need lessons in how to deal with women, you'll be the first people I ask. But until then – be good chaps and shut up.'

They grinned good-naturedly. I was a bit of an outsider, being older, and with a university education. They treated me with affectionate pity, like an idiot relation, because I spoke differently and thought differently from them, but there was no malice in it. When there were no tarts, bints or skirts on the horizon, we had very pleasant evenings together in the mess or the local pubs, playing darts and swapping unlikely stories.

I went on getting ready, and they left me alone after that, and started talking about football. I was so absorbed with my recollections of the day and my anticipation for the

18

evening, I barely noticed when their voices dropped and their heads came together in a conspiratorial way, and certainly I attached no importance to it. Even their too-innocent *adieux* when I left did not make me suspicious.

I arrived at the pub dead on eight o'clock. I expected her to be late, going on past experience of dates, but as I parked the car on the other side of the road I saw her walking across the forecourt towards the saloon door. I flung the car door open and shouted, 'Hi!', discovering only then the disadvantage of not knowing her name. But she turned her head and, seeing me, stopped and waited.

I crossed the road to her, feeling my insides churning with a sort of adolescent excitement I had not felt for years, not since I first took a girl to the cinema and sat there in the panting dark, timing my moves, oblivious to the film.

She looked luminous in the twilight, wearing a short-sleeved dress, her arms and legs pale brown and bare. Her hair was loose to her shoulders, curling softly there with its own natural shape, not teased and frizzed into fashion. As I stood in front of her, I found myself looking down into her face, and realised how much shorter than me she was. She was as small as the child I had first thought her.

'I'd sooner look down on you from horse-back,' she said, as though she had divined my thought. 'It would give me more of a sense of power.'

'You have all the power you need,' I said. 'Any more would make you too dangerous.'

She wrinkled her nose a moment, as though deciding whether to accept the compliment or not. Then she smiled and said, 'All right, you can talk prettily to me if you like. Just until we get used to each other.'

'What will happen then?'

'We'll talk sensibly, of course,' she said, and turned to lead the way in. I followed, think-ing it was not so far anything like any other date I had been on; and admiring the way she walked, with a free, graceful stride, so different from the usual female high-heeled totterings. I bought drinks, and we went through into the parlour and sat down oppo-site each other across a small table, with an air of mentally rolling up our sleeves.

I wanted most of all to ask her name, but it seemed too prosaic, too unromantic just to blurt out the question. Instead I said, 'The other fellows at the camp don't believe you exist. They think they know all the local girls.'

'Who thinks?'

'Well, Evans especially,' I said.

'Oh, Evans,' she said dismissively. 'What's your name?'

So much for the romantic approach, I thought. Perhaps I should already have known better. 'George West,' I said, feeling faintly embarrassed as one always does saying one's name aloud.

'That's a nice, plain name. It suits you.'

'Is that a compliment or an insult?' I said.

'Neither. It's merely—'

'An observation, I know. What's your name?'

'Josella Emily Grace. Age seventeen,' she said in declamatory mode, showing that she was not as much at ease as she tried to pretend. 'Height five feet two and a half inches. Colour of eyes—'

'All right, I'll take that little lot to be going on with. What do I call you – Josella?'

'Whatever you please,' she said. 'But I shouldn't try anything just yet. Wait until a name slips out, and then you'll know what really works best for you.'

'That sounds like good thinking,' I said. I was beginning to get the swing of her conversation. It was rather like speaking a foreign language you have learnt at school: suddenly, while talking to a native, it clicks and you find the whole idiom at your tongue's end.

'I'm always rather surprised to find that soldiers have so much free time. I imagine them under orders twenty-four hours a day, never let out of barracks. I suppose that was the war-time army.'

'I wasn't in the army during the war. I was too young.'

'You're not a regular?' It was hardly a question.

'National Service,' I said.

My tone could not have been as impartial as I meant it to be, for she said, 'I expect you mind it. But there's no need. Anything you really want to do can wait. There's plenty of time.'

I was almost amused at her offering wisdom and comfort to me. 'You may think so. But it's a big piece taken out of your life. You're starting two years behind the other fellow. It puts you at a disadvantage.'

'Only if you let it. Everything in your life is under your own control, ultimately.'

'Barring accidents,' I said, and saw a shadow pass across her face.

She said, as though changing direction slightly, 'Why aren't you an officer?'

'I didn't want to be. I refused.'

'Oh, that must have made you unpopular with the brass,' she said with an impish grin.

It had. I said, 'You seem to know a lot about the army.'

'How can you not, living here?'

My attention was drawn from her at that point by the hideous sight of Horrocks and Smart leering at me through the window. I made a furious gesture at them, and Smart responded by pressing his face against the glass and making a horrible grimace. Weddell's fat cheeks crammed themselves in below the other two, his eyes goggling. Behind them Evans was ducking and stretching, trying to see in, and waving his hands at me, mouthing something with an urgent expression.

She looked to see what I was looking at, and was startled by Smart's distorted flesh and crossed eyes. 'What on earth—?'

'They must have followed me, blast them. Go away!' I mouthed at them with exaggerated clarity.

'Your friends?' she asked.

'Hardly that,' I said bitterly. 'The army makes strange bedfellows.'

She laughed. 'How right you are,' she said, as though it meant something different to her. 'Shall we go somewhere else?'

'That *would* give them something to talk about.'

'Let's, then.' She stood up and led the way, walking with an impervious dignity that royalty might have envied. Outside my four oppos were waiting, but such was her presence that they fell back and let her pass without a word.

But as I drew level with them, Smart grabbed my arm, almost jerking me over, and hissed, 'Do you know who that is?'

'Do you?' I countered, taken aback by his

vehemence.

'Evans does,' he said with grim triumph.

Evans, looking worried, said, 'That's the Grace girl.'

'I know,' I said.

'As in *Colonel* Grace,' Smart concluded, with an air of one laying four aces on the table.

'Oh,' was all I could manage. I shook myself free of them and followed her out into the pellucid evening.

We drove out to Chaldon Herring, to the Sailor's Return, a quiet pub where the soldiers did not go, and there we talked of other things. She knew that I knew, but we did not speak of it. It gave her an air of good-natured omniscience which suited her. I was already half in love with her, fascinated by her every movement, gesture, word. I could have sat looking at her for ever, and not grown tired of it.

Afterwards we spent a long hour sitting in the car on a cliff-top looking over the moon-lit sea. A romantic setting *par excellence* – but such was her spell over me I did not kiss her, did not even touch her hand. Perhaps she wanted me to; perhaps she was disappointed; thought me a poor fish. I don't know. Far away in another world I could imagine Smart and Co jeering at me for being slow. But this did not seem the time for all that, though a deep swell of confidence in me told me such things *would* happen, in their own time. For now, I was content with what I had; and at the end of the evening I felt more intimate with her than if we had lain together a hundred times. Somehow she had become part of me – or perhaps I had, of her. When the owl eats the fieldmouse, there's no separating them again.

I, in case you have not 'sussed' it, was the fieldmouse in this instance.

Chapter Two: 1964

What had happened to the world? It went to bed one night well muffled against the clammy cold that had held it immobile since November, and woke at sunrise the next day sweating, to a sky of powder blue and sugar pink like a baby's blanket. In one night the weather had passed from February to May. Of course, as it was really only April, the bare trees hadn't had time yet to catch up, but the privet and forsythia were coping pretty well; and the birds, of course, claimed that they had known about it from the beginning.

She emerged from her bedsitter that morning feeling like Rip Van Winkle; or one of the victims of Rhyannid, whose birds put you to sleep for a hundred years with their song. Except, of course, that the witch would not have bothered with a female victim.

She caught the bus in Brompton Road and took the front seat on the upper deck so that she could get a good view of the first day of summer. People in surprising numbers had decided to walk to work. The girls, released from their fur-lined boots and winter coats, looked as leggy as fillies. Bus queues spread themselves out and lounged gracefully, where only yesterday they had huddled like Dartmoor ponies with their heads turned out of the wind. What made it seem even stranger was that it was only mid-week. Office workers were occupationally unfitted to accept anything starting on a Thursday.

With deep regret she went in out of the sunshine to the office, and into the gloomy cubby which housed the switchboard. It smelt of dusty carpets and old files, which was mostly what it was full of. The window was set high and had frosted glass halfway up, so that she could only see a strip of blue sky at the top. She glanced with distaste at the ink-marked board, the leaking biro, the scribbling-pad with the page of old messages and doodles, and looked forward with no delight to another day of business jargon, set

26

replies and a sandwich luncheon.

Of course, it could have been worse. She liked working switchboards, especially the doll's-eye sort, for it made her feel clever when the board was busy and covered with a seemingly impenetrable tangle of red and black cords. As offices went, this was not such a bad one. There was always someone ready for a chat. The men from the drawing office liked to bring her cups of coffee and lounge in the doorway talking in instalments, breaking off while she dealt with a call, and resuming seamlessly when she pushed the mouthpiece of her headset to one side and turned her head towards them again.

She had been lucky, too, to get this assignment for the whole winter. Usually when she did temporary work it was a few days here and a week there; and sometimes it was typing, or even filing, which she hated. However, she thought as she took off her coat and put it on the wooden hanger on the back of the door which would not close properly; however, she thought as she put her handbag on the windowsill and sat down on the swivel chair that swivelled at an angle, ready to tip the unwary into the wicker waste-paper basket; however, she thought grimly as the metal hatch over the first line dropped down to announce that somebody somewhere had resumed their labours a lot more promptly than those at Mason, Peabody & Ptnrs; however, she thought, there is lucky and lucky, and today it was the second sort she craved.

She banged the headset on, stabbed the plug into the socket, flicked the switch forward and said in the bright, impersonal tone of the telephonist, 'Mason Peabody – good morning?'

'Hello Josy, thou angel of light and embodiment of efficiency.'

'Yes, Mr Sanders. What can I do for you?'

'Don't tempt me, darling, not so early in the morning. Is the Quare Feller in?'

'I doubt it. It's only just nine.'

'Thank God for that. I'm an accomplished liar, but there's something about old Hart that shrivels the words in my mouth. I'd far rather spin the tale to someone else.'

'I take it from that that you aren't coming in today,' she said, amused.

'Angel, would *you*, with the sun shining away like this? Oh, well, obviously you would, since there you are, but for less high-minded souls like me—'

'Temporaries don't get sick pay,' she said briskly.

'You're breaking my heart. However, I'd better get my story told before I forget the corroborative detail. Who's in?'

'I can offer you a nice line in off-the-peg typists, or if you prefer bespoke there's Mr Mark or Mr Mason.'

'I'll take Mark. He's almost human.'

'Trying to connect you,' she trilled, plugging into the extension and ringing; and added, just as Mr Mark lifted his receiver, 'And may the Lord have mercy on your soul.'

'I beg your pardon?' came the voice of Mr Mark, startled.

'Mr Sanders for you, sir,' she said sweetly, and restored her switch.

'Good morning, Miss Grace.' That was Mr Hart, the senior partner, pausing at the door on the way to his office. He was a large, distinguished-looking man in his late fifties, with thick grey hair and mutton-chop whiskers, who affected an old-fashioned type of bowler hat with a curly brim. It always made Josy think of a hansom cab driver. His courtly, old-world good manners subdued even the cockiest young draughtsman, and he ran his office as he had run it in the thirties, eschewing both modern business methods and the half-American jargon that was so prevalent these days. His secretary, who was an English graduate, said that his letters were a pleasure to type, gloriously free from 'further to yours of the 21st inst' and 'we beg to advise' and 'your goodselves'.

'Good morning, Mr Hart. What a lovely day,' Josy responded, turning round on her chair and politely removing her headset.

'Did I hear you say that was Mr Sanders

on the telephone?'

'Yes, sir. I put him through to Mr Mark. He asked for you, of course.'

'Of course,' said Hart, with a twinkle of complicity. 'He is unwell?' The 'again' hung unspoken on the air.

'I imagine so. I didn't ask.'

'Quite so,' Hart said kindly. He glanced at the window. 'I suspect the sunshine will give rise to quite a few obscure maladies today.' He smiled at Josy, and she could see why Sanders had not wanted to speak to him. 'Perhaps you would kindly ask Mr Mark to come along to my room when it is convenient to him.'

'Certainly, sir.'

He turned away towards his office, and then paused and came back into the doorway. 'I wonder, Miss Grace, if you would consider joining us as a permanent member of staff. You have been here now for – five months, is it? – and you seem to have settled in very well. If you would be interested in a position, I am sure we could make a satisfactory arrangement about your remuneration.'

That was nice of him, she thought. It meant he knew that temporaries were paid higher wages than permanent staff, and was willing to make up the difference to her. Yesterday, when it was winter, she might almost have been charmed by him into accepting; but today, ah, today summer had come in April, and it was long past time for the geese to fly north.

'Well, sir,' she began.

He sensed her refusal. 'No need to give me an answer now,' he said quickly. 'Think about it, and come and see me at half past five.'

'Very well, sir,' she said. It would be churlish not to give him the opportunity to try and change her mind.

The hatches of the first two lines dropped together and buzzed in unison, and Hart left her, with a suspicion of a bow, to her labours.

Mrs Marshall, the tea lady, came round at eleven with her trolley. She usually did Josy last, just after Mr Hart, when she had time to be expansive, for she found her a good captive audience. Other people had the habit of saying, 'Yes, of course, Mrs Marshall, but I must take this file up to Mr Mason right away,' before she had properly got into her stride; but Josy had to stay put, tied by the head, as it were, to her position.

'Well, glad to see *you're* in, at least,' she said, plonking down a cup of tea and two Custard Creams next to Josy's bank of switches. Everyone else got Morning Coffee in the morning and Rich Tea in the afternoon, but she always saved Josy a couple of what she gave Mr Hart. 'Fine lot of people not in today. It's the weather. First bit of sun, and you'd be amazed at the excuses. Weddings, frunerals, backache, stummercake – it's all the same to them.'

'Um,' said Josy. It was all that was needed.

'Wasn't like that before the war. If we'd've skived off then, we'd've got the sack, no messing. And likely not've got another job, no. Not that we would have skived anyway. We fought ourselves lucky to *have* a job. We remembered the hard times, y'see, the Depression an' that. We took what we could get, and grateful. If you were lucky enough to have a job you stuck to it like flypaper.'

'Um,' said Josy.

Mrs Marshall spread her weight a little more evenly and got dug in. 'I wanted to thank you, dear, for what you did for my sister, filling in them forms for her. Of course, her Stan used to do all that sort of thing, but now he's gone, well, she couldn't make head nor tail of 'em, and you know what the people up the Rates Office are like – dot every "i" and cross every "t" just right, or it's back you go and come again next week, thank you very much for nothing. Little 'Itlers they are. But it's all come out right now, thanks to you, and she got the letter yes'd'y morning, so thanks again, dear, for taking the trouble.'

'It was no trouble,' Josy said.

'Well, there's not many would've bothered,

I can tell you that, so Vi and me, we're very grateful to you.'

'Don't mention it.'

Mrs Marshall did not like to talk in a vacuum. Finding her quarry a little distracted, she changed tack, and tried another line and a direct question.

'Bless me if I know how you work that thing,' she said, peering at the switchboard. 'Black strings here and red strings there – regular cat's cradle. How do you know one from another?'

'Oh, it's easy, really,' Josy said, clearing down a line and letting the cords run back into their holes with a fine snap. 'If you put them up, you naturally know where they all go.'

'So you say,' said Mrs Marshall. 'Sooner you than me, though. Too much messing about with Electric for my liking. Get a lot of shocks, do you?'

'Oh yes. Well, this is an old board, so you're bound to get a few. You don't notice them, though. You get used to it – like an immunity. Telephonists can take shocks that would kill a normal person,' Josy went on, playing to Mrs Marshall's round eyes. 'The only trouble is, when you shake hands with someone, you tend to give them a bit of a jolt.'

'Well I never,' Mrs Marshall said with respect. 'What'd your boyfriend say about that? Wouldn't like it much, I dare say?'

This was a regular theme with Mrs M. Josy said patiently, not for the first time, 'I don't have a boyfriend.'

'What, still? That'll never do. Never mind, I reckon that young Harris from Drawing is a bit sweet on you.'

'What makes you think that?' Josy asked with a private smile. Office romance was meat and drink to Mrs Marshall.

'Well, I'm always seeing him hanging around in here.'

'The others send him down for their stationery,' Josy explained. The stationery cupboard was in the telephone room. She had been startled, during the first few days, by the number of young men who appeared in her doorway asking for paper-clips. Now they didn't bother about an excuse for a 'chin', unless one of the managers happened to pass while they were leaning on the door-post.

'Well I never,' said Mrs Marshall, and was reminded of another long-standing grievance. 'Couldn't fetch their own stationery, I suppose. Wonderful how some people seem to lose the use of their legs. Those girls up in the typing pool, for instance, they won't bother to put their cups out. Oh no, I have to go round every desk to get 'em back, sometimes have to go down on my knees to pick 'em up off the floor, and me with *my* back. It wouldn't take 'em a second to put all the

34

cups on the tray by the door where I could just pick 'em up on my way back down, but oh no, not them. "That's your job, Mrs M," they say. That's as may be, but there's no harm I ever heard of, making someone's job a bit easier, especially when they're my age, and worked hard all their life. But not them. Waited on hand and foot, that's what they expect. Little madams.'

Josy made a sympathetic noise, and Mrs Marshall softened.

'Of course, it's different for you. Can't leave that contraption of yours, I do see that. And there's only one of you. But you take the Drawing Office, for instance—'

'Hullo-ullo-ullo,' said Danny Wilson cheerfully, appearing behind the tea trolley and winking at Josy over the top of Mrs Marshall's home perm. She and Vi did each other's once a month. 'Had a puncture, Mrs M? I heard a rumour that Mr Mark was hoping for seconds, what with all these people being away, not to mention an extra biccy.'

Mrs Marshall swelled. 'Mr Mark can wait, same as anyone would have to, till I've got round the first time. And if there *was* seconds, Mr Hart would get first call, what's only right, him being the boss. Not but what Mr Mark *would* wait, having better manners than some people I could mention,' she added, slapping Wilson's hand away from

35

the biscuit tin. She backed her trolley, did a neat three-point turn in the narrow corridor, and hurried back to the lift. She had a soft spot for Mr Mark almost amounting to a crush.

'That was wicked,' Josy said sternly when she was out of earshot.

'Think nothing of it,' said Danny Wilson, waving a magnanimous hand. 'Maidens Rescued, Dragons Slain, Damsels Delivered, by our fully trained representatives, in the comfort of your own home. No mess. Satisfaction guaranteed. Why Let a Tea Lady Ruin Your Life? Call now for a Free Estimate.'

'She's all right.'

'She isn't.'

'Then you should feel sorry for Mr Mark.'

'Not at all. He has his own method. As soon as he sees her in the doorway he asks for a long-distance call. Any minute now his number will show up. Just watch.'

'Don't be silly. He only uses the switchboard for internal calls. He has his own direct line for calls out.'

'Well, that's me told,' said Wilson, and hitched himself down on the radiator.

'You'll get piles,' Josy warned.

'Charming sentiment. Romance is dead. Still, I shall rise above it. I'd suffer any discomfort for five minutes of your company. Miss Grace, will you marry me?'

'Don't you know that bigamy is a crime?'

'You have the most lacerating use of language.'

'Only to save you from fifteen years in jug.'

'It'd be worth it. You are my dream-girl, my pin-up, the golden voice at the end of the line. When I hear you say "Number please," my collar studs melt. I'm transported along the throbbing wire to a better place, where blueprints always come out right, and pencils never wear down.'

'You'll be taking your wife along with you, of course?'

'She supports me in every decision. She believes that behind every great man is a capable wife.'

'She's probably right. How many great men weren't married?'

'Why do you women always stick together?'

'Why do you men always lump women together? Generalisations are always false.'

'Including that one.'

Josy laughed, leaning back comfortably in her wonky chair and admiring his Grecian good looks. She didn't need to watch the switchboard. Every change on it was accompanied by a faint click, almost inaudible to the untrained ear but heard by the telephonist through any ambient noise, traffic, pneumatic drills, or the most fascinating conversation.

'I don't know why you don't respond to my advances, though,' Wilson went on.

'Because you'd be horrified if I did,' Josy said. But, though he had spoken with mock peevishness, she had a sinking feeling that he was serious.

'Not at all,' he said. 'You're a very attractive woman, you know.'

He *was* serious. She tried to keep the light-teasing atmosphere going, but with diminishing hope. 'That's a man's most patronising remark, and the reason women don't respect them.'

'I mean it. I find you very attractive. Will you come out to dinner with me?'

Oh God, he was going to be a bore, Josy thought. 'How kind. Is that with or without your wife?'

'Why do you keep bringing her into it? It's you and me I'm talking about.'

'And I'm trying not to.'

'But why?' He sounded genuinely puzzled. It simply didn't cross his mind that she might not find him desirable – and, of course, basically he was right.

Josy sighed. He had crossed over the line from teasing to serious, and now all sorts of horrid complications loomed. She'd have to get serious too. 'Look, I don't want to go out with a married man,' she said.

'Oh, come on! Just because I'm married, doesn't mean I've got two heads. We could have a lot of fun together.'

'Until someone got hurt.'

'No-one will get hurt. We're mature people. We both know the score.'

He was looking at her with that gleam of calculation, like the greedy child watching the cake plate, having calculated there would be one éclair over. A little extra. Something for nothing. Yes, she knew the score. She was out of her place here, according to people like Danny Wilson, and by a bizarre species of reasoning, that meant she was 'up for it'. She didn't play by the same rules as everyone else, which must mean she was available for any kind of proposition.

She had to use the knife. 'Don't you understand, I don't want to go out with you. You're not my type,' she said, firmly enough not to be misunderstood. Now, of course, he would be offended. He would have to cover up his hurt pride, and she would have lost an amusing work colleague.

'Well, of course, I didn't mean to force my unwelcome attentions on you,' he said stiffly. 'I thought you fancied me.'

According to the script, she should now jump in with some emollient phrases, regrets about what could not be, wistful compliments that would allow him to retire with dignity, his masculine pride intact. But a spirit of irritability rose up in her. If he insisted on being a bore, he could jolly well stew

39

in his own juice.

'You thought wrong,' she said coldly.

'Well, you certainly gave that impression,' he retorted. He removed himself from her radiator, and at the door turned to deliver his parting barb. 'All I can say is that you shouldn't lead people on, if you don't mean it. Men don't like that sort of thing. There's a word for people like you, and it isn't a nice one.'

He thought he had slapped her face, but the words were so hackneyed they tickled her sense of humour. Her irritation faded before laughter. That made things worse, of course. His face went crimson.

'I didn't realise I was so very amusing,' he said tautly.

'Oh, but you are, you really are. Call me a prick-teaser and be done with it. A man contemplating adultery shouldn't be prudish about words.'

He turned on his heel and stalked away. Laughter faded and she felt annoyed with herself. She shouldn't have done it. She'd left him with nowhere to hide. It would be all over the office by lunchtime, and in a form so filtered by Wilson's hurt feelings she would not recognise it. She answered a call, and then sat staring out of the window, daydreaming, feeling inside her the familiar rising of the sap that told her she had been in one place long enough. It had come late this year, subdued by the weather, perhaps, but it had come. She imagined that hibernating animals felt like this in their sleep when it was time to wake up. The migrating birds felt it in their season. Perhaps some other humans felt it, and didn't recognise it for what it was, or tried to sublimate it by buying new clothes, or washing the curtains, or growing a moustache.

Or perhaps they did know what it was, that undefined yearning, the prickles of restlessness that attended the first fine weather of the year, but couldn't act on it. In fairness, not many were in her position. She felt suddenly sorry for all the people who couldn't go; who had to thrust down their rearing spirits and stifle the urge with another batch of invoices; listen to a tiresome customer instead of that pining, insistent voice.

It was time to go. In her mind she was already out there, in the sun, on a train, across the country, somewhere else – that was the requirement, to be somewhere else. Perhaps the only requirement. She answered calls with some mechanical part of her and was hardly aware she was doing it.

Lunchtime brought the first of the gossip-hounds snuffling into her cubby-hole. Eric Morse, junior draughtsman and bosom buddy of young Harris, came to ask her if she wanted any sandwiches bringing in, and having received her negative reply, settled himself on the radiator with folded arms to get the facts.

'So what happened to old Wilson? He came up with a face like thunder, and old Ma Marshall says you were talking to him thick as thieves when she left.'

'I thought you'd have got it out of him by now,' said Josy.

'Well, I got one version,' he admitted. 'I wondered what really happened.'

'How do you know his version isn't the right one?'

'He seemed upset. Anyway, he said some – well – uncharitable things about you, so I bet it wasn't.'

'I'm touched by your devotion.'

'No, go on, tell. What really happened? I'll spread your version. I like you better than him.'

'I'd sooner everyone forgot it.'

He was not going to let a promising scandal drop that easily. 'Did he make a pass at you?'

'What delightfully old-fashioned language you use,' Josy laughed.

'So he did! The old dog! And him married, too. And you knocked him back?'

'Why do you conclude that?'

'He wouldn't have come upstairs looking like thunder if you'd said yes. Well, good for you! About time he got his comeuppance. But, I say, you must have said some pretty stiff things to him. According to him we've got a real scarlet woman in the telephone room, no better than she ought.' The thought came to him, and he glowed with creation. 'A real switch-bawd!'

'Eric, please, do me a favour. Don't make a big thing out of it.'

'You can't stop gossip in an office like this,' he said reasonably. 'If you can't beat 'em, you might as well join 'em.'

'Well, you can talk about me until your heads fall off, as far as I'm concerned, but wait until I've gone, will you?'

'Gone? Gone where? You aren't leaving us, are you? Oh, come on, not just because of old Loverboy Wilson?'

'Of course not.'

'What, then? Another job? You're not getting married?'

'It's spring, that's all. I want to go somewhere else, see some new faces, live in another town. Don't you ever feel like that, that you've just got to move on?'

Eric's nice round face looked even rounder with surprise. 'No, never. What's another town going to have that London hasn't?'

'It'll be different, that's all. I need change. That's why I don't take permanent jobs, because I always move on in spring. I come to London in winter because it's convenient – somewhere to hibernate. But come spring, I've got to be off.'

The romance was getting to him now. His eyes dreamed a little. 'Just like that? It sounds terrific. But don't you ever get homesick?'

'I have no home to be homesick for.'

'God, it sounds marvellous. I wish I could come with you.'

She almost said, 'Why don't you?' But he didn't really mean it. He wouldn't go. Most people wouldn't – and a good thing, too. The country would break down if everyone followed his whim. But in any case, it would be a horrible bore to have someone trailing along with her. She couldn't move quickly unless she was alone.

'So when are you going to tell Mr Hart? He won't like it. He's got a soft spot for you.'

'I've got to see him at five thirty.'

'Tell him the truth,' he advised. 'He'll probably envy you. I reckon he was quite a goer when he was young. Ah well,' he slid off the radiator, 'better go and get the sarnies or they'll be sending out search-parties. Shall I have cheese or ham today? Or shall I go really fancy and have chicken? You've given me a taste for the exotic, with your talk of faraway places. See you later!'

He went off, whistling, aware of a pleasantly nostalgic feeling that Josy had stirred up in him, vaguely redolent of unspecified things far away and long ago. He had a chicken sandwich and, yearning for a taste of tropic isles, lashed out on a tin of pineapple chunks which he shared with Harris, dip and dip about with a teaspoon pilfered from Mrs Marshall's trolley.

'Ah, come in, Miss Grace. Please sit down.'

Mr Hart's office was cool. His carpet was not dusty, and his window was clear glass all over, so you could see a tree waving its hands about gently, and the marvellous speedwell sky. She sat down on a leather chair, folded her coat across her lap and studied the charming, handsome face across the desk from her. It was a face of easy authority, but the lines in it were gentle, as though made by pleasurable experiences. It was a face of a man who had loved and been loved. He had a wife, a home, a business. What more could he want? Life was so easy for a man, she thought. Eric Morse was wrong – he would not envy her for a second.

'Have you thought about my proposition?' he asked at last. 'Before you answer, let me elaborate a little. I am quite aware that your ambitions cannot stop at being a telephonist. You have too much about you for that. I have been thinking about how we might best use your qualities, and what I propose is this. I should like you to spend a few weeks in each of the departments, so that you fully understand the company in all its aspects. Then, when Mr Pickford retires, which will be in a few months' time, I should like to make you office manager.'

She looked her astonishment. This was far beyond anything she had expected. 'I don't know what to say,' she began.

'Don't say anything just yet. Let me explain further. You see, I am quite well aware that I am seen as something of an old fogey – no, no, don't trouble yourself to deny it. I hear all the gossip, despite my splendid isolation up here. It is true, I like the formality and grace of the old ways. But some of our ways are perhaps now too old. I am not averse to change, if it is beneficial and applied discriminatingly. I believe you could do that for the firm. You could bring in modern efficiencies, without sacrificing the traditions and – shall I say – the *tone* of the company. You have intelligence, and you have sensitivity. You could get changes through without offending people.'

'It's a most generous offer,' she said.

'It doesn't end there. Join this company, and there need be no limit to your ambition. We have had a good deal of work coming in from France and Germany lately, and there will soon be the need to open a continental office, most probably in Paris. Your ability to speak French—' How the devil did he know that? – 'would make you a natural candidate for running it.'

Josy was stunned. It was a position few

women could aspire to. Girls became secretaries – and, yes, sometimes they were as important to the company as any executive, more or less running things, though it was never acknowledged. But girls did not become managers; girls were not offered their own branches to run. It was an offer to jump at, and a tremendous compliment to her. 'Are you sure I have the right qualities?'

'I should not be saying these things if I did not.'

She looked into his face and imagined herself as perhaps he saw her, a female executive, a woman in a suit, holding meetings, making decisions, giving orders, meeting other businessmen on their terms. Responsibility. Respect. A salary – probably a large one – and expenses, travel, her own office – her own secretary? To work in Paris! She should jump at it. Why wasn't she jumping at it?

In her mind there was another image, that of the train she had planned to take, the countryside flying past its windows, the dear, shabby places she stayed in; of the peace, the ease of her life as it had been, the freedom to be where she wanted, and only for as long as she wanted. Hart's offer was a gilded prison, and she feared it.

Girls were secretaries, or they got married. They were secretaries *until* they got married. Implicit in his offer was that she would not get married. He had not asked her, he had assumed. But he knew nothing about her. If she stayed, if she took the job, he would come to know about her. It was inevitable. Along with security (the cage) came know-ledge. She could not allow that. Her precious anonymity! And freedom! She must be free.

'It's the most wonderful offer,' she said, 'and I'm very grateful and deeply flattered that you thought of me—'

'I sense a refusal coming,' he said, creasing his brow with gentle distress.

'It's difficult to explain,' she said. 'I want to travel—'

'And so you shall, once we open the Paris office.'

'I know,' she said. 'But—' Phrases formed themselves inside her head, and were re-jected. It sounded so silly in the context of Hart's quiet, well-appointed office. How could she explain to an elderly, respectable, powerful businessman? 'All my life, since I left home, I have come and gone as I pleas-ed. I've been free – no home, no luggage, just moving from place to place as and when I pleased.'

She saw he was trying to understand, and failing. 'It sounds a lonely life.'

He might have said pointless. She was grateful for that. 'Perhaps it is. But at all events, I'm not ready to settle down yet. I'm still restless.'

He shook his head; it was beyond him. 'Well, if that's your decision—?'

'It is,' she said. 'Thank you, but I must go.'

'When do you intend to leave?'

'At the end of the week. I hope it won't inconvenience you.'

'We can get another temporary,' he said. There was just a hint of hurt in his choice of words. If she would not be his protégée, she was just another temp.

'Of course,' she said, and stood up to go.

He let her almost reach the door. 'Just one thing more.' She turned. 'If you do decide you want to settle down, come and see me. There will always be a position of some sort for you in this firm.'

'Thank you,' she said. He was most extraordinarily nice. 'Goodbye.'

'Good luck,' he said, and she left, feeling rather guilty, but on the other hand enormously relieved.

George was already there when she got home to her bedsitter. He was sitting on the bed – there was nowhere else – reading one of her few permanent books, *Brideshead Revisited*.

'Oh good, you're nice and early,' she said.

'I'm not early – you're late,' he said.

'How did you get in?'

'The man in the next room was just

coming in as I arrived, so he let me in.'

She dumped her bag and coat on the floor and went to him to be kissed. He was very thorough about it, pushing her down full-length so as to give her the attention she deserved. When he'd finished, she sat up, pushed the hair out of her eyes, and smiled. 'You must have missed me.'

He pulled the crushed book out from under her and restored it to the bedside locker. 'I've read this one before,' he explained.

'How you surprise me.'

'What happened at work today?'

He was always amused by her anecdotes, so she told him all about Danny Wilson's approach to her, embroidering it to make it funnier and more outrageous.

He laughed, but there was a shadow in his eyes. At last he said, 'Poor bloke.'

'Poor bloke?' she said with mock outrage. 'What about poor me? Didn't I tell you he insulted me?'

'All the same, one feels sorry for the poor booby. You take quite a bit of getting used to. He must have seen you as a siren.'

'I ain't a syreen, honey, he jest thought I was.' She looked towards the window, a natural movement of escape she was not aware of. 'Phew! What's happened to the weather? Where shall we eat this evening? Somewhere on the river would be nice.'

'It can't be too far away. I've to be back earlyish – work to finish for tomorrow.'

'The river runs through London,' she pointed out.

He thought. 'All right, how about the Festival Hall? The restaurant there is supposed to be good.'

'Lovely. I've always wondered what that was like. It looks so nice when it's all lit up. It will make me feel expensive.'

'Not too expensive. Remember it's the end of the month.'

'Oh George, don't be a pooh! I'll choose the cheapest things.'

'You needn't. Festival Hall it is. It's nice to think there are some things you've always wanted to do and haven't done yet,' he said.

'That sounds a tiny bit sour-grapesish.'

'*Mea culpa*,' he said. He looked into her face. 'When are you leaving?'

She stared in surprise, but in the end she didn't ask how he knew. He was George, after all.

'Tomorrow. Tomorrow night, if you'll spend the evening with me. Otherwise I'll go straight from work.'

'I suppose,' he said slowly, 'there's no point in asking you not to go.'

A tiny worm of panic formed in her guts. He wasn't going to try to stop her, was he? He never had before. He mustn't try to stop her. She had to go – *had* to.

'No,' he said, 'I see there isn't. Take the night train, then, and I'll see you off.'

'Lovely,' she said, though with a faint reservation. He had never seen her off before, either, agreeing with her that standing around on a station waiting for the train to pull out was an embarrassing bore. There was something going on in his mind and for a moment she studied his face, trying to work out what it might be. He was staring out of the window, absently, a small frown between his brows. Then his focus changed and he met her eyes, and she found hers sliding away automatically.

He put a hand on her knee, and said lightly, 'At least I'll get some work done, with you gone. You distract me too much.'

She laughed, everything back in its usual place. He took her into his arms, and they began kissing again.

Chapter Three: 1954

It wasn't difficult to get her to talk about herself. Her family seemed much on her mind, and it was natural enough for me to mention her father, that second time I took her out. I made no mistake that time, by the way. I picked her up in the car, by the war memorial, early enough in the evening for it to seem to Smart, Horrocks and Co that I was just going for a drink on my own, and took her away from the neighbourhood, so we would not bump into them. We stopped at a pub in Owermoigne, and there, overheard only by the large and somnolent cat couched on the windowsill, I brought up the subject.

Colonel Grace was no longer a serving officer, but it was not possible to belong to that regiment even for a few weeks without hearing his name, and learning a bit about him. He was their most famous colonel of recent history, hero of many a lovingly polished war story, spoken of with affection. His portrait was hung in the entrance vestibule of the officers' mess. I had seen it when sent there with a message, and had been kept waiting long enough to study it in some detail. He was almost a legend, and it was no wonder that Smart and Horrocks had urged me not to see the colonel's daughter again. Weddell had gone so far as to offer helpfully to 'cut them off' for me right away, to save the colonel the trouble of doing it later when he found out a bog-standard squaddie was after his little girl.

I wasn't to be put off by them; nevertheless, my first question to her, when we were comfortably ensconced, was whether she was really the daughter of *that* colonel.

'Yes. What of it?' she said indifferently.

'You know quite well what. Colonels don't like their daughters being courted by private soldiers. I could get into trouble. You should have told me.'

'I didn't tell you because there was no need. I shouldn't have gone out with you if it meant trouble for you.'

'Easy for you to say—'

'Oh, look,' she interrupted impatiently, 'he doesn't know where I am, and even if he did, he wouldn't mind. Daddy's not like that.'

'Where does he think you are, then?'

'He doesn't think anything. He's always shut up in his study in the evenings, reading or writing, and he doesn't like to be disturbed. He's writing a history of the regiment.'

'What about your mother?' I asked

'My mother's dead. So there's only Daddy, and it would never occur to him to wonder where I was.'

I doubted that, but left it. After all, here I was, of my own choice; and I didn't want her to stalk off in a huff.

'Is there just you?' I asked. 'I mean, have you any brothers or sisters?'

'One brother – darling Rob – but he's much older than me. He's in the army, too, but a regular. He's in the Engineers. He's hardly ever home. It's been just Daddy and me for ages, and I promise you, he's not a bit stuffy. I got rather a crush on a private once – years ago, when I was fifteen. You know what it's like when you're that age – I was desperately in love – and Daddy took pity on me and invited him home to tea. The poor soul thought he was for it and sat there all through tea with his teeth chattering, while Daddy tried to be nice to him. He never came again,' she concluded, 'but it didn't matter. I'd gone off him anyway, after that.'

I wondered if there was a message for me there.

Later she talked about her mother. 'I could never understand why Daddy married her. She wasn't his type at all. He's so sensible and intelligent and funny, and Mummy was just very silly. Flighty, I suppose, is the word. She used to be an actress. Not a very good one, I shouldn't have thought. Daddy fell for her when he saw her on stage once, playing a maid in some play or other. So he went backstage to meet her. She was struck by him at once. Well, she couldn't often have had men like him coming to see her – tall, handsome, distinguished – even the leading lady could hardly have expected a man like him in her dressing room. So after he'd called a couple of times, and he asked her out to supper, she went.'

She frowned. 'It was a bad start, really, for him to be adoring her from afar like that, because it must have given her high ideas of herself. She *was* very pretty, but, as I said, very silly. She led Daddy a terrible dance, saying yes one minute and no the next, until eventually Daddy wouldn't be pushed any more and he got tough with her, and said either she should marry him or he was off. So then, of course, she said yes at once, because he was a terrific catch for her, and poor Daddy's goose was cooked.'

'Isn't that rather a harsh thing to say?' I protested. I was made a little uneasy by her language. It didn't seem right in those days to hear a child criticise its parents in such robust terms.

'Not at all,' she said unconcernedly. 'She was a terrible wife. She didn't do *anything*, except lie about the house all day in a negligée, talking on the telephone, or get dressed up and go out and spend Daddy's money.'

'Perhaps that's all he wanted her to do,' I suggested; but she had definite ideas about it all.

'Daddy isn't that silly. Of course, he didn't expect her to cook and clean, he had servants for that, but there are other ways of making a home for a person. She didn't like any of his friends, she wasn't interested in any of the things he liked, and she complained every time the army made him move. She hated the army and said she was bored all the time. So he made her have a baby. That was Rob. Everyone thinks his name is Robert but it isn't, it's Robin. The only books Mummy ever read were historical romances. She loved them, and she named him after Elizabeth I's Robin. He hates it, so he always makes people call him Rob.'

'And did that work?' I asked.

'Work? Oh, I see what you mean. No, only for a bit. Mummy soon got bored with the baby and started being silly again. She flirted with other officers. It made life very difficult for Daddy. So he tried again, and that was me.'

I stirred uneasily. 'Did he tell you all this, your father?'

'He told me some, and Mummy told me some. Their stories hardly ever agreed, but I pieced it all together, bit by bit. And of course, Rob remembers more than me, because he's ten years older. Rob's a darling – you'd really like him,' she added, and her face glowed when she spoke about him.

'Well, anyway,' she resumed, 'then the war came, and Daddy had to go away. You'd have thought Mummy would have got something useful to do, some war work or something, but she didn't. She just kept on spending, and going out to dinner and dancing with whoever was in London. I think the war frightened her, and she wanted to forget it. Then the London house got bombed and we had to move to the country and she hated that. She had weekend parties – I remember *them*, a bit – but it wasn't enough. There was all the rest of the week to get through, you see. So she took lovers.'

I almost laughed at the preposterous word coming so glibly from her mouth, but controlled myself in time. She seemed almost to be telling a story from one of her mother's romantic novels. I said, 'I'm sure you're just guessing now.'

'Oh no,' she said simply. 'It's the truth. I'm sure Daddy knew all about it, because when he came home on leave he treated her very distantly, and he looked so sad when he looked at Rob and me. They had a terrible row once – I heard them shouting in another room.'

She paused for a while, frowning in thought. I prompted her.

'What happened after the war?'

'Oh, that was even worse. Because, you see, Daddy could have retired, but they were so short of officers they asked him to stay on for a bit. He was posted to Kenya and he insisted Mummy and I went with him. Rob was grown-up and gone by then. Well, Mummy was furious. She only ever wanted to live in London – or possibly New York. Anyway, *not* in the countryside, and *definitely* not another country, most of all Africa. She hated it so much. She nagged and complained and she and Daddy had more rows. She took lovers there, too, which made it very awkward for Daddy because, of course, it was always someone he knew. And then soon after we got home Mummy died.'

I made sympathetic noises.

'Oh, don't mind it,' she said. 'Mummy never had time for me. I don't think she liked me much. I think she thought I had ruined her figure – having me, you know. Well, I suppose when you're a sort of woman like her, bird-brained, with nothing to fall back on but your looks, it must be pretty terrible to lose them. But she loved Rob – especially when he became a soldier.'

'I thought you said she hated the army.'

'She hated army life, but she liked soldiers – at least, when they were away from camp. She thought they were exciting and brave and dashing. I suppose that's why she fell for Daddy in the first place.'

'So, after your mother died, your father brought you up?'

'Yes, and it's been much better than when she was alive. Everything was always fun with Daddy. He was always interested in everything one did. We had lovely times, lovely outings. And when he retired he decided to take up horses, and I always loved horses, so we had that in common, you see.'

'I see,' I said.

'I just wish Rob was home more. But he writes to me, and he always comes home when he gets any leave.'

'He's not married?'

'No, he's married to the army.'

I remember her voice, so young, so certain, plucking apart the fibres of an elaborate tapestry of lives and emotions with forensic indifference. I can see her in memory, with her bell of shining hair and bright eyes, sitting up so straight, full of a clear light, like a candle flame when there is no draught to sway it. I think I laughed at her a little, with the part of my mind that had decided that nothing was that simple. I saw myself as so much older and wiser than her. She would change as she grew older, I told myself; she would grow less direct, less positive about everything, less sure of herself. But though I laughed, I envied her. None of us would have our paintings smeared if we knew how to preserve them when they were wet.

The pub began to fill with the evening trade, and we left, wanting to be alone together. We drove around for a while, and then parked the car and went for a walk along the cliff tops. For a while we watched the moving lights of ships, the static ones marking out the black whale-hump of Portland Bill, and the spangled curve that was Weymouth, and then I took her hand for the first time. It was small and warm and felt amazingly alive, like a bird. It had not been like that with other girls, whose hands I remembered as seeming mere awkward appendages. I stood still and marvelled at it for a while, and then I turned her towards me and kissed her. Her mouth was cold, but started to warmth as it touched mine, and she kissed me with easy passion, as if we had been doing it for months.

I was twenty-two and full of the juices of life. I wanted to have her, there and then, on the invisible turf under the impossibly starry sky, but I could not. Of course I couldn't – but I don't mean only that. I felt ... afraid. Of what, I don't know. It was easy to feel superstitious on that great empty cliff top and under those stars. It was like being drawn towards something dangerous and only half perceived.

We kissed for a little while, and then walked on, still holding hands. I felt warm towards her now, and confident, as if some guarantee had been made that everything would be all right.

We talked about me, then; about my childhood in Bournemouth – so different from hers in every way. My father had been a railway worker, and we lived in a small terraced house among countless others identical. My parents were devoted to each other, and to me, their only child, and though we had little money to spare, there had never been any conflict or quarrels, and we were as quietly happy as any small family in England.

Though my childhood was without material luxury, I still knew I had been brought up soft, with never any shortage of love or security or friends.

I was a bright child, and my father wanted me to 'get on'. He subscribed what seems to me now a preposterous amount out of his weekly wages to an encyclopaedia which was issued in parts, and his pride was to come home of an evening and see me reading it, or consulting it while I did my homework. Being on the railway, he did not go away to war, but he became a volunteer firewatcher in his spare time. Bournemouth did suffer some attacks, and the only unhappy moments in my childhood were when they coincided with my father's firewatching, for though I was immensely proud of him, I knew my mother was afraid, and feared with her. From our blacked-out town you could see Southampton blazing on the nights the Luftwaffe targeted it. You could hear the crumps of the falling bombs, too – it was only about twenty miles away. And my mother would look up from her knitting, as I scribbled away at my homework, and say softly, 'Southampton's catching it again, poor things.'

Despite its proximity to Southampton, Bournemouth was much safer than London, and for the latter part of the war we had two evacuee children billeted on us. One hears horror stories about evacuees, but once they settled down, ours were perfectly nice children. I remember the five of us having long, comfortable games of Monopoly on grey Sunday afternoons. Mother was never much good at it, being too soft hearted. When any of us, impoverished, landed on her property she would defer or even try to forget the debt. I, likewise, loved her too much ever to demand payment from her, and had we played alone our games would never have been concluded. But Sam and Tommy played to win, and Father was a demon at it, and perfectly unscrupulous, in a straight-faced, twinkling way. It was not until I grew up that I discovered you could not build houses on the stations.

Near the end of the war there was an incident involving my father. A bomb fell on the marshalling yard where he was working, setting fire to a tool shed. Two men, caught out by the raid, were sheltering there, something known only to my father, who had seen them run in. At great risk to his life he had rescued them, suffering painful burns to his hands which laid him off work for many weeks. It was all written up in the papers, to my mother's intense and silent pride, and a benevolent society took up a subscription for him and had a medal pressed, which it sent it to him, along with a cheque for the first lump sum of money he had ever had in his life.

After long deliberation, he used the money to buy Betsy, the small Morris motor car, then ten years old, which was now mine. Petrol shortages meant that she spent a great deal of time sitting out in front of the house, to the pride and wonder of the whole street, but on the occasional fine Sunday he would take us all out for a ride into the country, for a walk or a picnic. It was the one extravagance of his life, and it had the true qualities of luxury: it was utterly pointless, and it gave him huge pleasure. I'm not sure my mother approved of it as a way of spending the money: I think her mind would have run towards a new carpet, mattresses, shoes, or the famed Rainy Day. But at the time I was thrilled, as any boy would be, by this mechanical acquisition; and later I felt I understood why he had done it, after a lifetime of carefulness and 'making do'.

Sam's parents perished in an air raid, so he stayed on with us after the war, which was some consolation to Mother when I won a scholarship and went away to boarding school. I already knew what I wanted to do. The destruction of so many buildings during the war nourished my latent interest in architecture, and five years amongst some moderately ancient stones only made it keener. Father died during my last year, of a worn-out heart. It had been hard, heavy work on the railways, and he was not a big man.

When school finished I went home to Bournemouth with the idea of finding a local job for Mother's sake, but she wanted me to follow up my advantage and go to university. 'It's what your father always hoped for,' she said. And when I won my place at UCL, with a bursary, 'He'd have been so proud.' Sam still lived at home, and had a local job in a garage, so I didn't feel too bad about leaving her, and went off to a new and exciting life as a student in London. I did well there, and took a good degree. My call-up was waiting for me when I gradu-ated, but even there, as I've said, I struck pretty lucky. My life had been so easy – why, then, did I feel so much older than Josella, so much more worldly-wise, so much less idealistic? Perhaps it is because, contrary to all adages, hardship in the emotional sense makes one less, and not more, aware of reality.

She was as fascinated by my life as I was by hers. We could have walked and talked all night, but I began to worry about the colonel and to feel guilty about keeping her out. I insisted on taking her home, and she didn't argue with me, but just looked at me in a certain way which made me feel she had consented only to humour me. Unneces-sarily, I added a further argument. 'Anyway,

Jo, I have to be up early tomorrow.' That was how I discovered what I was going to call her. As she had suggested the first evening, it just slipped out naturally, and I never called her anything else, though she had many other names to other people.

When we parked at the war memorial she agreed to come with me to a dance in Weymouth the following Saturday, accompanied by Horrocks and his girlfriend, and Smart, if he could find a partner.

'And one Sunday you must come to tea and meet Daddy,' she added.

'Are you sure?' I said. I didn't relish the prospect, no matter what she said about her father being nice.

'Definitely definitely,' she said.

'All right, then. Where to now?'

'I'll walk from here,' she said.

'Alone? And in the dark?' I protested.

'Don't be silly. I've lived here almost for ever.'

'What would Daddy think?'

'What he won't know, won't hurt him.'

I didn't like it, but she was adamant, and in the end I had to let her go. I arranged to meet her at the war memorial again for the dance, and she kissed me briskly and got out. Then she waited by the plinth until I had driven off, so that I should not see which way she went.

Chapter Four: 1964

Towns there are that are a joy to arrive in at four in the morning; towns that offer warmth and sustenance to the miserable wayfarer, that cheer his night-worn spirit with noise and bustle. Edinburgh is not one of them. Joey felt, as she arrived, that she should really have thought more about it. She had remembered arrivals of other years all right, had just not given them sufficient weight; with the result that here she was again, climbing stiffly off the night train at four thirty-two ack emma and flinching as the icy Edinburgh air thrust knives up her nostrils. Tears of protest sprang to her eyes, and she was forced to stop and blow her nose before passing through the ticket gate.

Most of the people who had travelled up with her were being met by sturdy citizens in warm tweeds, with rosy, sleepy faces like children, who would whisk them off in motor-cars to hot porridge, crisp bacon and belated bed. Joey could scent and taste it; she could even feel the sense of unreality that creeps over you when, having been coldly and uncomfortably wakeful all night, you relax at last in an armchair in front of a fire, sip tea, and smoke your twentieth cigarette too many, while the rest of the world wakes up for the first time outside your windows. Not for her those joys. She watched the soldiers she had sat with through the night trudge away to a waiting lorry, and then headed herself for the waiting room. The ladies waiting room first. Ah, as she had expected, there was no room there, unless she sat on the table, which was worse than useless. All around the benches – deliberately designed too narrow to lie on and too low in the back to sleep on sitting up – the early comers had disposed themselves and were dozing with one ear pricked for the step of the 'pollis'. There was nothing for it but to go to the general waiting room in the main hall.

Like a cathedral, it was, and about as comfortable. She chose a seat on one of the leather-covered benches where she would not have to sit too close to one of the filthy old vagrants whose home this was. Having turned up her collar and thrust her hands into her pockets, she settled down to endure. Outside, under a frozen black sky, Edinburgh lay sunk deep in sleep. Nothing stirred, not even a cat, and the citizens slept the moveless sleep of the righteous, or champed their way like horses through the chaff of dreams. There would be no more trains until the seven ten to Glasgow, and a singing silence settled itself on Joey's cold ears.

At five the duty policeman came round, and Joey watched the progress of his chequered hat through the slit of her eyelids.

'Waiting on a train?' he asked as he stopped in front of her. She shook her head. 'You'll have to move on, then,' he said inexorably.

She made the routine protest. 'I've just got off one. There's nothing open until seven.'

One corner of his mouth curled up in acknowledgement of this truth, but he said nothing, only stood aside for her to go. She sighed and stood up, picked up her carpet bag and trudged away up the exit slope. He knew she would come straight back down the entrance slope, and she knew he knew, but it didn't really matter. The game had to be played. He would come and move her on again at six, for it was his duty to move vagrants off the railway property, and if she didn't have a ticket she was a vagrant. By the time she got back down he had gone, and she settled herself back in her old seat to wait.

What a city! she thought. In London you could always find something open, somewhere to get a cup of tea and a sandwich at least. She thought longingly of the steamy pubs of Smithfield market, and hot pies; the greasy caffs of Covent Garden, and coffee made with bottled syrup and boiled milk, too hot to gulp. But the capital of Scotland closed down at midnight with stern Presbyterian propriety, and thereafter opened its eyes for no-one. She watched the hands of the clock not moving, felt her feet going dead, and a pagan longing for dawn seized her. She stared at the tiny bit of sky she could see until her watering eyes closed without her volition, and she slept. She woke with a jerk to find that her head had fallen forward and her neck ached bitterly; but at least dawn had broken at last, in a strip of pink between bands of purple cloud. It was even colder than the night had been; but the worst was over now. There were a few people moving about, the odd cleaner and a porter or two, with the bright-eyed aloofness of people who have slept in a bed; and out in the starving streets a little traffic was starting up. At seven the tea trolley arrived, and she hastened to join the queue. The attendant was as cheerful as a missionary, discussed the weather with his customers in an accent of purest Corstorphine, rubbed his hands, grinned a toothless grin at them. Joey wrapped her frozen fingers round the plastic beaker and blinked in the steam, feeling her nose tingle with the buzz of returning blood.

Now there were noises, normal, daytime, station noises of trains and porters and trolleys. The early business travellers came down for the Glasgow train and bought newspapers with their ink still damp. The cleaners slapped down their pails of hot water and sloshed around with dirty mops. The shutters of the W.H. Smith stall went up with a wooden rattle that could be nothing else. Now the hands of the clock woke up and moved at normal speed towards seven thirty, when the milk bar on the corner of South St Andrew Street would open and Joey could get breakfast.

She walked for the second time up the exit slope and paused for a moment to take in the Scott Monument, black against the ice-blue and lemon of the morning sky; the fairy-tale castle slightly misty, as if interrupted in the middle of some transformation; the familiar purple buses gliding along Princes Street; the black taxis with their owners' names written under the nearside front window. She smiled with satisfaction and walked on to the main road. A leisurely breakfast, a tidy-up in the bus-station ladies' room, and by that time Guy and company would be stirring, or at least be not too disagreeable to waking up and opening the door to her.

The Transom Theatre occupied one of the enormous flats – 'houses' in Edinburghese – in the Old Town, at the top of the Royal Mile. The theatre itself was nothing more than a very large room, created by taking out most of the dividing walls, with everything, floor, ceiling and all, painted black. There were rows of chairs round three sides, leaving an acting space with a blank wall behind it. There were no flats or backdrops, and scenery was limited to a few items of ordinary domestic furniture; lighting had to do the job of setting the scene. But the company, performing a mixture of old, new and controversial plays, was regarded as excitingly avant-garde, and had a devoted following among the students and intelligentsia of the city.

On the same level as the theatre, the original 'house' had been knocked through into the house next door to provide a bar and small restaurant: the Theatre Club, which had become the venue of choice for the Bohemian set; and in the flat directly above the theatre, the Company actors lived. Guy Lomax, Ann Blythe and Roddy Mc-Phaill were the permanent members, but there was always a changing cast of extras there too – other actors brought in for plays with larger casts, and various friends and hangers-on, sleeping on sofas or camp beds or on the floor.

It was after nine when Joey arrived outside the door at the top of the close, whose steps were so worn with age they were dish-shaped in the middle. Knowing that no-one got up much before eleven, she had brought a peace-offering of a dozen morning-rolls from the tiny shop in Lawnmarket. It was Ann who opened the door to her, tiny, neat, dark-haired Ann, dressed in the trailing red-and-gold silk Chinese dressing gown that was all her husband left behind when he ran away to America with a drama student from Lamda.

'Oh, hello, Joey.' She didn't seem particularly surprised to see her. 'I wondered who it could be at this time of the morning.'

'Peace-offering,' Joey said, holding out the bag of rolls, 'for dragging you out of bed.'

'You didn't really,' Ann said, rubbing her eyes and yawning. 'I was just going to the kitchen to make some coffee. But thanks anyway. There isn't anything else for breakfast.'

She padded barefoot back into the dark recesses of the flat, and Joey followed her, shutting the massive door behind her with a shove of the foot. The flat had been modernised, so that the kitchen was now a part of the living room, divided from it in the new, American style by something like a bar counter. The curtains were still drawn, and in the submarine light Joey counted three people asleep on the floor in tangles of blanket, and one on the sofa. It seemed almost as cold inside the flat as outside – it always took Joey a few days to acclimatise herself to unheated Edinburgh living.

'I'll introduce everyone later,' Ann said, stepping over bodies. In the kitchen she turned on the light that hung over the sink and filled the kettle – with some difficulty, for the sink was piled high with dishes and cooking pots waiting to be washed.

Nothing had changed, Joey thought with a smile of satisfaction. 'I think I remember some of those plates from the last time I was here,' she said.

Ann smiled. 'Could be. I wish Roddy's wife would come back. She was an awful bore, but at least she kept the place reasonably tidy. No-one else will bother.'

'I'll give it a going over later,' said Joey. 'Pay for my keep.'

'You don't need to.'

'I know. That's why I'll do it.'

'Och, too early for philosophy,' Ann said, yawning. 'You'll need to keep it simple until I wake up properly.' She lit the gas under the kettle, and leaned against the sink, blinking sleepily, waiting for it to boil. 'Staying long?' she asked at last, with an effort.

'Couple of months, I expect,' said Joey. 'What are you doing at the moment?'

'A new play – written by one of the students, as a matter of fact. Terrible rubbish, but it seems to be going down all right.'

'Good houses?'

'Have been so far. It's been on a week, and

74

we've been sold out every night. If it stays popular we'll extend the run, so Andrew says.' Andrew Cole was the producer/director. 'Suits me,' she added. 'Pinter's next on the bill, and I hate the bloody old bore.'

'You can't call England's greatest contemporary playwright a bloody old bore,' Joey laughed.

'I bloody well can. They don't pay me enough to be literary as well.'

'Poor Ann. What a life you lead!'

Ann grinned unwillingly. 'Ach, I know. I could go elsewhere, but I like it here. And I always get the female lead.'

'Better to reign in Hell than serve in Heaven?'

'Big fush in a wee pond, that's me. I suppose it's a matter of courage, really. I know where I am here. Everyone would like to do what you do, but mostly people are too scared. I know I couldn't face the insecurity.'

'My life isn't as insecure as it looks,' Joey said. 'I mean, I never go anywhere unless I know I've got somewhere to stay. I'm always full of admiration for those people who go to foreign countries where they don't even speak the language. I could never do that. I'm a coward too.'

'Well, if you're a coward, I don't know what that makes me,' Ann said. The kettle boiled, and she turned away to snatch it off the gas at the first shriek. She rummaged out some mugs, and Joey picked up the jar of Maxwell House and dumped a spoonful of coffee powder into each.

'There won't be enough water for everyone,' Ann said. She filled five cups and put the kettle back on to boil again, and then sugared the ones she had made. 'No milk, of course. It went off yesterday and no-one got round to buying any more.'

'Who are these for?'

'Those two – do you mind? Roddy's got a girl in with him. Would you just knock at his door and let him come out for them?'

Joey went back along the passage. Leading off it were two large bedrooms – Ann's and Roddy's – and the bathroom. Guy slept in the smaller bedroom that opened off the living-room – a common arrangement in Edinburgh 'houses', she had found. Joey shared the room with Guy when she was in Edinburgh. She had known him for years, and was commonly accepted as his girlfriend, but though they were very fond of each other, she had never been, as was generally supposed, his mistress. When they slept together, it was just that. He was always admiring of women, and had an easy way with kisses and hugs, which made him very popular with them, but he had never, to Joey's knowledge (and Ann's, for they had discussed it more than once) had sex with anyone. Ann said he must be a neuter, like a

76

mule. Joey never thought about it, never supposed him to be anything in particular. To her he was just Guy, and that was the way he was.

She thundered on Roddy's door and yelled, 'Coffee's up!' and having heard a pre-historic sort of grunt in reply, went back to the kitchen. The bodies on the floor were stirring now. One of them, hermaphroditi-cally long-haired and clean shaven, sat up, looking disagreeably tousled, and rubbed its eyes.

'Morning,' said Joey.

'Who the hell are you?' it said unpleasantly.

Joey decided it was male, but still too young to need to shave every day. 'I'm the angel of light who's about to bring you a cup of coffee,' she said, and he moaned at the mention.

Ann, mixing a fresh batch of life-savers, made introductions. 'This is Alex, a friend of Roddy's. Came for one night on his way up north, got sloshed, been here ever since. This is the most articulate I've seen him. Alex, this is Joey, old friend of the company.'

Alex made a noise that could have meant anything, but Joey charitably took to be 'pleased to meet you'.

Ann continued. 'The bundle next to him is his girlfriend Irene, who came down from Aberdeen to rescue him and got entangled in our mesh as well. On the mattress by the window is Paul – you probably remember him. He used to do children's theatre in Liverpool. He's taking the fourth part in our current production. And lying in state on the sofa is Andrew, of course.'

Joey had not recognised the top of his head, all that was showing from under the blanket. Andrew was grown-up and married and had his own house out at Silverknowes, but he often stayed over at the theatre. Joey thought he probably didn't really like being grown-up very much. The theatre didn't need him to be there half as often as he was.

She helped Ann carry round mugs. Irene seemed a little put out at being woken by a strange woman. Paul was either rude or still drunk from the night before, or both, for he only stared at her, but Andrew sprang amazingly to life as if he had never been asleep, and kissed her in a friendly way. 'Hulloo! You again! You weren't here last night were you?'

'I've just arrived. Came on the night train.'

'Thank God. Thought I was losing my mind for a minute.' He looked round indulgently. 'This place gets more like a doss-house every day.'

'There's no more room on the floor,' Paul grumbled. 'She's not having my mattress.'

'You've your own wee hoose to go to,' Andrew reminded him. 'You'd no need to stay here at all.' And to Joey he said, 'Pay him no mind. He's all right once he's woken up

78

properly.'

Ann put a mug of coffee in her hand. 'D'you want to take Guy's in to him?'

Joey stepped across the bodies to the door of Guy's room. Inside it was like an animal's burrow, hot, dark and feral-smelling. He slept all night with the electric fire on and the shutters closed to keep the heat in, and the airless furry warmth smelled of him. His bed was a mattress on the floor at the far end, and he was curled up on it, wound into a cocoon of blankets and as impervious to the approach of day as a hibernating bear. Joey put the mug down on the floor and shook him gently. He rolled over at least onto his back, smacked his lips a couple of times, open his eyes – and smiled at her. He had never been known to wake up bad-tempered.

'Coffee,' she said informatively.

'Good,' he said. After a moment's thought he said, 'Hello, Joey,' and pulled her down to him to kiss her. Then he propped himself on one elbow and she put the mug into his hand so he could sip his coffee. She sat on the edge of his mattress waiting for him to come to.

'Just arrived?' he said at last.

'Night train,' she answered, as economically.

'Poor you.' He sipped a little more. 'You must be tired. Why don't you crash out here,

79

sleep while we're rehearsing?'

'I might do that. This must be the only warm room in Edinburgh.'

He nodded. 'Is it raining?' he asked next.

'No, it's sunny, it's a lovely day. And I brought morning-rolls with me,' she added, remembering.

'Ah, you're a lovely woman. In that case, I'm getting up, before they all go.'

He bounded up, mother-naked, and began shrugging himself into a pair of tight and faded jeans, and a shapeless sweater. She watched him, unembarrassed. His was a stocky figure, well-muscled, with a mane of thick, healthy hair. Not handsome, exactly – compelling, was perhaps the word. With his smooth face, friendly, sleepy eyes and slow smile he could have been any age from twenty to forty. Joey had never asked him how old he was. She knew very little about him, in fact. She knew that Guy Lomax was a stage name, but what his real name was she had no idea. He likewise had never, from the day she first walked into his life, asked her anything about herself. Their relationship stood firm on mutual esteem and common ignorance.

They came out together from his room to find all the bodies upright and folding away their bedding. The disagreeable Paul stared at Joey, and when Guy draped a friendly arm over her shoulder said, 'I might have known it. Another bloody hanger-on.'

Guy only smiled. 'As long as she's not hanging on you, why should you mind?'

Ann turned to Paul with a sweet smile. 'You must learn to curb this hatred of the public, darling. All famous actors have their devoted fans. It's part of theatre life. But what am I saying? You know that of course.'

He snorted and turned away. Ann was always ready to take down a peg anyone who got 'uppity' in her presence, but as she turned her tongue as often on herself few people took offence. She had been down and borrowed a stick of butter from the theatre restaurant and was now buttering the morning-rolls. Joey and Guy went to help her. Guy produced his own jar of Rose's Lime Marmalade, to which he was addicted, and smeared it on generously, and everyone came and took one and sat down to come to life slowly.

Roddy came in, tall, furrily fair-haired, wearing a yellow felt dressing gown that was perilously too short for him, and accompanied by a pretty girl, fully dressed but looking as if she needed half an hour to herself in front of a mirror.

'Morning,' Roddy greeted the company at large, and then, 'Hello, Joey. Back again?' He stretched his endless arms upwards in a yawn, then clenched his hands together and cracked his knuckles explosively.

'God! Don't do that!' Ann winced.

'My word, what's this? Actually something to eat?' Roddy grabbed a roll and went with it to the window to open the curtains, and stood there staring at the houses warming in the sunlight while he ate. His partner of the night before took her coffee and retired hastily, seeming embarrassed at the number of people who had witnessed her arising from a bed of sin.

'Bit young for you, isn't she, Rod?' Andrew asked when she was safely out of the room.

'Oh, I like 'em young,' Roddy said. 'They're grateful for the notice. And easily impressed.'

'You mean she thinks you're an actor,' Ann said kindly.

'Exactly,' said Roddy imperturbably. 'Why else, my darling, do we all stay here, playing to houses made up largely of students?'

'So tactful, Roddy dear, considering Alex is a student,' Ann reminded him.

'Won't be much longer, unless he tears himself away from us and goes home,' Roddy said. He gave Alex a stern, fatherly look, and suddenly shouted, 'Go home, boy!'

Everyone winced, and Andrew stood up and said, 'That does it. Me for the bathroom.'

'Don't hog,' Ann called after him.

A drowsy silence fell over the room, and Joey sat beside Guy and adapted herself to the new surroundings that would be her home for the next couple of months. Each place she lived in was entirely different, but each within a few hours seemed as inevitably familiar as if she had lived there all her life.

By noon Roddy's girlfriend had gone home, and Alex and Irene had been urged as far on their way as going down to the station to find out if they could exchange their now expired tickets. The rest of them walked down to Deacon Brodie's for their usual lunchtime pint of draught Guinness – Deac's speciality. In the upstairs room they took their usual table, spread themselves out with the papers, talked to the other regulars and discussed theatre news and each other at random.

Joey was glad to find herself sitting beside Andrew, who had always interested her. He was her idea of the Perpetual Student, a man of education and ability, who ran the theatre and the theatre club with an intermittently iron hand and considerable financial flair which, she always thought, could have elevated him to the boardroom of a large company or the Cabinet if he had been minded that way. He was tall and handsome in a very English, lean, slicked-down fair way. His wife, she had heard, adored him, but she must have been a patient and supremely self-confident woman to allow him to waste his time playing at theatres, especially as it meant he was always surrounded by girl students and would-be young actresses who fell for his grave charm and fluttered for his potential power of advancement.

'So, what's this play you're doing?' Joey asked him, as he drank deep of his obsidian pint.

'Eh? Oh, it's called *The Ghost*,' Andrew said, emerging with a cream moustache. He licked it away delicately. 'It's written by a student but it's actually very good. In fact, I think it's bloody brilliant. I've got a man from the BBC coming down to see it next week. Don't tell the others that,' he added, glancing around to check he was not overheard. 'It'll make them nervous.'

'Ann thinks it's terrible.'

'Ann thinks everything's terrible. She thinks Shakespeare shouldn't have bothered. But this chap's really got talent. He's doing an adaptation of Bram Stoker's *Dracula* for us for the Festival, and I want to make sure he gets it done before someone discovers him and whisks him away. Ann'll love that – swooning about in a white nightie covered in blood.'

Joey pictured it. 'Should work well in the theatre, against those black walls.'

'Exactly. And *The Ghost* is just right, too – a sort of Oresteian tragedy, very stark, all words, no need for scenery or costumes.'

'I can see how Ann wouldn't like it. What's it about?'

'It's about a man in ancient Greece who thinks he's killed his father, the king, and he goes into exile and wanders the earth being pursued by the Furies. But in fact he hadn't killed his father at all. It was all a mistake. But when he ran away, his father thought he was abandoning him because the kingdom was about to be attacked. So he curses his son for cowardice and ingratitude. That's why the Furies are pursuing him. But of course he doesn't find that out until it's too late.'

'Well, that does sound jolly,' Joey said.

'Oh, it's great stuff, lots of hair-tearing and wailing and breast-beating. The writing's brilliant. And the audiences have been loving it. The misunderstandings make for terrific theatre – dramatic irony and all that. The audience knows what the hero doesn't. Great tension.'

'Why is it called *The Ghost*?' Joey asked.

'The writer says that a ghost is anyone out of his own world. The hero is a ghost while he's in exile, and can only become a real person again by going home and facing his fate.' He smiled at Joey. 'There's an awful lot of that sort of stuff in it. But it's very effective. The Beeb are going to love it.'

Joey smiled back. She doubted there would be any benefit to the company out of calling in the BBC man. Andrew was doing it purely to advance the playwright, who he thought had talent and deserved a chance. What a nice man he was.

'Any plans while you're here?' Andrew asked, after a second long sup.

'What, me? When did I ever have plans?' Joey answered cheerfully.

'True. Silly question, really. Well then, to the point – I need a barmaid for the club. Fancy it?'

'Why not? One job's the same as another to me. What do you pay?'

'A pound a day, plus lunch and dinner from the restaurant. But you must promise not to ruin me by giving this lot free drinks. Everything they have goes on the slate.'

Ann had overheard that. 'You malign us,' she said. 'Do you think we'd cheat you of our hard-earned pay?'

'Any time off?' Joey asked.

'It's two sessions a day, but you can have Sunday evening off, if you like. I don't mind standing in then. Might even get a relief in.'

'Okay. Thanks,' said Joey.

'Good girl. Start tonight?' Andrew said.

'If you like.' Joey was quite glad to have got something settled so quickly. She would have had to get a job anyway, and at least this would allow her to stay around the theatre and fit in with the company's times. A lot more congenial than filing in an office, too.

The theatre bar was always full of interesting and lively people and she'd enjoy talking to them. The pay wasn't much, it was true, but she would have no expenses to speak of, with her meals and accommodation covered. Probably he had taken that into account. There were no flies on Andrew when it came to money.

Having finished his drink, Andrew stood up. 'Rehearsal in ten minutes. Finish up,' he said, and walked briskly out.

The company stirred itself. 'Oh woe, woe, thrice woe!' Ann declaimed. 'There, that's me done.'

'She's the Greek chorus,' Paul said. 'You know what a Greek earns?'

'For God's sake, get it right,' Ann said, as Roddy sniggered. 'The line is, "What's a Greek earn?"'

'That's what I said,' Paul said stubbornly.

Joey turned to Guy. 'I think I'll take you up on that offer of sleep. I'm beginning to feel my age.'

'All right, darling,' Guy said, and kissed her lavishly. 'I'll come and wake you up when we finish.'

'How touchingly domestic,' Ann said. 'You two ought to get married.'

'Good idea,' said Guy. 'Would you like to marry me, Joey?'

'When?' Joey asked gravely.

'Oh, tomorrow some time?'

'Terribly sorry. I'm all tied up tomorrow.'

'Don't ring her, she'll ring you,' Roddy said, grinning. 'I hope you thrive on rejection.'

'See you later,' Joey said, and took herself away. The key to the flat's front door was under the doormat as always, and she let herself in and wandered along to Guy's room. Sleepiness was coming over her in great waves now. The electric fire was still on so the small room was almost hot, the one warm spot in all Scotland, she thought. She dragged off her clothes and flopped down onto the mattress, drawing the blankets over her. They smelled of Guy – a nice, clean-animal smell. Outside it was still icy cold. With a sensation of utter comfort, she drifted off to sleep.

Chapter Five: 1954

After the dance in Weymouth, Smart, Horrocks and Co did not rag me any more about Jo. They were impressed with her. Frankly, so was I. It had been a potentially awkward situation, but she had handled them wonderfully, meeting them on terms of easy comradeliness, which nevertheless gave them no room for over-familiarity. She addressed them as equals, but in a way that was somehow completely sexless. They had never before met a female who talked to them openly, joined in all the conversations, had something fresh and interesting to bring to every topic, and yet was not trying to impress them.

Back in barracks afterwards, Smart said, 'Nice girl,' and Horrocks said, 'Very bright upstairs,' and they left it at that. After that she was not mentioned, proof of how strongly she had affected them.

She affected me, too. I had never met a girl like her. Women, so far in my experience (and probably in Smart's and Horrocks's too) came in two varieties. There was the sort that my comrades usually dated, the teetering, lipsticked, hair-primping, giggling and slapping sort; and then there was the sort I had taken out once or twice in the past, the respectable, proper, knees-together girls whose parents waited up for them when they went out and lurked behind the front-room curtains on their return to check for any possible snogging in the porch.

Both sorts operated by a code which, while it was different in detail one from the other, was equally rigid in both cases and had the same purpose. The result was that you never took out a girl who behaved naturally. Everything they said and did, every word and gesture, was nicely calculated for its effect on you: would it make you more, or less, likely to propose marriage? Every girl wanted to get married – *had* to get married. It was the mark of their success or failure as human beings. At first meeting they would size you up, and if you would 'do', the game began.

Smart's 'bints' had a slightly different method. They knew they had to give something, bait the trap. The Smart/Horrocks element knew a snog was certainly on at the end of an evening, after two or three gin-and-oranges. Early attempts to step up the game would be met with giggling protests, slaps and 'Get off', or 'Don't be daft'; but a snog there certainly had to be, if there was ever to be a second date. After that it was a war of attrition between bint and bloke. The bint had to calculate to a nicety how far the bloke could be allowed to go without spoiling her chances. If he was allowed to go too far, too soon, he might perhaps accept that he had been trapped, and propose, but on the other hand he might merely think she was 'too easy'.

I found it all rather depressing to observe – though Smart/Horrocks seemed to enjoy the battle of wits, and played with relish. Their philosophy was 'you don't know if you don't try' and 'you get a lot of slaps but you get a lot of kisses'.

But middle-class girls were just as regimented, and they didn't even feel they had to give you anything. You might go out for half a dozen dates before even getting a peck on the cheek. Most of all, I found it boring to be with someone who, when you asked her a question, would try to work out what you wanted to hear before answering, would pick the answer most calculated to bring you a step nearer the altar.

Why did we do it? The girls couldn't help it, poor things – they were brought up to behave like that, and after all, marriage was the only contemplatable future for most girls in the 1950s. But why did we men go through those awful motions? I suppose the biological urge to mate is too strong to resist, even at the cost of so much boredom.

But Jo was different. She was natural, eager, conversable. She said what she thought, laughed when she wanted to, argued if she disagreed. She looked you straight in the eyes when she spoke to you – she never knew how rare that was in anyone, let alone a woman. She didn't simper, giggle, flatter, or take umbrage over supposed breeches of etiquette. She *had* no etiquette. She always made me think of a wild animal, not in the sense of something fierce or untamed – though she could be both those things – but in the sense of a creature that behaved without artifice, driven by simple response, without fear of consequences. I suppose I was a fool to think that. I was pretty young myself. No-one is entirely free from the effects of the society in which they are reared. But she was unlike anyone I had ever met, and the more I saw of her, the more I wanted to be with her. I was fascinated by her, entranced, mesmerised. When I was away from her I thought about her all the time – not analytically, but in a sort of dream of adolescent bliss which elevated her above the human.

I spent every moment I could with her, and she seemed, marvellously, to be always available when I was. Sometimes it was a stolen half-hour, when all we could do was walk up one side of the lane and down the other. But when I had longer, we would get in the car and drive away from the camp, from Lulworth, from people in general. Dorset was wonderfully unpopulated in those days. Cars were few and we had the roads almost to ourselves; and wherever we stopped there was nothing to prevent us walking where we wanted. We could be alone, and we felt free.

We conversed all the time, about everything. I can't at this distance remember what we talked about, because there seemed no limits on it. All topics were equal, and despite the difference in our ages, we had an equality of mind that made it exciting and liberating. I knew more about social structures than her, politics, civics, the ways of man, the conventions of society. But she knew more about the physical world. She could tell me the names of all the flowers, the birds, the insects, the trees. She knew the ways of the fox, the badger, the owl, the hawk, what birds made their nests of, how crickets sang and glow-worms lighted themselves. When we wandered through fields or over clifftops, she was my guide. Bournemouth was not exactly inner-city, but nothing in my busy and blameless upgrowing had given me this sureness of touch and quickness of eye when it came to the land we lived in.

Holding hands we would brush through a waist-high field of grass and flowers, and she would point to some crimson winged thing on the end of a stem and tell me some fascinating story about it. Creatures seemed attracted to her: insects would obligingly crawl onto her finger to be closely observed; butterflies would settle on her hair as on a flower; birds didn't mind her; cows would come hopefully towards her across meadows; and every dog in Dorset seemed to know her, and would stop and smile and exchange a wag or two as we passed.

In this world of nature she gave off a flame of eagerness that lit a response in me. She shone gold with it, and I reflected her. All our days together rang with her. I lived in her wonder, and lost count of time. I hoped that she loved me as I was beginning to love her. But I never asked, or spoke of my feelings. There was something in her that I felt without having a name for it, or understanding it: a sense of tension somewhere deeply hidden but basic to her. If, through quietness and patience you somehow coaxed a wild deer to come stepping close, if you got it to trust you enough to eat out of your hand, you would still know that an incautious movement or sudden noise would have it bounding for cover. It would be gone before you had even registered the alarm. That was the feeling I had with her, that though she was happy in my company, something inside her was still alert for flight.

The Sunday arrived when I was to go to tea with her at her father's house. Since she had first suggested it, I had dreaded it. Meeting a girl's father was always a trial – but to meet the colonel himself! On the day, my oppos treated me with the silent sympathy reserved to a man condemned to be hanged. Sometimes I caught them watching me out of the corners of their eyes and discussing me in low voices, with sad shakes of the head. They avoided contact with a tart's family at all costs, for it was a recognised capitulation in the battle not to get married. They thought me a sap – but they also saw how it could have happened. She was different. How would you know what rules to play by with someone as different as that? As I prepared for execution, Horrocks cleaned my shoes for me, Weddell cleaned a spot off my tie, and Smart leant me his cut-throat, because the blade in my safety was past its best. Then they sat on their beds and watched me gloomily as I dressed with meticulous attention to detail.

At length Smart said, 'What are you going to say to him?'

'How should I know?' I said. 'It depends on what he's going to say to me.'

'Probably, "How dare you go out with my daughter?"' Smart suggested.

Horrocks said, with a nervous giggle, 'Suppose he says, "Are your intentions towards my daughter honourable?" You'd never have the nerve to say no.'

'Your goose is cooked, mate,' Weddell agreed sadly. 'That's what comes of dating posh tarts.'

'But she didn't seem posh at the start, that's the trouble,' said Horrocks.

'Not as posh as all that,' Smart agreed. 'Well, it's too late now.'

'We'll have a whip-round, help you buy the ring,' Horrocks suggested.

I told him where he could put his whip-round.

'It might not be half bad, you know, being married into that family,' Smart mused. 'Plenty of oscar, anyway.'

'I'm only going to tea,' I reminded him.

'Only!' Smart scoffed.

Horrocks hummed a few bars of the Dead March. 'Want the blindfold?'

'Maybe she won't be there,' Weddell said, as if offering hope.

He shouldn't have put it into my mind, for it bothered me all the way to the war memorial. But there she was, waiting for me, sitting on the monument's steps with her hands in her lap, as no other girl waiting for her date would have sat; not got up regardless (she was wearing a simple cotton frock that left her brown arms and legs bare), not fussing over how she looked, just waiting as you might wait for a friend. At that point it did not worry me that she might only see me as a friend. It was all too rare and precious to be anything but delightful and exciting.

I pulled up beside her and she smiled and climbed in next to me. 'Hello,' she said.

'Hello. Where to?'

'Straight on.' She settled herself with one foot up under her, her favourite position. No knees-together proper deportment for her.

'I feel rather nervous,' I said.

'There's no need for that. Daddy's a lamb.'

'A colonel lamb,' I pointed out.

'He'll love you.' She glanced sidelong at

me. 'Have your friends been getting at you?'

'They've been suggesting terrifying things he might say to me.'

She laughed. 'Don't worry, Daddy doesn't even own a shotgun.'

'Uncanny how you always know what I'm thinking.'

'Not uncanny at all,' she said, laying her hand over mine on the gear-stick. 'All you need is imagination. And love.'

As a young man, one was trained by one's contemporaries to shy away from that word, flinch at the mention of love. But I had been in love with her for weeks, and it thrilled rather than alarmed. And she said it so naturally, without fluster or archness, that I was more intrigued than gratified.

'Do you love me, then?' I asked.

She didn't look at me. 'I love everyone,' she said. 'Until they prove they're not worth loving. Of course I love you. You've never done anything to stop me.'

She had evaded the question. That wakeful eye inside her had made her jump away from my hand. I knew that, but I was not experienced enough to know why, or in what particular direction. There was a silence as I drove, and she gazed out of the window with that fresh interest in everything that she never disguised with world-weary sophistication. Once or twice she waved at people as we passed, and they waved and smiled back.

'Oh,' she said suddenly, 'I forgot to say – there's a special treat for you when we get home. Rob's home on leave. He arrived late last night – he was home when I got in. So you'll be able to meet him.'

Wonderful, I groaned inwardly. Not just a colonel father but a doting brother to inspect me. But she said it so much as if it really were a special treat that it made me smile all the same.

'I hope they'll like me,' I said. 'I should hate to let you down.'

'Of course they'll like you,' she said, sounding a little annoyed. 'Don't make such a fuss.'

'All right, I won't,' I placated her. Her warm, living hand crept over mine again and squeezed it, and we drove like that for a while.

Then she said, 'This is it. The white gate on the right.'

A sign, black lettering on a white board, said 'Roselands'.

'Just drive in – it's all right.'

There was a short, gravelled drive and then a sweep in front of the house, where I pulled up and parked in front of a long, white-stuccoed house. At first glance I took it for modern, nineteen thirties perhaps. Then as I got out and took in the proportions and the long windows I realised it was a genuine Regency villa, a rarity in this part of Dorset, and rather a lovely one.

'Do you like it?' she asked, watching my face as I stood back and scanned the façade.

'It's beautiful. The porch had me fooled for a moment – that's not original.'

'I know,' she said, 'but I'm glad you do.'

'And those shutters are all wrong.'

'The originals rotted, and Mummy had them replaced with those. She liked them. They don't close of course – they're just for show.'

'I know,' I said, 'but I'm glad you do. Was it a test?'

'You did say you'd studied architecture.'

'Nasty, underhand girl.'

She laughed. 'Come in and meet everyone.'

We trod up the two shallow steps to the front door, which was open, and passed through the inner glass door into the hall. At once a small, wiry woman appeared, wearing a neat print dress with an apron over it, her sandy-grey hair carefully 'permed', her face wreathed in smiles and dusted with freckles.

'Right on time,' she said, 'as usual.'

'Jean, this is Mr West. George, this is Jean, Daddy's housekeeper for years and years, and my friend.'

'How do you do, sir,' Jean said, shaking my hand with one small, hard and shiny from kitchen work. Her accent was Scots. She surveyed my face quickly but comprehensively as she did, and seemed to find me not too disappointing, for she smiled with what seemed like genuine warmth.

Jo watched this with a look of broad satisfaction, and then asked, 'Where is everybody?'

'They're in the drawing room. Go on in, now. I'll just bring in the tea.'

'Come on,' said Jo, catching at my hand with a child's eagerness to drag me away. She took me into one of the most pleasant rooms I've ever seen. It was long, with several windows and two pairs of french doors piercing one wall, looking onto the sunny garden. The floor was of parquet, covered in the middle by a dark blue Chinese carpet. The walls were of panelling painted plain white, except that round the top, between panelling and ceiling, ran a strip of plaster like a frieze, on which had been painted pretty rustic scenes of a Bouchard sort, which I longed to examine more closely. The colours were soft and faded and I guessed they had been done a long time ago. The furniture that stood around the room was solid and comfortable and rather pleasantly shabby – wing-back chairs with faded chintz covers, an enormous and much scarred leather chesterfield, useful tables and footstools placed for comfort. The furniture was well dusted and polished, but there were no flowers, ornaments or 'feminine touches' anywhere to be seen. It was a man's room – almost a bachelor's room: spacious, solid, unpretentious, comfortable.

The colonel rose at once from a chair, setting aside the newspaper, and advanced to meet me. I knew the look of him from his portrait, though he was quite a bit older now. He had a broad, fair, handsome face; clean shaven, which was unusual in those days for a man of his generation, and particularly a military man. The lines in it were the lines of authority, now softened by retirement, the mouth was firm, the gaze level. His eyes were dark, and his hair, though grey, was still thick – in his portrait it had been dark red-brown like the pelt of a fox. Though pouched with tiredness, the darkness of the eyes gave the face a vitality and almost animal magnetism that made it impossible to look away. Though the colouring was different, I saw Jo in his face and his air.

What I also saw, as he held out his hand to shake mine, was something akin to anxiety. I had expected sternness, a sort of forbidding scrutiny that asked me to prove my worth, that kept me on probation until I had shown I was worthy to know the colonel's daughter. I had not expected to have to smile reassuringly, as though the power were mine, and even as I did so, and placed my hand into the broad, warm palm, I understood, and liked him for it. *She* had not brought me home on probation: I was already hers; he had no veto, and he had known it. He had only feared lest she had given her friendship to someone who might hurt her, some callow adventurer who had deceived her extreme youth and inexperience.

There had been times in the past when I had wished I looked a little more raffish, a little more daredevil, quite a lot more Rhett Butler and a great deal less Ashley Wilkes. But now I blessed the plain, honest face my parents had bequeathed me, as the colonel scanned it and decided, endearingly visibly, that whatever else I might be, at all events I was not a poodle-faker.

'I've been looking forward to meeting you, Mr West. Josella described you as her friend, and since we seem to share the same taste in people, I was sure we would enjoy the occasion. My son, Robin.'

I had barely had a chance to notice the other figure that rose at the same time from a sofa across the room. Now as he advanced towards me and I was licensed to turn and look, I marvelled how such a person could be overshadowed even by Colonel Grace. Jo's Rob was tall, taller than his father, and gave an impression of slenderness, though he must have been muscular enough to be a serving soldier and an engineer. His skin was the same faint, clear gold as Jo's, his eyes the same pellucid grey; his hair was hers, soft and silvery as moonlight – though his was a little darkened with the preparation he had used to keep it down. She always had soft little tendrils escaping, but he was a soldier, and had to be neat. He shook my hand, and his eyes, which had that same long, far-horizon stare as hers, yet scanned me as probingly as had the colonel's; but his face gave away nothing of what he had expected or now thought. I knew from what Jo had told me that he was ten years older than her, but he looked much younger. The smooth, impassive face, the clarity of the skin and eyes – above all that marvellous beauty, made him seem at once ageless and almost boyish. It would never have occurred to me before to talk of a man's beauty, but the word came into my mind unbidden. His was that fragile beauty of the youth just passing into manhood, which is somehow heart-breaking, as if one knew it was doomed.

He said, 'How do you do,' and did not smile, but I sensed no hostility from him, only caution.

Jo went to each of them, and hugged and kissed each as if she had been gone years rather than minutes. It was charming to me, coming from a class that was sparing with embraces. My father and mother had been devoted to each other, but I did not remember ever seeing them touch each other: that was for when they were alone together.

My mother kissed me goodnight when she tucked me into bed as a little boy; my father had sometimes ruffled my hair in passing. But that was it. Perhaps if I'd had a sister... At all events, I liked it that she kissed them, and even more that they kissed her back.

She turned, pulling Rob's arm round her shoulder like a cardigan, and faced me.

'Well, didn't I tell you about Rob? Isn't he simply stunning?'

'Don't embarrass your brother,' the colonel chided, but smilingly. 'When will you ever learn proper manners?'

'If you mean pretending Rob is ordinary, not till I'm dead,' Jo responded.

'Mr West, please sit down,' said the colonel, and we all sat, Jo balancing herself on her brother's chair arm. 'You'll forgive the over-enthusiasm of a sister.'

'I never had a sister,' I said, 'but if I did, I hope she'd care for me as much.'

It seemed to have been the right thing to say. The colonel smiled. 'Josella tells me you studied architecture?'

'At university, yes,' I said.

'Is that what you want to do when you've finished your National Service?'

I had no chance to answer, because Jo interrupted, 'Oh Daddy, don't question him like a Victorian father. What do you think of this room, George? Isn't it heaven?'

'I like it very much,' I said, 'but architecturally, it puzzles me.'

'It used to be the orangery,' the colonel said. 'One of the owners long past changed it into a ladies' sitting room and the Victorians built the second storey above. The drawing room proper is on the other side of the house, but we found it too dark, so we've never used it. We always call this the drawing room.'

'Yes, I see,' I said. Everything was now clear. 'Have you lived here long?'

'It hasn't been in our family for generations, if that's what you mean,' Rob answered for him.

'I bought it in 1920, when I married,' said the colonel. 'One of the difficulties of army life is that one moves around too much to put down proper roots. I bought this place so that my children at least would have a place they could regard as home. It's an interesting house. I took some trouble to learn its history. You noticed the frescoes, of course?'

I nodded, not liking to point out to him fresco meant something specific that these were not.

'Come and have a closer look,' Jo said, jumping up.

'They were done by one of the ladies of the house in about 1850,' the colonel said. 'Poor thing, she was confined to the house, and it was for her that this room was made a sitting room. She passed her time with painting and sewing, and the frescoes were some of her work. I don't suppose they are particularly good work, but one thinks of her, you know, doing them.'

'Was she ill?' I asked.

'I don't know,' said the colonel.

'It doesn't say anywhere that she was, only that she was confined to the house,' Jo said at my side. 'I think she was probably mad and locked up, like Caroline Lamb.'

It didn't look like the work of a mad-woman. The paintings were soft and pretty, wistful, perhaps one might say. Not out-standing work, but good enough.

'This is my favourite one, with the dog,' she said. In a garden scene, a King Charles spaniel frisked after a rather out-of-propor-tion rabbit.

'I suppose that was her dog,' I said. 'The mad lady's.'

'But if it was, she'd have surely painted it more than once. No, I think it was a dog she'd had once, long ago, and lost. Don't you think? See how unsubstantial he looks – a ghost dog.'

'You talk more nonsense, child, than anyone I know,' said the colonel.

The housekeeper brought the tea in just then, on a trolley. It was the sort of tea you read about in books, with little savoury sand-wiches, hot buttered toast, and two kinds of cake. I was impressed. Jean poured out and Jo handed round and then we sat round, Jo and Rob side by side on the leather sofa, looking ethereal, like two Olympians paying a visit to earth; the colonel and I faced them in two armchairs. Jean looked around to check everything was in order and then disappeared, and a silence fell.

The colonel cleared his throat. 'Well, well,' he said. 'Awkward business, meeting people's families for the first time. Difficult not to be formal.'

'Jo told me not to be nervous, but she'd talked so much about you I was terrified,' I said. I cursed myself for it at once – what a daft thing to say! – but the colonel didn't seem to mind it.

He smiled. 'Thought you'd find an adoring father and brother sizing you up and finding you falling short of the mark?'

'Something like that,' I said, feeling my blush subside a little.

'You were right about the adoring father, at least, but as to the rest – well, one has learnt to trust her taste somewhat.' Though he said it, he sounded as though there were a doubt in his mind somewhere.

'Please don't talk about me as if I wasn't here,' Jo said. 'Rob, how long are you staying? I haven't had a chance to ask you yet.'

'A week,' he said. 'I'll have to go back next Sunday.'

'I think Jo said you were out in Malaya?' I said.

'That's right. Construction work at Port Dickson.'

'I was in Kuala Lumpur last year,' I said. We chatted a little about conditions out there, and I saw it put both the men at ease, this reminder that I was a soldier too, even if only temporarily. Jo watched, her eyes going from face to face, with an air of amusement, as if she had engineered the whole thing. The conversation slid from there inevitably into politics, the left-overs from the war, Palestine, Korea, Suez. Jo began to look bored.

'If you've finished with tea, do come out and look at the garden,' she said, jumping up, and we put aside our cups and plates and obeyed, as one would the importunings of a puppy. Beyond the french windows was a wide sweep of lawn, edged by beds of perennials, the sort of garden one sees on jigsaw puzzles and chocolate boxes, with roses and hollyhocks and lavender and delphiniums. The air was soft and golden, thrumming with bees, and we strolled and looked at the flowers, and Jo told me the names of all of them. We hadn't had much of a garden back home, and all my life that I remembered, the small space had been crowded with cabbages and carrots and runner beans. Garden flowers were a mystery to me.

'How sad,' she said, when I told her. 'I

know vegetables are practical, but there ought to be room in everyone's life for beauty as well.'

'I dare say my father thought a cabbage just as beautiful as a cabbage-rose,' I told her, and then, afraid I might have offended the colonel, I added, 'But this is lovely. Someone has taken a great deal of trouble with it.'

'Not me, I'm sorry to say. It was planned and planted like this when I bought the house. We've had to simplify a little, over the years, of course. The park's all gone now. I do a little mowing and weeding from time to time, but nowadays it's mostly Jean who takes care of it. She loves to potter about out here.'

'She says it's a change from sweltering in the kitchen,' said Jo.

'But I do often think I ought to start taking an interest,' said the colonel. 'It's a suitable occupation for an old gentleman.'

'Old!' Jo cried, mockingly, but I saw her brother cast a quick glance in the colonel's direction. The sunshine, which lit Jo to a glorious, healthy glow, only showed up the pallor and weariness in her father's face.

The colonel took out a cigarette case and offered it round. As he breathed out the first cloud of smoke, Jo drew near him, holding his arm and sniffing happily.

'I love the smell when you first light it.

After that, it starts to smell horrid.'

'Turkish,' said the colonel, examining the burning end. 'Robin brings them back for me. I believe you can get them in London, too, but out here in the back of beyond—'

'Don't insult Dorset,' Jo warned him. 'I love it here. I never want to live anywhere else. George takes me out in his car and shows me all the wonderful countryside. You love it too, don't you, George?'

'You know Dorset well?' the colonel asked.

'I was born and bred in Bournemouth, and never came here until I was posted here. The places I drive to are as new to me. It's Jo who shows them to me.'

'Why do you call her Jo?' Rob asked suddenly.

I was startled. It sounded like a criticism. 'I don't know. It just happened that way.'

'A creature of many parts, is my Josella,' the colonel said. 'Everyone seems to have a different name for her. I've never got used to it, myself.' He smiled down at her. 'Don't you find it confusing?'

'No,' she said. 'I feel different with different people, so it seems natural they'd have different names for me. When I'm with you I feel like Josella, and with George I feel like Jo. And with Rob—'

'You've always been skinny-malink,' he completed for her. It must have been an old tease, for she flew at him. He ran away, laughing, and they chased round the garden like children.

I strolled on with the colonel, feeling, because of the division, oddly aged. He began to talk to me about the regiment and camp affairs, and we conversed comfortably on those subjects until we reached the end of the walk and turned back. Jo and Rob were still frolicking on the far side. The colonel narrowed his eyes against the sun to study them, and said, 'It hasn't always been easy, bringing up a girl without a mother.'

'I imagine not,' I said, and was about to say he had done a good job, when I realised that would sound both proprietorial and patronising.

'I believe in young people being allowed to make their own mistakes. That's the line I've always taken in my commands. Now I'm trying to take it with my own children, too. But it's much harder when it's a beloved daughter. Then one finds one can't prevent oneself stepping in.'

Was he stepping in now? Was I unsuitable? I found my mouth dry at the prospect of being warned off. Not only the embarrassment and shame of it, but the thought of not seeing her again.

He looked at me, holding my eyes. I made myself return the look steadily.

'We are alike in some ways, Josella and I. We make up our minds quickly about people. She told me you would do, and I agree with her.'

Relief made my legs feel weak. 'Thank you, sir,' I said.

He smiled, a different sort of smile from before, a colonel's smile, with a bit of steel in it somewhere. 'The man who doesn't let me down has nothing to fear,' he said. It interested me that he said it that way round, rather than the obvious corollary – the man who lets me down has much to fear. Was he a man who preferred to promise rather than threaten – or was it because I wasn't actually serving under him, so in point of law he couldn't threaten me?

'I think the world of her,' I said, rather weakly, but he nodded as if that was enough.

Jo and Rob had come back to join us. Jo looked quickly from one of us to the other, as if trying to gauge what had been said, before saying, 'I think we should all go riding next Saturday, before Rob has to go back. The four of us.'

'Oh, do you ride?' the colonel asked me.

I caught Jo's eye and answered, 'Yes.'

'That's better,' she laughed approvingly. It pleased me that we had an esoteric joke already.

'But I don't have any riding clothes,' I added.

'That doesn't matter. We won't dress up,' Jo said. 'You must have jeans.' What young man did not? 'Jeans and a sweater will be all right.'

'We only have two horses,' Rob pointed out.

'Why don't you and Mr West go, Josella?' the colonel suggested.

'Oh, don't bother about me,' I said hastily. 'Jo should go with her brother while she has the chance.'

'The point is,' Jo said patiently, 'that I want us all to go together. Horses aren't a problem – goodness, the place is *littered* with them. We can borrow Vanguard from Sir Hugh. You can ring him tonight, can't you, Daddy? And I know Mrs Weldon will lend us Secret. She never manages to give her enough exercise.'

'Well, if you insist,' said the colonel.

'I do. George can ride Secret,' Jo added with an air of innocence.

The colonel looked at me quizzically. 'I don't know if that's a compliment to your horsemanship, or if Josella is planning a practical joke. Secret is the most difficult horse in the district.'

'In the county,' Jo laughed. 'Especially when she hasn't been out.'

'Hot as Hades,' Rob mentioned.

'It's a practical joke,' I said. 'Definitely.'

'Very well, then, my girl,' the colonel said grimly, '*you* shall ride Secret, and I hope you can't sit down for a week.'

Soon afterwards I took my leave, and Jo said she would ride down to the bottom of the hill with me, for the sake of the walk up. The men parted with me on pleasantly friendly terms, and as soon as we were in the car and out of earshot, I turned to her and said, 'What was all that about, the riding?'

'I want to do it. Besides, it will consolidate you with them,' she said. 'Make them see that you're the right sort of person.'

'Not if I fall off and make an ass of myself,' I said. 'I haven't ridden since I was about seven.'

'You won't fall off.'

'Anyway, right sort of person for what?' I caught up with her remark.

'To associate with Miss Josella Emily Grace, of course. Daddy worries about me so, poor lamb.'

'Your father is not a poor lamb,' I advised her firmly.

'Oh, but he is. You don't know the half of it. But they like you already, don't worry. I knew they would. Well, I knew Daddy would. Rob is slower to take to people, and he's very jealous of me – just as I was about his girlfriends. They had to be good enough in my eyes. But I could see he liked you.'

'You could see more than me.'

'I should hope so, with my own family.'

We were at the bottom of the hill. I stopped the car, and she twisted round in the seat to face me. 'Kiss me,' she commanded.

I complied, and it drove everything else out of my thoughts, including any possible dread of the following weekend's trial. When at last we broke apart, she stared at me a moment with a sort of drowned look, and then snapped back into normality.

'Bye!' she said briskly, and jumped out of the car in one movement. She was halfway back up the hill before I had even got into gear again.

Chapter Six: 1964

Joey was a success as a barmaid, and so she was happy, for there was nothing she liked better than doing something well. When she was working switchboards, she liked people to watch her, so that she could feel how complicated they thought it was. So now, she loved to have customers leaning on the bar watching her pull pints and flick caps off bottles with a twist of the wrist. There was never any shortage of audience for her. The bar was crowded most nights of the week, and she was good-looking and lively and enjoyed a chat, which was all a barmaid needed to be.

She had settled in with the company now, and even Paul had accepted her presence and no longer regarded her as a hanger-on. She usually got up around eleven, did some superficial tidying-up, made coffee and toast for everyone, which they ate sitting around the living room and yawning, and then, having done the washing-up from the night before, she would leave them to come back to life slowly and go downstairs to the bar, in time to open at twelve. Ann, Roddy, Guy and Paul always went to Deac's at lunchtime, so she didn't see them again until the bar closed at two, when they came back for rehearsal. When she had cleaned up and washed the glasses she would slip through to the theatre to watch. Andrew liked her to be there, because there were always little jobs for her to do: fetching and carrying, helping with the scenery and props, prompting. When they did the first read-through of the new *Dracula* production, she read-in the other female part, for which he would have to import another actress. And she was the only person apart from him and the electrician, who only came in the evenings, who knew how to work the lighting box.

Making herself useful made her feel more a part of them, gave her the justification for hanging round, and joining them when they went to eat or for a drink. She wanted most of all to belong. After rehearsing, the company went through into the club for a meal, and then sat round in the bar drinking and talking to each other and the few privileged members and friends who were allowed to use the bar out of hours.

The club officially reopened at five thirty, and was always busy, for the students had no restraints on their time at that hour of the day. The performance began at seven thirty, and apart from the brief moment in the interval when one of the actors would come in to collect their drinks, she did not see the company again until the performance ended. Then, when they had changed and cleaned off their make-up, they would come through and drink bottled Guinness until closing-time. After that, when Joey had cleared up, they would take a couple of bottles of cheap wine and ascend the stairs to the flat with a few friends, to play records, drink, talk – sometimes even play games – until the small hours. Joey loved these times best of all. It was as though life were a perpetual party. The company was young, and in love with itself and its own humour; it had all the time in the world, and was – or seemed – ignorant of the strain and rush that held the rest of the population in thrall seven days a week. Even the fact that she had prescribed working hours did not seem to have the same significance as it did when she was in London.

At last, when the drink ran out, and everyone grew sleepy, and the dead cold of three in the morning gripped them with its lassitude, the talk would thin and stop, and someone would give in and yawn and say they were going to bed. Then the party would break up. Any hangers-on would be given blankets, and the rest of them would go to their rooms. Joey would wander with Guy into the grateful warmth of his little animal den, strip off quickly and jump into his bed where, snuggling in to his shoulder, she would fall instantly and deeply asleep. Guy was a comforting person to be with – always loving and affectionate, full of easy kisses, smiles, little pats and kind words – but never demanding. With him she could have the unparalleled physical comfort of being hugged and cuddled as often as she wanted without any of the tiresome complications of passion – the misunderstandings, quarrels, questions and doubts. Always when she came here, she was sure she would never go away. Where could life ever be better? Where could she ever be more comfortable?

April in Edinburgh was not a good month for weather, tending to bring sheets of icy rain and sleet beating in from the east on Siberian winds. There were just two afternoons nice enough to go out. One they spent sitting on Castle Rock; on the other they went to Silverknowes in Andrew's car and sat on the beach where, though sunny, it was still too cold to sit long, and they were soon driven to take shelter in Andrew's blocky little modern house, where his glorious wife gave them tea and crumpets. For the rest, Joey hardly left the environs of the theatre. There was nothing to go out for. It held all she wanted – companionship, food, and belonging.

When the new month came, the company was to take the play to Glasgow, to its sister theatre, for a fortnight, while a commercial company used the Transom Theatre. Joey felt so much a part of the company that she assumed without even thinking about it that she would be going with them. So, apparently, did the others, for when Roddy broke the news, which he had learned from Andrew, they were indignant.

'Of course Joey must come!' Ann exclaimed. 'She does as much as anyone – dressing, make-up, lighting, scenery. We couldn't manage without her.'

'I know that,' Roddy said. 'Don't go on at me. I want her to come, too.'

'Who's going to take charge of the properties?' Guy said. 'Joey's acting unpaid props manager for this show.'

'And we're going to be reading *Dracula* while we're there,' Ann added. 'Who's going to read Mina?'

'Andrew's getting Helen Burns from the Cit's in to do the part, and she'll be rehearsing with us,' Roddy said. 'Look, I feel the same, but Andrew says she's bar staff and that's that.'

'Andrew's a BF,' said Ann. 'As if he could not get some student to stand in at the bar for a week. We need her much more.'

'Andrew doesn't like hangers-on, that's the truth of it,' said Paul wisely.

Joey sighed and said, 'I really wish I could go with you, but there's nothing to be done about it. Andrew's the boss, and what he says goes.'

'Not if we went on strike, it wouldn't,' said Guy.

There was a silence, as everyone stared at him, and then Joey said quickly, 'Don't be silly, you can't do that.' All the eyes came round to her. The scenario was clear in their heads – them standing up to Andrew, him shrugging and saying in that case he'd get other actors in. The power was all with him, and even though he behaved like a student, he was a businessman at heart. The chronic but justified insecurity of actors vied feebly with their loyalty to Joey, and she hastened to stop the struggle before it was lost. 'I wouldn't let you do that,' she said firmly.

They did not quite sigh, but she saw the relief in their eyes that she was not going to take Guy up on his unguarded suggestion.

'After all, we've managed without her before and we'll manage without her again,' Paul said reasonably.

'You could always come over on your own if you want to,' Roddy said. 'No-one can stop you walking out of the job.'

'I couldn't do that,' Joey said. 'Andrew wouldn't let me stay with you if I let him down here. No, I'll just stay here. It's only two weeks.'

When they had gone, Joey quickly slipped into a new routine, going to bed as soon as she'd closed up the bar, and getting up early. In consequence she had a lot of time to herself during the day. She took to wandering about the city, revisiting old haunts, trying to find old friends. In the last she failed: people she had known before were part of the town's shifting population, students, or young people trying out life away from their parents for the short time before they went home to Perth or Ayr or Jedburgh and settled down and married. She sat in cafés: Brattisani's and Rossi's, the milkbar at Surgeon's Hall, the café in Buccleuch Street where the lorry drivers stopped for tea and mutton-pie and beans. She wandered over the Meadows and George Square Gardens, she strolled along the Grassmarket and Leith walk; she looked in at the billiard hall in Manse Road and the common room in the Old Quad; but nowhere could she find any familiar faces, nowhere did any voice hail her, 'Joey! Long time no see! What're you doing here?'

Life – that species of it known generally to its prisoners as Real Life – had claimed them, while she had remained free. Little houses and jobs, marriage and children, cars and respectability and bridge and dinner parties had happened to them. The males were joining golf clubs and the females were getting perms. She became aware of an extraordinary feeling, which after some thought she tracked down as loneliness. How strange! She had rarely felt it before. It made her glad to go back to work, to the warm, noisy atmosphere of the bar where her acquaintances of a week would always greet her with the ready affection of the young and fluid. Some of the young males, knowing that while she was generally thought to be 'Guy's girl', he was both notoriously easy-going and absent, tried to get off with her, asked her out for meals or drinks. She was not in the least tempted, though to assuage their pride she would sometimes stay on after closing for half an hour for a chat before yawning and making her excuses.

After all, it was only two weeks. And at last the company was back, flowing like water back into the spaces they had occupied, full of themselves and of the events of Glasgow.

Long practice had made them adept at drawing the last ounce of conversational value out of the smallest occurrence. Joey went upstairs with them after closing-time on the first evening back, carrying two bottles of the usual Spanish 'plonk', and felt strangely left out.

'I thought I was going to die when you dried in the last scene,' Ann was saying to Paul. 'Whatever were you thinking about?'

'Well, actually, I was thinking about fishing,' he answered. 'There's a lovely rod in a shop in the Mile, but it's way too expensive, but I've seen a similar one in a junk shop, and I was wondering what condition it would be in.'

'You really are the limit,' Ann said, laughing.

'*You* should complain! How do you think I felt when I came back from mentally rebinding it and found myself facing you on a stage and no idea even what *play* I was in, never mind what my line was!'

'I thought your eyes were going to fall out, they bulged so much,' Guy murmured.

'Yes,' said Ann, 'but I'd just gone through two pages of passionate build-up, worked myself up to screaming pitch, turned round ready for you to stab me, and all you did was stare at me with your mouth open. Talk about falling off a cliff.'

'You shouldn't take it so seriously,' Roddy

drawled, throwing himself down across the sofa. 'The play is such a piece of crap, you can't get worked up about a scene like that.'

'That's just the point,' Ann said, clasping her hands behind her head. 'To get any sort of pace you've got to get yourself worked up, otherwise the whole thing becomes a farce.'

'It's a farce anyway,' said Paul. 'Did you hear the laughter last night when I stabbed you?'

'Actually, with a bit of rewriting, it could make very good comedy,' said Guy. He was acting as barman, and carried two glasses over to where Joey was sitting, handed her one, and perched on the arm of the chair with the other.

'I don't remember any stabbing in *The Ghost*,' Joey said.

'Oh, this wasn't *The Ghost*,' Guy said. 'It didn't go down terribly well over there, so after the first week we changed the programme, and revived *Mirror for the Mad*.'

'Oh, gosh, yes, I remember that,' Joey said. 'You did that last year.'

The others were still talking about Paul's dry. 'Actually, I think it worked quite well,' Roddy said. 'It just looked as though you were so stunned by her screaming you were frozen with rage, or horror, or something.'

'Make your mind up,' said Paul.

'Anyway,' said Guy, 'Pinter next, so we can forget about *Mirror* – until the next time.'

Ann groaned. 'Oh, Pinter! Don't remind me.'

'You've got some great lines,' Guy said. 'You succulent old washing-bag, you.'

'All right for you,' she grumbled. 'You're not going to be stuck in this dead-end hole for the rest of your career. I'm going to grow old and wrinkled in thrall to Andrew and his students.'

'You'll get married,' Paul said. 'There's always your fan in the front row.' This was a strange little man in glasses and a peculiar taste in ties who bought a ticket for every performance and gazed at Ann in rapture the whole way through.

'God! I'd forgotten him,' Ann said. 'It was so nice in Glasgow, not having him leering at me.'

'He doesn't leer, he adores,' Roddy laughed. 'I think he's working himself up to a proposal. He'll do it at the end of the Pinter run – you know how the sight of you in a head rag inflames him—'

'And then he'll propose every night for the rest of your life until you accept him out of desperation,' Guy concluded.

'All right for you!' Ann said again in impotent fury. 'Golden boy!'

'Director's pet!' Guy retorted, laughing.

Joey listened, with nothing to contribute as they rambled through their fantasies and finally came back to real events and discussed the Pinter, the new girl Helen Burns, the return of an old colleague, Toby Salmon, for *Dracula*, the costumes for it, and Andrew's parsimony – a perennial subject. It was basic theatre talk, such as she'd heard hundreds of times before; but suddenly it seemed flat to her, uninteresting. It had lost its magic. Guy was sitting beside her with his arm round her shoulders, but the arm was only so much meat – she could draw no warmth from it. She felt he had put it there out of habit, and that he was hardly really aware of her presence.

Later they retired to bed, and as she sat on the mattress and watched him strip off, he must have noticed that her expression was not as usual, for he suddenly stopped what he was doing, sat down beside her half-dressed, and said, 'What's the matter, Joey? Don't you feel well?'

'I'm all right.'

'But you're very quiet. You hardly said a word all night.'

'I didn't really have anything to say. How could I? You were talking about what happened in Glasgow, and I wasn't there.'

'True,' he said, and stood up to continue to undress. His thought processes were not swift, but when he was naked and had climbed into bed and turned off the light, he said, 'Were you sulking about that, then?'

'I wasn't sulking,' she denied, a little

annoyed. 'I never sulk. It was just – that I felt like an outsider.'

'Well, you are an outsider,' Guy said reasonably.

He didn't mean to be hurtful, it was just his way. And yet only a fortnight before he had been arguing that she was as much a part of the company as anyone. Never expect logic from an actor, she told herself.

'I suppose I am,' she said. She was silent a moment, and then something else occurred to her. 'What did Ann mean when she said to you, "All right for you"?'

'Did she?'

'She said it twice. When she was talking about growing old and wrinkled in the Transom. She said it was all right for *you*.'

'Oh. Yes,' he said vaguely. 'I dunno. Maybe she meant because I've got a telly.'

'What?' She was stunned. To 'get a telly' was the ambition of them all: it was the chance of a big break, the chance to get on, to get noticed – to get decent pay, for that matter. Paul had had a couple of tellys: one had been an advert, where he had played an animated, dancing carrot destined for soup; but the other had been a tiny part in a hospital drama series. He'd been a patient in a hospital bed, and he'd had two lines: 'What are my chances, doctor?' and 'Oh God! I can't believe it!' Sometimes the others would chant them at him, just to annoy him. But however inglorious, a telly was a telly, and Guy must have been thrilled and delighted with the news. She couldn't believe he hadn't mentioned it to her.

'What telly?' she asked. 'When did you hear? What is it, an advert?'

'No,' he said, his voice sounding furry with pleasure in the darkness. 'I heard about it last week, in Glasgow – my agent phoned Andrew.'

'I didn't know you had an agent.'

'Course I have. Everyone has. But she doesn't often get me stuff. But this time, she came up trumps. It's a new drama series on BBC, about the police. There are two teams of two coppers, and they follow one team on alternate weeks. It's going to be very up-to-the-moment and topical.'

'It sounds exciting. And what's your part?'

'Well, there are these two teams, like I said. Four leads – and I'm one of them.'

She was stunned into silence. She had expected him to describe a minor role, perhaps a walk-on, or perhaps with a few lines. A few lines would be terrific. But this – a lead in an ongoing series? This was huge!

'That's fantastic,' she said at last.

'Yeah,' he said happily. 'She – my agent – reckons it could be really big, the series. There's been nothing like it before. It's not going to be cosy, like *Dixon of Dock Green*. Controversial, she said.'

'And controversial can make you famous,' Joey said. 'I can't believe you didn't tell me.'

'I'm telling you now,' he said fairly.

'When do you start?'

'End of July, the filming starts.'

'Well, it's fantastic,' she said again. 'Congratulations.'

He grunted in reply, because he was falling asleep. He always slept easily, slipping out of consciousness with the simple innocence of a child. But she was wide awake. She pictured in her mind his smooth, impassive face and kindly smile, which looked for her exactly the way it looked for everyone else. Around the theatre they said she was 'Guy's girl', but was she? She hunted through memory to find anything he had ever said or done that would suggest that he was aware of her being her, and not anyone else. He had just had the best news of his life, and he had not thought to tell her.

'What do you think about me?' she asked aloud.

'Hnngh?' he answered.

'Did you miss me last week? Do you think of me as your girl?'

His voice was blurred with sleep. She could hardly catch the words.

'—think of you at all—'

And then he was gone, without a sigh; peacefully asleep, snoring softly and rhythmically.

She lay with her head on his shoulder, pressed close to him for warmth. *I don't think of you at all* – was that what he had said? He didn't mean it unkindly, she knew that. He never meant to be unkind to anyone. He probably was fond of her, as fond as he was of anyone. He was inscrutable – that's what Ann said about him. But she had thought she belonged, and she didn't really. It didn't make any difference to Guy, to any of them, whether she was here or not. Well, that's what she had always said she wanted, wasn't it? To come and go without remorse, to be anonymous, to have no entanglements, to be free.

It was May, and down south the weather would already be warm. It was time to move on. As soon as she thought that, her feelings eased. Movement was the antidote to all poison of the mind. Feeling bored, feeling miserable? Move on, move on! Travel, trains, journeys that never ended, because they were only stages of a longer journey that never resolved itself into any conclusion; new faces, new places, new conversations – always new. That's what she needed. Yes, it was time to go. She would leave tomorrow – why wait? Do what you want, when you want. That was the way to live. The only way to live.

Comforted, she drifted off to sleep, her mind already plotting the journey and envisaging the movement. But the last thought she was aware of before sleep claimed her was that Edinburgh and the Transom Theatre were finished for her. She would never come back here again.

Chapter Seven: 1954

It took all my willpower to make myself go to the meeting place that afternoon when I was to ride with the Graces. Smart, Horrocks and Co were all at the regular football session, in which I had fortunately long established that I had no interest. They left me reading on my bed as usual, saying that I might go out for a drive later. I had not dared tell them the truth, because I knew they would think I was stepping out of my class.

I thought so too – or at least, I thought I was doing an unwise thing and would end up with egg all over my face. The Graces had doubtless been riding since being put onto their first pony by their nanny at the age of two. It was in their blood. They had probably hunted and everything. I didn't come from the sort of people who had things in their blood. I was a boy from a back-street terrace in Bournemouth. I had only been on a riding-school pony a few times, and a beach pony a few times more.

Look, about this class thing: it wasn't a big deal with me. I had been brought up the son of a railway worker, with the robust and level-headed views of the respectable working classes. My father was a Union man, but not a militant one: he offered respect and courtesy to all people, and subservience to none. It wasn't that I thought the Graces were better than me. I had no inappropriate feelings of deference towards them. Nor – it might as well be said here – did I think *I* was better than *them*. That's the modern snobbery, and quite as bad as the other sort, in my view. No, it was just that we were different, and there was no getting away from it. Because of my scholarship to boarding school and then my time at university, I had moved a little away from the sphere in which I was born. I could meet and talk on terms with anyone. I was quite capable of going to tea with the highest in the land, and I had no deep-seated insecurities about cutlery. But going riding was an entirely different kettle of fish.

I thought long and hard about cancelling. I didn't want to make a fool of myself. But if I cancelled, I felt that Jo would know why, and she would despise me for a coward. Perhaps she would refuse to see me again – and when I contemplated that possibility, I knew that I very much did *not* want to lose her. All right: so look on this as a trial; the Gauge of Love, the Chivalric Ordeal you have to go through to deserve the lady.

In jeans and a sweater I drove to the war memorial, and the sight of Jo in neat jodhpurs and boots and a yellow flannel shirt did nothing to calm my fears.

'You said you wouldn't dress up,' I accused her by way of greeting.

'I'm not. But jodhs are so much more comfortable for riding than jeans. It would be foolish to be uncomfortable for no good reason. After all, you *know* I own riding clothes. You've seen me in them.'

'Piker,' I said. I let her into the car and leaned over to kiss her.

'None of that,' she said. 'Equitation is an activity only to be followed by the pure in heart. Besides, you'll get lipstick on you.'

'Lipstick!' I saw it now. I had never seen her wear any kind of make-up before. It was one of the things that made her look younger than she was.

'Just a touch. I usually do, in riding clothes. To stop me looking too mannish.'

'Yes, you should worry about that,' I assured her gravely. Her hair was in its thick plait, the fronds around her brows escaping silkily; her breasts moved under her soft shirt

133

with her breathing. My pulse was unruly, and I felt such importunate stirrings I wished we were going anywhere but to meet her father and brother.

They were waiting for us outside the front door, and I noticed with relief that Rob, more considerate of the outsider's feelings than Jo, was wearing jeans and a polo-necked jumper. The colonel was in breeches and boots, though one could hardly have expected him to be otherwise; but even he had topped it with a sweater rather than a jacket.

'All fit?' the colonel greeted me as I stepped out of the car. Perhaps I looked my doubts, for he said, 'Do say if you want to change your mind. Riding is meant to be a pleasure, not a toil.'

'No, I'm really looking forward to it,' I said, and meant it now – more or less. 'But I haven't ridden for so long, I'm afraid I shan't be able to keep up with you.'

'I shan't be doing anything dashing today, I assure you,' said the colonel kindly. 'If those two want to tear off, they can, but you and I can bring up a leisurely rear and enjoy the scenery. An amble on horseback over the downs is all I want at my age.'

'That sounds good to me, sir,' I said.

We walked together, crunching over the gravel, around the house and through a small walled kitchen garden at the back. It was neglected and unplanted, the marked-off beds rampant with weeds, and the tall, brittle ghosts of seed-heads. The paths were blurred with greenery, the espaliered fruit trees shapeless. A blackbird rocketed out of a thicket of untamed raspberry canes with a wild cry of annoyance. Climbing roses waved lethally clawed shoots at us as we passed, trying to catch our hair and scratch our faces. Thoughts of *Sleeping Beauty*, and *The Secret Garden*, filled my mind.

The colonel saw me looking and said, 'It's a shame, but you need two full-time gardeners to keep up a place like this. We only have one, and then only part time.'

'Besides,' said Rob, 'if you kept it up, what would you do with all the produce? You never entertain any more.'

An arched gateway in the further wall took us into the stableyard. Here, too, there were signs of neglect. It was a large establishment with room for about twenty horses, but was obviously only partly used. One whole range of stables was falling into ruin, and only the end two boxes of the other range looked well kept, with fresh paint on the doors and no grass in the gutters. There were horses looking over the half doors of the two boxes, and two other animals, fully tacked up, were tied to rings in the wall next to them. I recognised Mistral, looking over one door; from the other box a lean white head stared out with pricked ears and large, dark eyes. The tethered horses were both bays, one considerably larger than the other.

'I thought you'd do best on Tambour,' the colonel said. 'He's very nicely mannered, and he's had plenty of exercise this week, so he should be quiet.'

I was relieved to discover this was the smaller of the bays. Rob went to him and tightened the girth, then untied him and held him courteously while I prepared to mount. It seemed a long way up, and jeans being made of inflexible material, I wasn't sure I would be able to get my foot up high enough to reach the stirrup. But as I hesitated, Jo came up behind me and said, 'Bend your leg, and I'll throw you up. You can't mount properly in jeans.'

I bent my knee, felt her cupped hands under it, and then she counted to three and flung me briskly up as I jumped. I managed to get my leg across and settled myself with rather a thump in the saddle. The horse, to my relief, showed no resentment of my ineptitude, other than turning its ears back at me. Rob quietly questioned me about the length of my stirrups, altered them for me, checked the girth again, and left me with a reassuring smile and a pat on the horse's neck. I felt stiff and awkward and too far off the ground. Tambour sighed deeply and seemed to go back to sleep, which suited me just fine.

The colonel, meanwhile, had untied the larger bay – the borrowed Vanguard – and got himself mounted. Rob brought Mistral out from his box and, despite what Jo had said, mounted like a bird, jeans or no jeans. Then cocking his left leg forward over the horse's shoulder he proceeded to tighten the girth while mounted, an exhibition of casual expertise that impressed me far more than if he had jumped a five-bar gate on the beast.

Meanwhile the owner of the white head had been beating an impatient tattoo on the loose-box door with a forefoot. Jo went inside, the head vanished, and there was a lot of clattering and some muffled exclamations. Then the door banged open and Jo reappeared, towed out at speed by a small white horse freckled all over with brown and black. The horse had its head up and its ears back, and once outside began to waltz round in tight circles while Jo revolved with it, trying to pull down the stirrup. I watched in wonder as somewhere in the fifth revolution she shot up into the air and by the middle of the sixth was in the saddle, adjusting the reins and finding the other stirrup by feel.

'Hot as Hades,' Rob observed. 'She's a nice mare but she doesn't get anywhere near enough exercise.'

'Mrs Weldon ought to sell her,' Jo said rather bumpily as she was swung round and round.

'Not to you, please God,' the colonel murmured, watching.

'I hope you're all ready,' Jo flung over her shoulder, 'because I'm going to have to let her go.'

With that warning she shot past us on the grey, regained control, and went out of the gate on the other side of the stable yard at a jarring trot. My horse threw its head up excitedly, but fortunately did not try to run off. Rob took Mistral through the gate after her, and then the colonel smiled and said, 'After you.' I gathered the reins and administered a jab of the heels and my horse – oh kind, beautiful horse! – obeyed me and walked forward eagerly but not *too* eagerly. The colonel followed me, and we clattered out.

The softly rolling hills rose straight up from the track beyond the gate. Jo was circling her mount, and then I saw her give a great grin to Rob and turn it at the steepest part of the hill. The grey went up it at a canter, moving like a coiled spring, seeming to fight for its head all the time, wanting to go faster. Rob sent Mistral after, and soon overhauled her. Mistral and Secret reached the top neck and neck, were silhouetted for a moment on the crest, and then disappeared over it.

'Bad horsemanship,' the colonel said, 'to canter straight away. We won't emulate them, if you don't mind.'

The two bays were jogging and pulling, not liking to be left behind, but it was not unmanageable. I checked my horse without difficulty, and at once felt much more confident. I was remembering things from my riding lessons – among them how hard a saddle was, harder by far than a kitchen chair.

'We'll ride round the bottom and meet them on the other side,' said the colonel.

I don't know if he did it for my benefit, but at all events it put me at my ease. We walked and then trotted side by side round the base of the hill and then up more gently rising ground, and by the time the colonel suggested a canter, I felt safe enough to agree. Cantering, as I now remembered discovering a lifetime ago, was easier than trotting – a smoother pace. Going uphill stopped the horses going too fast and took the first fizz out of them. When we reached the crest we pulled down easily to a walk, and saw Jo and Rob coming back towards us at a canter.

'Slowcoaches!' Jo taunted when she reached us. She couldn't make Secret halt, so had to prance round in circles to talk to us. Her body seemed moulded to the animal, no daylight anywhere between her legs and seat and the saddle. You could see how the legend of the Centaurs arose. It was lovely to see. Her face was flushed and exultant, and she and the horse seemed like one beautiful, supple, excited animal.

We walked our horses all together across the top of the hill – or at least we men walked ours, while Secret kept up a continuous slow dance, putting in three steps to every forward pace, her head turned sideways, feeling constantly for any loophole in Jo's control through which she could slip and dash off.

'She's nutty,' Jo said, not even breathless. 'She never learns.'

'It looks exhausting,' I said.

'Oh no. It isn't unseating. It's all show. She's like an armchair, really. I love riding her. Will you buy her for me, Daddy?'

'Absolutely not. I'd never have a moment's peace of mind,' the colonel said calmly.

At the far end of the ridge we stopped to admire the view. It was worth seeing, the hills and fields spread out under us in subtly blended shades of green, grey and brown, falling and rising like a gently billowed eiderdown, curving up at last to the hard green line that was the cliff edge. Beyond that lay the sea, quiet today, slightly misty; mauve-grey, fading into the faint, silvery horizon of the sky.

'I love England,' Rob said quietly. 'I'm glad I've travelled so much, I love seeing new places, but whenever I have time to stop and think, it's always hills and greenness I see in my mind. I always want to come home.'

'Aren't you happy in the army?' Jo asked anxiously.

He was somewhere else, and I saw him pull his attention back to her. 'Of course I am. Didn't I just say so? I wouldn't do anything else. But one can enjoy being abroad and be homesick at the same time.'

'There's nothing like this anywhere else in the world,' said the colonel, and his voice had a note in it that made me look at him. He was gazing at the view like a man saying goodbye.

Secret began to fret again, turning on the spot, and I saw Jo's face swing back and forth as she tried to look at her father. She had heard that note too, I thought.

'It's Daddy we ought to feel sorry for,' she said. 'You're away all the time, Rob, and now I'm going to be going as well, in the autumn. He'll be all alone.'

'Don't worry about me,' said the colonel. 'I have everything I need. I have Jean to look after me. And you always come back.'

'Yes, we always will,' Jo said, as if he needed assuring of that. And then, 'Come on, Secret's breaking my arms. Let's gallop. All right, George?'

I didn't have the chance to answer, for she let her horse go and with a flying leap they were off. Our horses caught the excitement and started jogging. Rob looked towards me questioningly and, not wanting to spoil everyone's pleasure, I nodded. Next moment we were all off in pursuit, and the four horses were stretched out in a gallop. Galloping was easier than cantering: the movement was level, less rocking-horse, more like being carried along at speed by a motor-bike. I found the occasional grab at the front of the saddle was all I needed for security. Vanguard and Tambour kept pace with each other, but Rob and Mistral drew away from us, eating up the ground with great strides. I remembered Jo saying he was the fastest horse in the county, and he looked it.

He quickly caught up on Secret. I don't quite know what happened next. I think Secret might have tried to bite Mistral, for I saw the big horse swing head and neck away in mid stride, stumble, and recover. Secret jerked her head about, trying to escape Johands, and then began to buck. Had they not been going downhill, all might have been well, but as it was, the momentum made the bucks ever bigger and faster, until she seemed in danger of going heels over head. I saw them part company, Jo flying over Secret's shoulder to slam into the earth, rolling. At the same moment the mare somehow lost her footing and fell, twisting as she did. Then for a horrible instant the two figures were mixed up as the great body of the horse rolled right over the small figure of the girl. The mare regained her feet immediately, and pulled back on her reins, which seemed to be caught somehow under Jo's body. She thrashed her head back and forth a moment, and then desisted and stood trembling. Horses hate to fall – it knocks the fight out of them. Jo was much slower to move, and for a breathless moment I thought she must be unconscious – or dead. Then she sat up slowly, and I saw she had kept hold of the reins when she fell, which was why the mare couldn't escape.

Rob reached her, flung himself off Mistral and took Secret's reins from Jo. 'Are you all right?' he asked her breathlessly.

The colonel and I arrived too, and halted. I looked at him for a lead as to what we should do. But he did not dismount, only sat looking at his daughter expressionlessly, but with the skin drawn tight about his eyes.

Jo was levering herself shakily to her feet. I gulped with relief that she could do so much. I had been trying not to imagine a broken back or broken neck. Her face was white, and there was a red mark on her cheek that looked as if it would turn into a bruise. But she was upright. She felt her left forearm carefully with her right hand.

'Are you all right?' Rob asked her again. He sounded shaky, as though, had he not been holding two horses, he might have enveloped her in his arms with relief. 'She rolled on you.'

'She was only on me for a second,' Jo said, and though her voice sounded a little strained, she seemed quite calm.

'Hold my horse for a moment, would you, George?' the colonel said to me. He gave me the rein and dismounted, and I thought: at last, some proper fatherly feeling. I wished I could go to her myself, but I was now handicapped like Rob. But to my surprise the colonel went not to his daughter, but to the mare, and began running his hands over her and down her legs. What kind of a father was he, I thought, to check over the horse rather than his child?

'That horse is dangerous,' I heard myself say, in a voice indignant with shock, and the recent anxiety I had felt for Jo.

It was she who answered. 'It wasn't her fault, poor darling. She lost her balance. Could happen to anyone.'

The colonel straightened up and turned to his daughter. 'She seems all right. How about you?'

'Not sure,' Jo said, still feeling her arm. 'I think I've sprained my wrist. It was underneath me when she went over. Don't think I've busted it.'

I was looking at the colonel. He was standing quite still, but I saw the small movement he made, instantly checked, of going to her. Then he drew himself up a little, and his drawn face assumed a mask of indifference.

'Fit to ride?' he asked indifferently.

'Yes, I think so.'

'You'd better take Mistral,' said Rob. 'I'll take Secret – you'll never hold her with one hand.'

In a few moments all were remounted and we were on our way again. Secret still jogged and pulled, but less violently, either because of Rob's greater weight and strength in the saddle, or because the fall had taken some of the fight out of her. Jo rode Mistral easily, one handed, the other hand tucked between two buttons of her shirt, to support the hurt wrist. Soon they began to talk and laugh again, but I found it hard to join in. I was dumbfounded by their casualness. I kept seeing, over and over in my mind, the image of Jo disappearing under the horse, and lying so still, a tiny, flattened figure pale against the dark turf. She might have been killed, I kept thinking. I exempted Rob, for after all brothers are known to be much more casual about their sisters, but I couldn't understand the colonel. To bring up sons to be hardy was one thing – but daughters?

When we got back to the stables, the colonel said quietly to me, 'Will you drive Jo to the doctor, to check on that wrist? We'll take care of the horses. I just want to be sure it isn't broken.'

I felt better at once. 'Of course,' I said, and for a wonder, Jo didn't argue with me. In the car I kept glancing sideways at her. The bruise on her cheek was darkening now, making her face look paler by contrast. Suddenly I realised she was looking at me, too.

'Don't look so funereal, George,' she said, smiling faintly. 'There's no real harm done.'

'I can't help it,' I said. 'I thought you were dead when you didn't get up.'

'I'd had all the breath knocked out of me,' she said. Then, 'I'm sorry, did it spoil the ride for you?'

'To hell with the ride,' I muttered angrily.

'Then what are you cross about?'

'I don't like you to be hurt,' I said.

'Oh,' she said.

I saw her move the injured arm carefully, and after a short silence to master my voice, I asked more normally, 'Does it hurt?'

'Only when I laugh,' she said, straight-faced; and so I had to.

I waited outside the doctor's house in the car, smoking nervously, while he looked her over. I was imagining internal injuries or delayed concussion. But when they came out they were both smiling, though Jo's wrist was bandaged and in a sling.

'Only a sprain,' she called out to me cheerfully. 'Nothing broken.'

'It'll take time to heal, all the same,' said the doctor, as if he knew her impatience. 'Rest it, don't use it – do you hear? And next time, choose a horse that can stay on its feet.'

She kissed his cheek goodbye, and he patted her affectionately before going back indoors.

I drove her home. 'You see, George, I'm perfectly all right,' she said.

She said it again to her father when we got back. I looked for some sign of relief in his face, but he showed nothing, and all he said was, 'That's good. You shouldn't have galloped her downhill, you know.'

'That was her idea, not mine,' she grinned.

She walked me back to the car when I took my leave. Glancing back I saw the colonel's eyes following her, their expression veiled.

'Poor Daddy,' she said when we were out of earshot, 'I'm such a trial to him. Oh George, don't look so mournful! It's nothing serious. I've fallen off a hundred times before. Listen, you should see the rest of me. That hillside was stony, you know. I'm all over horrid little black bruises where they pressed into me.'

I tried to be as cheerful as she was. 'Are you offering to show me?'

'Not on your life!' She reached up and kissed me on the cheek, and when I went to return the kiss, moved her face so that our lips met, and kissed me as if it was the first time.

'What was that for?' I asked when I had caught my breath.

'For loving me,' she said, and I had no answer to that.

I went back to the house the next day, because Rob had asked me, rather diffidently, if I would run him to the station. I was happy to be able to help, but I did wonder – especially since he said Jo was not to come – whether he wanted to get me alone either to run an elder-brotherly rule over me, or to warn me off his sister.

So I was there to witness his and Jo's farewells. From the way she clung to him I was afraid she would be inconsolable for the next few weeks, and wondered how that boded for me. Having gently disentangled himself from her, Rob extended a hand to the colonel, and they shook with, for me, an odd formality. Then the colonel put his arm round Jo's shoulders, as if to restrain her from further physical demonstrations. Her eyes were swimmingly bright, and fixed on her brother.

'Take care of yourself,' she begged.

'Don't worry,' he said.

'But I do. And don't forget to write.'

'When did I ever? Ready George?'

I walked round to the driver's door while he put his suitcase in the back, and by the time I had settled myself inside and looked back, Jo and the colonel had gone into the house and shut the door. Rob got in beside me, divined my thoughts, and said, 'Family custom. No long-drawn-out goodbyes.'

'I suppose you can't afford to keep doing it, with an army family.'

'Right,' he agreed. But as we reached the end of the drive and began to turn out onto the road, I saw him quickly glance back, as though he couldn't help it. I liked him the better for it.

'It's kind of you to drive me,' he said after a pause.

'Don't mention it,' I said.

'I wanted to have a chance to say thank you, for looking after Josella.'

'It doesn't really amount to that,' I said.

'And to ask you to go on taking care of her, for me.'

I felt awkward. 'She would never let me. And she'll be going away to university soon.'

'Yes,' he said, and sank into thought. 'It'll be the best thing for her,' he said at last, as if he had just come to the conclusion.

'I don't think she much wants to go,' I said.

'She can't stay here for ever,' he said, but almost more to himself than me. 'She shouldn't have been left here all this time.'

I wasn't sure what this meant, and wondered if it was about finishing schools and London Seasons. Such things did still happen among the upper classes, and I had no way of knowing, from my limited experience, how 'upper' the Graces were – though

I did know the colonel had a private income, whatever that might be. But then, if those were his concerns, why would Rob be asking a nonentity like me to keep an eye on her? Finishing school and London Season were aimed at getting a suitably rich and/or powerful husband for a girl, and he couldn't possibly have any doubt that I was neither.

He was still brooding, so I said comfortingly, 'Once she's settled in and makes new friends, I expect she'll like university. And it does create wonderful opportunities—'

He interrupted me, not rudely, but out of his own thoughts. 'It'll be the best thing for her,' he said again. 'I've sometimes wished I hadn't joined the army, so I could have stayed around and taken care of her; but I'm not sure now that would have been a good thing. The less she relies on me the better. She has to get used to being on her own sooner or later.'

'I suppose so,' I said doubtfully. There was something odd about the tone of all this.

'There's so much you don't know about her,' he said abruptly.

Warning me off, I wondered? A few moments ago he was asking me to take care of her. 'Of course, I haven't known her for very long,' I said, a little stiffly.

'She's a very different – a very special person.'

'I agree,' I said. I turned the car into the

station car park, eager now for this uncomfortable interview to end. What the devil *did* he want of me? I stopped the car and got out to retrieve his suitcase from the back. He got out on his side and came round to take it from me. For a moment we stood facing each other. He overtopped me by two or three inches, a tall, slender-looking man of deceptive, steely strength, with Jo's pale hair and level, clear grey eyes. A little breeze moved the silky hairs around his brow that he would have to Brylcreem to keep in check – he had not disciplined them yet, still on leave until he reached the other end of his journey.

'Well,' he said, and looked into my face searchingly, a slight frown of thought between his fair brows. He seemed in gestation of an idea; my mind was full of assurances and reassurances and questions which I longed and feared to put. For a moment, it seemed as though one or other of us would say something important and change the course of at least our personal history. But then he stuck out his hand, and the moment passed.

'Well, so long, George.'

I shook it. 'So long,' I said.

He turned and walked through the gate onto the platform, and out of sight.

151

Chapter Eight: 1964

The Boda twins, Francis and James, lived in a two-roomed cottage up in the village. It was called Rose Cottage and was as picturesque as its name, attracting as many visitors in the summer as any of the other features of the village and bay. It was almost doll's-house sized, so small and low a tall man standing in the tiny front garden could have touched the eaves. It was painted white, with silvery beams, and a long, deep thatch like a little blonde girl's fringe, out of which peeped the tiny upstairs window, about sixteen inches square and glazed with panes of thick, greenish glass four hundred years old. An extravagant pale-pink rose scrambled all over its face and tangled itself in the blonde thatch; and down the side, under the deep green of overgrown banks, ran a narrow tributary of the stream, which disappeared into a culvert under the road. Rose Cottage featured in many of the 'local views' postcards, and was the subject of many a visitor's snapshot. In the summer one could pass it at any time of the day and find a tourist posing by the gate, while a friend or relative crouched among the sea-pinks against the wall across the road, trying to get as much of the cottage behind into his viewfinder as possible.

Inside, the cottage was as primitive as the outside was pretty. The two rooms led off to either side of a narrow passage which ran front to back, and the twins had one each as a sort of bed-sitting room. The upstairs room, which was about five feet square, had originally been reached by a wooden staircase in one of the rooms, but its floor-boards were none too strong and the staircase had been removed in the interests of making more space downstairs, so no-one had been up there in twenty years. Neither twin could remember if there was anything in the upstairs room or not. The fore-and-aft passage had originally led straight out into the back garden, but now there was a lean-to across the back of the cottage, which housed the kitchen: a sink with a bucket under it, a tin drainer and a cold water pump, a double calor-gas ring on an enamel-topped table, and a lattice-fronted cupboard, which someone in a frivolous moment had painted pale milk-bar green. Half-hidden in the overgrown may hedges of the back garden was an earth-closet which, like the pump, had never failed. In the winter, the twins sometimes moved together into one room, the one with the fireplace, for warmth, and if the weather got very bad they closed the shutters and abandoned it altogether for the Bull's front parlour. But in the summer they lived there very happily, among the bird-infested roses, under the swallow-haunted eaves.

Boats were their line, and their life. In the summer they hired out rowing boats in the bay to visitors. In the winter they did a little boat-building and boat-repairing for the fishing fleet, such as it was, and lived off the summer's profits. They were handsome and happy and lazy, devoid of ambition, devoted to each other and to comfort, and the only trouble that ever seemed to come to them was the occasional worry of a broken-hearted female holidaymaker writing them impassioned letters during the winter. Even that wasn't much of a worry: having been orphaned at an early age and left to fend for themselves, they had managed to evade the loose net of the education system. They could read all right, if there was ever any need to, but they did not often see the need, and did it without pleasure. They might start to decipher a letter sent to them, but something else more important was bound to distract them after a few words. There was nothing they could not make or mend with their own hands, and Jim could add up figures inside his head with a primitive genius, and that was all they needed to get by.

Frank woke first, as usual, and reckoned by the state of the sun that it was time to move. There was no necessity to get out early at this time of the year, for though the weather was fine – almost like high summer today – the tourist season was as yet green and unripe. Whitsun would bring the first big batch down. He rolled out of bed, stretched his magnificent six-feet-odd of brown, naked body, scratched his unruly straw-blond head, broke wind, sighed, and went to poke his head out of the window. The warm, rosy air was gently stirred by a soft breeze, and on it was the sound of bees at work, sundry birds deep in the nearby hedges, and more distantly the first of the delivery vans coming down to the beach café. That would make it about half past eight. Time to get moving.

He pulled on a pair of sea-bleached jeans whose legs had been hacked off at the knee, buttoned the fly – it was safer not to wear zippered jeans when you had no underpants – and climbed out of the window. The door swelled up with damp in the winter, and was not yet properly dried out. But it was easier to use the window in any case.

The sky was still milky with earliness, but the moss-rimmed flags of the front garden were warm to his feet. Sometimes people in the village gave him and Jim bits of plants for the front garden – sometimes even came and tended it themselves, for the honour of the village – so there were usually a few pinks or marigolds or pansies here and there, and the old, overgrown lavender bush in the corner was always vibrating with bees. The swallows had already started their day-long swoop after insects, and when one returned to the nest he could hear the babies squeaking like mice above his head. The adults seemed quite fearless and darted almost under his bare feet. He vaulted the garden gate and walked down the middle of the road, enjoying the warm tarmac under his toes, towards the bay.

The road ended at the beach, and on its right at that point stood his boathouse, with others beyond, while on the left stood the Victoria Café, a much-buffeted wooden structure with peeling paint and salt-clouded windows, which supplied snacks, teas, sandwiches, ice-cream, rock and souvenirs to the visitors. It had no competition within twenty miles, so it did very nicely without having to charge fancy prices. It also fed Frank and Jim for nothing during the summer days, reckoning that the rowing boats were part of what brought people to the bay, and that the twins' customers worked up an appetite and a thirst which they pretty well had to bring into the café to assuage.

The green van of the baker was pulled up outside the Victoria, and Arthur, the baker, was carrying in trays of bread rolls. An early tourist was standing and watching wistfully – probably a camper whom cold and discomfort had woken at dawn, and driven out with the longing for a cup of hot tea and a plateful of bacon and eggs. Frank lifted a hand in greeting to the baker – who merely nodded, his hands being occupied – and turned towards the boathouse. A glance at the water-level at the jetty confirmed that the tide was almost full. He and Jim could have told you the state of the tide at any time of the day or night, without even thinking: it surged back and forth in their heads like the whisper of their own breathing. Then he stopped and stared, screwing up his eyes against the white dazzle of the early sun and its dancing reflection on the waters of the still bay. A slow smile spread itself across his face, and he changed direction and loped down the shingle to the jetty.

A winter-pale girl in shorts and tee-shirt was sitting on the jetty with her hands under her knees, her feet dangling into the water, staring out to sea with the placid immobility of one who has nothing to do and all day to do it in. She turned her head at the scrunchy sound of his approach and smiled at him without emphasis. He stopped at the water's edge and leaned his elbow on the handrail, one of his feet rubbing itself back and forth over the instep of the other. After a while he asked, glancing over her shoulder as if he didn't really want to know, 'How did you get here?'

'I came up out of the sea,' she said.

He snorted at her nonsense. 'Get away.'

'I did – see, my hair's wet.'

'Well – before, then.'

'Oh the train, of course. What did you think?'

'You don't change,' he observed. He scratched casually at his hard, muscled stomach. 'Been here long?'

'Since sun-up. I looked in at your window but you were fast asleep so I came down here to get warm.'

Frank nodded, and continued his disgusting scratching movement, pursuing an itch across his ribs with his fingernails. Josy watched him with an amused smile, knowing all his movements intimately; and being able to guess most of his thoughts with fair accuracy could anticipate what he would say next.

'Staying?'

'Uh-huh,' she nodded.

He gave a non-committal grunt, and then heaved his foot out of the sea-edge shingle where it had sunk and turned back towards the boathouse, saying, 'C'mon, then.'

Josy swung herself off the jetty and trudged up the beach after him, a little tenderly, for her feet hadn't hardened yet. She took the key from him and unlocked the boathouse to get the oars out, while he began dragging the boats down to the water's edge. In half an hour all was ready for the day's trade. The black-lettered white sign was on its post, and the perfect little brown-varnished row boats – all named devoutly after saints, except for three that were named *Josella*, *Emily* and *Grace* – were lying waiting just behind the high-water bank. Josy put her bag into the boathouse and shut the door, and then she and Frank retired to the Victoria for breakfast.

Jim joined them as they were taking their first mouthful of bronzed, fragrant sausage. He greeted Josy with much more open pleasure than his twin.

'Nice to see you again. You're staying?'

'If you'll have me,' Josy said, grinning with pleasure.

'Course. You don't have to ask,' Jim said. He sat down next to his brother, opposite Josy, and dug into his breakfast with all the righteous hunger of a man who had just got up after a hard night's sleep. 'You're early this year, aren't you?'

Josy shrugged. 'I come with the good weather. Like the swallows.'

Frank snorted again at her nonsense, and Jim said, 'I never really feel it's summer properly until you get here.'

He was the more articulate of the two, with more charm and conversation, and such a pleasant way with him that he never had any difficulty in competing with Frank for girls. Frank was generally considered the handsomer of the two. With his slanting, green, sleepy-cat eyes, his slow smile and his enigmatic silences, he drove the visiting girls crazy. Jim chatted nicely to them, Frank just gave them silent, burning looks, but honours remained about even – except for Josy. Josy had always been Frank's, since the first summer of her staying, even though it was Jim Boda she had remembered from her childhood, Jim she had first come back here to look up.

Frank gave her one of his long, penetrating looks now, and asked, 'What've you been doing all winter?'

'The usual sort of thing,' she answered, after a mouthful. 'I was in London most of the winter. Had a good job, in an office. They wanted me to stay on permanently and I almost agreed, it was such a good job. But then the weather changed and I got restless.' As she paused both twins nodded sympathetically, though they never got restless that way themselves. But they knew all about the seasons and the migrating habits of birds and beasts, so it seemed natural enough to them. Besides, they knew Josy. 'So I went to Edinburgh,' she finished.

'Ah!' said Jim, as if this was the one piece of information he had been waiting for. Perhaps it was. She did not always go to

Edinburgh with the first migration. Sometimes it was York. 'Theatre, was it?'

'Yes. They gave me paid work, too, this year.'

'Have a good time?' Jim asked.

'Yes.' Her mind offered her a quick vision and she pulled her thoughts away from it. She didn't want to think about it. That was over – in the past – done with. She searched for something to say. 'I ate and drank too much as usual. I'll need to work off some weight on the boats.'

Frank laughed at this, but typically would not explain what he found amusing. Jim gave his brother a sharp look, and then shrugged and smiled reassuringly at Josy. There was a strong friendship and affection between Josy and Jim; but Frank had had for her since their first meeting a sort of slow-burning passion she felt she could not disregard, and which had made her turn from Jim with a shrug of regret. The brothers had shared too many girls in the past ever to make one the cause of strife between them. So for the eight years she had been summering in the bay, she had slept with Frank only, and Jim had smiled and shrugged and looked the other way.

'It'll be a hot summer this year,' Jim predicted, carefully mopping egg-yolk with a corner of fried bread. 'Good thing too, after last year. Hardly made enough to live on last year.'

Josy remembered the days of endless rain. They had been happy enough days for her, hanging around with the twins, playing shove ha'penny with Frank, darts with Jim, or dominoes with both, in the bar parlour at the Bull; gossiping with the locals when they came in for their lunchtime pint; chatting to the disconsolate tourists and suggesting things for them to do until the rain stopped. But the twins had been worried, and at one time she had felt they were almost on the point of falling out with her, not so much for being an extra mouth to feed, but for not being sufficiently concerned by the inclemency of the weather. It had improved at last enough to avert complete disaster, but the experience had left Josy with a feeling of unease. She was doubly glad, therefore, that the weather was fine and looked to be set fair.

They had finished eating and were drinking tea when Jim, who was looking out of the window, said with a tone of faint enquiry, 'Customer?'

The three of them looked out at a young man in cotton trousers, plimsolls and shirt who was standing near the boats and reading the notice board that was stuck into the shingle. Reading the notice didn't mean anything – a person alone had to do something – but at last his hunched shoulders straightened with decision and he looked about him with the confidence of one about to pay money for a service. It was their cue.

'Yes,' said Josy and Frank both together. They looked at each other and smiled.

'Bringing us luck,' said Frank.

'I'll go,' Jim said.

'No, you haven't finished your tea,' said Josy. 'I'll go – earn my keep. Where's the book?'

'On the windowsill,' Jim said, gesturing towards the door. He had left it there when he came in.

She caught it up and swung out of the café, crunching down the beach towards the young man. First customer, she thought. She liked first timers. He looked at her hopefully out of his growing isolation and doubt, and she smiled and said, 'Boat?'

'Yes, please,' he said.

'Lovely day,' she said.

'Yes,' he said. He thrust his hand into his pocket and his change rattled. 'Er, do I—?'

'Pay when you come back,' she said. 'Done much rowing?'

'Oh yes, quite a bit,' he said. He was standing up straighter, expanding his chest, affected by her good looks, wanting to impress her.

'River?' she asked.

'Mostly. The Thames. At Marlow.'

'It's a bit different rowing on the sea,' she

said, but she smiled so as not to crush him. 'You'll need to dig a bit deeper. But it's lovely and calm today. You'll be fine.'

She gestured to him to go along the jetty, and took hold of the prow of the boat nearest to her – it was the *Patrick* – to tug it down to the water. They were stout little clinker-built boats and heavy, and it took quite an effort to get it moving – she would soon develop her summer muscles again. She waded into the sea pulling *Patrick* behind her, its shingle sulkiness changing to smooth eagerness as the water lifted its weight, and positioned it beside the young man, holding it steady while he climbed in. She watched him settle his oars, said, 'Keep away from the rocks over there – there's a current,' and thrust him off. The brown boat bobbed away over the flickering, glittering water, looking as alive as the seagull that hastily paddled out of its way. The young man dug in his blades and pulled for the bay mouth, trying to look coolly expert for her benefit.

She turned and waded back to the beach, marked the departure time next to *Patrick*'s name in the book, and then stood and looked contentedly about her. The small, crescent-shaped bay was closed in by cliffs, which ran up into the surrounding hills to make the place a sun and heat trap. In the height of summer the cliffs were gay with broom and heather, sea-pinks, wild thyme, rock roses; the brilliant two-toned yellow of eggs-and-bacon, the faint dusty mauve of delicate harebells, and the intense blue of viper's bugloss with its crimson tongues. But just now they were green, and looked rich and edible, marked only with patches of deep red and purple honey-clover.

Behind the bay the village snuggled down into a tree-lined bowl; before it the sea spread out like a silver plate, showing blue only in the shadows of the cliffs, and fading at last at the horizon into the mistiness of heat, where the great upturned bowl of the sky came down to it, or the sea came up to the sky – she had never been able to decide which it was. And above it all the gulls turned and glided, sliding down invisible wind-channels, mewing forlornly from great heights; others sat arrogantly on the cliff tops and bickered with each other, their curiously human-sounding voices echoing hollowly across the water of the still bay.

It was a beautiful place, for her almost a holy place. Here she could feel as nowhere else that immutable peace, that feeling one has in childhood that there is duration but no time. It was all the good of her childhood, without any of the bad – a place where, now, she was known and not known, safe with friends in her anonymity, at once held close and free to go. Those two incompatibles she craved, belonging and secrecy, met here.

Every time she came back, she felt she could not understand why she ever left. Her contentment spilled over into love, loving everyone and everything in the place, from the twins down to the last sticky-mouthed tourist child.

They went to the Bull in the evening, into the public bar, stone-flagged and cool like a dairy, dim in the twilight, with a high wooden bar that glowed darkly like the beer in the old-fashioned tall glasses. The welcome Josy received was simple but satisfying.

'Back again?' accompanied by a nod of approval.

The barman, who was also the landlord, was more expansive. 'We're always grateful to these two lads for bringing you here.'

Josy bought a round. The village's two oldest inhabitants sat one at either end of the high bar on stools, like bookends, always erect, disdaining chairs with backs to them, never speaking to each other, although they were cousins. She included them in the round. One, lifting his drink in a salute to her, said, 'Been gorn a long time this time, encha?' and as if this had been the local dialect version of 'Cheers!' he quaffed off half the glassful.

His opposite number glared at Josy from beneath the bristling overhangs of his eyebrows. He was the hedger and ditcher for the

Rural District Council, and it always amused Josy that his own facial hedges were so unkempt, not to mention the missed bristles that sprouted from the grooves of his chin.

'Cheers, Billy,' Josy saluted him.

A gleam came into his eyes. His soft, toothless mouth chumbled around over some merry quip, his shoulders shook in a soundless laugh, and at the end of it he heaved a sigh of content at his own inner wit and said, 'Ar!'

'Still riding that old bike?' she asked him on a burst of affection.

He went through his soundless routine again, but this one was too good not to be shared, and having shaken himself to a standstill he wiped his mouth on the back of his hand, hitched his bristling chins upwards into the smile of a satanic baby, and said, 'Bin waitin' for you to name the day, 'fore I gets a car.'

'What d'you think I am, a cradle snatcher?' Josy quipped robustly, and Billy sniggered into his pint happily.

'Funny,' said the Guv'nor musingly, 'how the weather always changes for the best when you come down.'

He seemed to have forgotten last year. Josy thought of explaining the connection between the weather and her appearance, but felt too pleasantly indolent and let it pass.

Will, Billy's cousin, said, 'I remember how

there was a cormorant like that in the bay, oh, years back. 'Fore the war, that was. You'd remember him, Fred,' he said.

The Guv'nor, nodded. 'That old bird'd fly in just about sunset, just this time o' year, and set down on topper the old boathouse, what used to stand behind where the Vic stands now.'

This was in parenthesis to Josy. It was a new story to her, though she thought she'd heard the whole of the Bull's repertoire by now.

'Any 'ow, he'd set down there, and wait until old man Boda, old Joe Boda, what was these lads' grandad, come in to the jetty. Then he'd fly down, and damn me if he didn't walk up the beach alongside the old man, yarpin' away just like as if he was talkin' to 'im.'

Josy made a sound expressive of astonishment and interest. Old Will nodded, and Billy put in, 'It's the truth, what he says.'

The Guv'nor took up the story. 'I remember how old Joe Boda used to come into the pub and say to me dad – I was just a nipper then, o' course, but I'd often hang around the front parlour and do jobs for my dad – he'd say to my dad, "Charlie," he'd say, "you can put your summer vest on tomorrow. My old Sooty's come in." That was the name he give it, Sooty.'

'What was old Mr Boda like?' Josy asked

with interest.

'Oh, he was a big man, big and black.'

'Black?' Josy asked, startled.

'Black hair, black beard, black eyes,' Will interpolated.

'And he had a big voice, too,' the Guv'nor went on. 'Used to make the windows rattle when he laughed.'

'But he had a shocking temper, too,' said Billy. 'Black Joe, we called him, or French Joe, 'cause he came from some foreign parts.' He chumbled a laugh around inside his mouth and lost it somewhere. 'He went for Charlie Booker with a knife once for calling him a Froggy. He said, "I ain't a Froggy, I'm a Beljik," or some such. And Charlie Booker says it's all the same to him. Made ole Joe mad as fire! Cor, he had a temper.'

'Died of it in the end,' Will said, nodding portentously. 'S'fact. Got his nets tangled up in some fella's moorings, out in the bay. Fella comes along and starts laughing, and it made ole Boda so mad he just turned black in the face—'

'—and dropped down dead!' Billy finished for him, slapping his hand down flat on the bar top by way of demonstration. His laughter spilled out in short bursts like steam, hissing between his empty gums. 'Thass why we called him Black Joe Boda – not cos of his hair.'

Will snarled in silent fury at having his

story's best line stolen. 'Didn't oughter tell that story in front of a lady,' he addressed the mirror behind the bar.

'So what was the twins' father like?' Josy asked, to keep the peace. The twins were cleaning off the board for a game of darts on the other side of the room.

The Guv'nor answered. 'Jim Boda? He was a decent sort of chap. Dark, like his dad.'

'Book learned, he was. Even wrote poetry,' said Billy. 'S'fact. He could read anything that was wrote.'

'So the twins don't take after him?' Josy said.

'Not a bit. Take after their mother.' The Guv'nor glanced across at them, to make sure they were out of hearing. 'She was a pretty little thing, fair hair and blue eyes, but she couldn't even spell her own name.'

'I wonder why he married her?' Josy mused.

'Lonely, I suppose,' the Guv'nor said. 'Jim wasn't much of a man for mixing. Sort of – gloomy. Well, not that so much. He could laugh with the rest of 'em, but he sort of liked being on his own.'

'Writin' poetry,' Billy put in – the wonder of it!

'She was just the opposite – always fun, fun, fun for her. Never one to be washing and scrubbing and mending. Well, they say opposites attract.'

'I sometimes wonder what Jim Boda would have said if he could see his lads like they are,' Will broke in sadly.

'What happened to him?' Josy asked.

'Didn't the boys tell you?'

'I never asked,' Josy said.

'Well, their dad, he died of a stroke, like his dad before him,' the Guv'nor said. 'The twins'd be about seven. Their mother—'

'Mary Rose, her name was,' Billy put in. 'Named that cottage after her. Used to be called School Cottage before that, 'cause it was at the ender School Lane.'

'Their mother,' the Guv'nor resumed, 'she wasn't much of a housekeeper. Never had been. And she'd no head for money. After Jim died she couldn't manage. The boys used to go about dirty, with great holes in their clothes, and not enough to eat. Well, they used to get by, a bit here and a bit there, with the village women feeling sorry for 'em, so to speak. But Mary Boda, she couldn't beg off her neighbours, and she was too proud to ask for help. So she just went hungry. Then, time the twins were about ten, there was a very bad winter that year, and she just popped off.'

'Fell off the twig,' said Billy, 'like a sparrer. Pewmonia.'

'So how did the boys manage?' Josy asked.

'Oh, they brought themselves up some-how,' said the Guv'nor. 'Course, it was war-time, so they sort of fell through the net. No-one would've seen 'em starve, but otherwise...' He shrugged. 'And of course they never went near the school. Not that they were much for books at the best of times. Took after their mother that way.'

'But how did they live?'

'Well, they inherited the boathouse from their father, the boat, fishing-tackle, and a bit of money. That tided them over. Then there was a boat-builder in the village at that time, name of Henry Thorpe, and he had the idea of taking over the boathouse, which was more convenient to him, being closer to the water, and teaching the boys the trade.'

'Instead of rent,' Josy said, seeing the point.

'That's right. And when he died, he left the boys his business, which was worth a bit. So they pulled down the old boathouse and put up one bigger, built them little rowing boats, and set up in the tourist business.'

And that was how she remembered them, Josy thought, from her childhood – the young men with the rowing boats. She glanced across at them, playing darts now, two fair-haired, brown-skinned young men, supremely relaxed and unhurried about life, and tried to fit them into the story she now had of their childhood: the dark, gloomy father and the fair, blowsy mother. Wouldn't there have been rows, the father shouting, the mother crying, the sounds filling that tiny cottage? She imagined the twins lying awake – upstairs, in the tiny room under the thatch? – listening. Coming home from their roaming, would they have paused outside to gauge the mood, hearing the arguing coming out through the windows into the dusk, an accepted background to their lives like the hiss of an oil lamp or the grumble of the sea on the shingle?

She imagined the sudden huge gap where their black father had been, and their red-eyed, snuffling mother growing more frowsty and hopeless, while they ran wild, abandoning their uncomfortable home for a headier freedom – until she was gone, too, just fading away like colour bleached out by the wind and salt and sun of their world. Yet once she had been loved – Mary Rose, pretty enough to have a cottage named after her. Had he written poetry about her? And read it to her in the firelight, while she listened, admiring and uncomprehending? Josy felt a pang of pity for them both, for all men who marry brainless women and find they can't love them, and all women who find they cannot please their husbands and don't know why. And for the children of such unions, always orphans, whether their parents are alive or dead.

'How about another round, Fred?' she said to the Guv'nor, reaching into her shorts pocket for the money. Someone out at the back – the Guv'nor's wife probably – turned on the lights, and the bar warmed suddenly in the yellow-as-butter glow.

Chapter Nine: 1954

It was one of the beautiful, clear summer nights that seemed so plentiful that year, and we were sitting on top of the cliffs some-where beyond Durdle Door, watching the moonlight over the quiet sea. We had been silent for some time, Jo staring out at the water, and I staring at her, only half aware of the romance of the scene, but absorbed with her presence and her beauty. She sat with her knees up and her bare brown arms clasping them, her silvery hair loose to her shoulders, with the light airs from the sea playing with the soft fronds around her brows. The same airs caught under the full skirt of her dress so that it billowed and kept up a restless movement, so different from her stillness. I gazed at her profile, cut out against the dark sky – the moon was so bright there were no stars to be seen – and felt I could happily sit here and look at her for ever.

At last she said, 'I wish I didn't have to go away. It's coming soon, you know.'

'Not so very soon,' I said, comforting her, without really thinking.

'Yes, soon. In September, and it's August now. The summer goes so quickly. I don't want to go away.'

All sorts of automatic responses shuffled towards my tongue – don't go then, it won't be for long, you'll be back soon, it's all to the good – but this time I stopped them and thought about it. At last I said, 'Why do you have to?'

'Daddy wants it. He's quite determined.'

'Is it a family tradition?'

'Goodness, no. We're an army family,' she said, as if that answered everything. 'But I'm pretty good at school, and if I get a degree I'll be able to get a better sort of job. He says I must have a career.'

This still sounded a little odd to me. 'I would have thought,' I began, and paused to seek the right words. 'Do you really have to earn your own living? I thought, well, that your father was pretty well off.'

'He used to be,' she said. 'But things started to get difficult before the war. There used to be a farm, you know, and a park. He sold off all the land, bit by bit. And now, people like him have suddenly got quite poor since the war. I don't understand why, but it seems to be the case.'

I remembered the abandoned walled garden, the derelict stables. And, yes, I knew it was the case that people with private incomes were badly off these days. A lot of things suddenly made sense.

'He says we only get by because of his army pension,' she went on, 'and obviously he can't leave *that* to me. Rob's provided for, but he worries about me, poor pet.'

'You'll get married,' I said, surely.

She didn't respond to that at all, only continued to stare at the moon-path on the sea, with that same little thinking frown between her brows I had seen on Rob. She looked very like him just then.

She went on, 'When I was very small, there were servants. Now there's just Jean, and the gardener two half days a week. We don't even have a groom. We can only keep the horses because I look after them. Daddy says he's going to sell them when I go away. Imagine, no more riding!' The last burst out of her as if it were a thing of horror. Perhaps it was to her, not just in itself, but because of what it represented.

But to go to university still seemed to me to be a privilege, not something to be dreaded. 'Well, I'm sure you'll love university when you get there.'

'I shan't,' she said, with unemphatic, mournful certainty. 'It's the end of everything.'

'It's not the end, it's the beginning,' I said. 'It's a great opportunity. Your horizons will expand.'

'I don't want to grow up and change. I want to stay here, like this, for ever.'

'But life *is* change,' I said.

'I know. But people always seem to think change must be good, just in itself. That change is always for the better. But look at the way people are, all around us. I don't want to be like that. I don't want to stop caring about important things and start caring about stupid ones.'

There seemed an obvious flaw in the logic of that. 'But you'll always think the things you care about are important, whatever they are.'

She turned her head just a little to look at me, a quick glint of light as the moonlight caught her eye. 'You don't understand.'

'No, I don't,' I confessed.

She turned her head away again. 'This, here, is everything that matters to me. The rest of the world—' She paused, and went on in a lower voice, 'I'm safe here.'

'Safe from what?'

Another pause. 'Everything. Oh, I can't explain. You never knew my mother. That's in my blood as well.'

As well as what? But I didn't ask it. She was so troubled, and I didn't know why, and feared to make it worse with the wrong words.

'Don't you feel it?' she asked, with a sort of miserable urgency. 'That all we have is this, here, and if we let it go, we'll never find it again.'

I reached for her hand, and brought it back to my lap. I found it cold, where it had been resting on the grass, but hard and live in mine – so unlike any other girl's hand: leathery and strong from years of controlling horses, not soft and limp and merely decorative. It was like an extension of her personality, almost a creature in its own right. It curled round my fingers eagerly in response.

I sought for the right words. 'I know change isn't always for the good, but it isn't always bad either, not by any means. The world is full of wonderful things. You should look forward to finding out about them. They're something to enjoy. They're not a threat.'

'Not to you,' she said, very low. And then she sighed, and her hand gripped mine hard. 'Oh George! You're one of the things I don't want to leave. And we only have a little while left.'

'Then we'd better make sure we don't waste any of it,' I said, and drew her to me. She folded into me with the natural ease of a bird in its nest, and we kissed. We could never have enough of kissing, and in kissing she seemed to forget her melancholy, and grew warm and pliant, so that afterwards when we talked again she seemed happy, and laughed, and was lively in her ordinary way. We kissed and talked until the moon had gone round and left the sea in velvet darkness, and then we grew chilly and went, arms wound round each other's waists, back to the car.

It came and went, this mood of sorrow, over the next weeks; though it was infrequent. Mostly she seemed as she had always been; and I was as fascinated as ever. She was full of talk and laughter and energy, her mind enquiring, her interest seized by every new thing. I never knew what she would say next. Though we did not speak about university again, I could not see how she would not love it once she got there, and get on very well.

But suddenly it was her last day. She was to be leaving in the morning, and I was invited to spend the evening with her and her father, at home. The colonel seemed in a quiet way as upset as I knew she was, though he showed it only by being rather more silent than usual, and by the way his eyes followed her whenever she moved away from him. But each of them seemed putting on a brave show for the other, and I guessed that my presence there was to add an air of festivity

179

to what otherwise might have been as solemn as a wake. So I did my best, and whenever a silence fell dredged around in my mind for a topic of conversation that would keep things going. It was all rather strained, and not helped by the evident tension that hung around Jean. I had always eaten there superbly, but the meal she served that evening had symptoms about it of a mind elsewhere; and afterwards, when we had retired to the drawing room, she came in every so often with questions about packing and what time Jo wanted to be called in the morning, and each time her eyes flitted from the colonel to his daughter and back with an expression of concern that was almost apprehension.

At last the whole thing seemed to overwhelm Jo, and she stood up abruptly and said, 'I must get a breath of fresh air. Coming, George?'

I wasn't sure if this was a subtle hint to me, so I said, 'I ought to be getting back, really.'

'Oh no, it's early,' she said. 'I want a walk first. You don't mind, do you, Daddy?'

'Of course not,' the colonel said. 'But don't get chilly. I think you ought to take a coat.'

'I will,' she said, and with another abrupt turn went over to him and hugged him with brief vehemence. 'Don't worry about me.'

'If it's all right with you, sir, I'll go straight off afterwards,' I said. 'Thank you very much for inviting me.'

He stood up to shake my offered hand. 'Don't think that you need to stay away, just because Josella's gone,' he said. 'I've enjoyed your company these past months, and I'd be delighted if you'd drop in from time to time – if you can spare the time, that is.'

The last was added rather guiltily, as if he had just realised I was a young man with all a young man's interests, and probably no desire to spend my leisure hours with an old man. I'd have had to be a brute to refuse him. I said, 'I'd like to come, sir. I've enjoyed my evenings here.'

He brightened, so I must have sounded sincere, as I meant to. 'Good, good. Well, perhaps you'd like to come to dinner next Saturday? We could have a hand of cards afterwards.' He had discovered that I knew how to play piquet. 'If it wouldn't be too dull for you.'

I caught Jo looking at me with a sup-pressed smile. All my leisure time for months had been hers. How could I have a date arranged already for the first Saturday of her absence? 'No, I'd like that,' I said.

'Excellent. Eight o'clock suit you?'

I agreed.

Jo tugged importunately at my arm. 'Come on. Do come on.'

'I'm coming,' I said, wondering at her impatience. I supposed it was all part of her feeling unsettled. 'Until Saturday, then, sir.'

'Yes. Goodbye, George. Don't stay out too long, Josella.'

She more or less dragged me out. When we were in the cool darkness of the lane she said, 'I'm not sure I like the idea of you and Daddy getting together to talk about me while I'm not there.'

'Conceited little whatnot,' I said. 'Why should you think we'll be talking about you?'

'Daddy will want to,' she said. 'And I can't believe you'd stop him. No, whatever you think you'll be discussing, you'll get round to me before the evening's out. And I won't be there to hear.'

'Since we wouldn't do it if you *were* there, you won't miss anything,' I pointed out.

'It's not conceit,' she said abruptly. 'It's just that it's so difficult to know what people really think. Whether they really – love you. It just would be handy to know.'

She was silent for a while, walking beside me with her hand on my arm, but rather to guide me than through affection. I glanced at her. There was no moon, and the faint starlight hardly parted the darkness, but I could just see her profile. She walked with her head up, boldly, staring straight ahead as if in defiance of the world. It was her usual walk. She seemed so fragile and yet so brave that I could not have helped loving her, if I had not already. What she had to need to be brave about I had no idea then, but the feeling persisted.

She found her way with ease in the dark, having run about these lanes for so long that she knew every step, even when the equivalent of blindfold, so I felt easy about not being able to see the ground before me, and let her guide me, trusting her to keep me out of ditches and ruts. I was happy just to look at her, faintly gleaming in the starlight, glad to have this time alone with her, when I had thought we would be constrained by the presence of her father all evening. We were nearing the bottom of the hill, where the trees crowded closer on either side of the lane, so that we seemed about to enter a dark tunnel. I was about to make some remark to that effect, when I saw something glitter on her cheek, just for an instant before she turned her head away. She put her free hand up and dashed the tear away with the impatient, simple movement of a child, annoyed with herself for having given way. I found it unbearably touching.

'Are you really so sorry to be going?' I asked her.

We entered the tunnel, and her hand slid from my arm down to my hand. 'I can't explain to you,' she said, so faintly I only just heard her. In the blackness she moved automatically closer to me. 'It's like the end of everything, as though I were going to die.'

My normal robustness of mind rejected this as ridiculously over-dramatic; and yet in the blackness of the tree shadows I felt a chill on the back of my neck, and I couldn't say what I felt I ought to have said. It seemed suddenly too serious to be scoffed at.

She went on, 'I think of you all carrying on without me, still living in the sunlight while I'm lost in the dark. That's how it seems to me.'

I stopped and reached out for her, turned her towards me and pulled her close. I bent to kiss her, and in the darkness missed her mouth the first time, and found instead the wet salty curve of her cheek. There had, as I suspected, been more tears. My mouth slipped in them, and her lips came round to meet mine, and we kissed with passionate intensity. Then she buried her head in my chest and I held her close until I sensed she had stopped crying; at least, the little jerkings of suppressed sobs had stopped, and she rested quietly against me.

'Better?' I enquired tenderly. 'All done now?'

'Yes,' she said. 'I'm sorry, George. I won't do that again.'

'Don't be sorry,' I said. 'My chest is always at your service.'

She laughed – a little shakily, but it was a beginning.

She pulled herself away from me and felt

around for my hand, caught it, and led the way forward. 'Come on,' she said, with a note of purpose.

'Come on where?'

'You'll see.'

We walked, she surely, I stumbling a little. The mothy, leaf-scented night was mild – milder now, and darker, by which I knew that the sky had clouded over, obscuring even the stars. I have reasonably good night vision, but there was nothing to see now but black on black. Staring hopelessly downwards in the hope of seeing my footing, I had no idea where we were going. We turned aside from the lane onto a narrower track, and I tried to remember from daylight visits what there was there. It led slightly uphill, and a scratchy hedge brushed at my arm, while tussocky grass caught at my feet.

After a long walk she stopped. 'Here,' she said. 'Don't make a noise.' She had turned at right angles and was pulling me into the hedge. Sensing my confusion she added, 'There's a gap. Feel.'

She let go of my hand and I reached out and felt the twiggy mass and the space, with her body bending to pass through it. I followed clumsily, feeling it catch in my hair. Then we were through, and into a space of uneven ground, still very dark – I felt the loom of large trees all around. She led me forward, and my feet struck against what I took to be rocks, or ledges of rock. Then she stopped. By the brush of her movements I understood she was taking off her coat; she bent and spread it on the ground, which was lighter in colour just there. Then taking my hand again she folded herself down onto it, and drew me with her.

It was hard under her coat: we were lying on a flat outcrop of rock. With both hands she drew my face to hers and kissed me. The touch excited me, I responded, and then we were kissing fervently. Her arms went round me, holding me tightly to her; she kissed me with a kind of desperate passion.

In the darkness, all things seemed possible; or rather, the impossibles melted away. I was a young man, and I was in love with her. My passion mounted, at every step met as an equal by hers. I struggled out of my jacket, and she helped me pull it away, without taking her mouth from mine. Her body was hot and very near, scorching me through my shirt and her cotton frock. A wild, abandoned joy rushed through me like sweet, hot liquid. And yet some sentinel still watched in my brain, for when I found my hand cupped over her small, hard breast, I was still able to feel shocked with myself, and to pull my mouth away from hers, though it was agony to do it.

'No, George, don't stop,' she said, arching her head up for my mouth again.

'We mustn't.' I heard my words, blurred with desire, moan from me.

'It's all right. I want it. Don't stop. I must have you.'

Her hard, pointed tongue slid between my lips, and it was like a bolt of heat slamming into my brain. I fell then beyond control, into the starless dark of sensation. Her hands were already fumbling with my belt. I could not have stopped now if the earth had split in two – or so it seemed. So it always seems at such moments. Her clothes seemed to come off without effort – I realised later that she must have been helping me. Her body gleamed before me, just visible in the darkness, and where I touched it, it felt hot, stinging hot as if she had been sunbathing. I kissed her lips, her face, toeing off my shoes; wriggled somehow out of my trousers, too exalted with desire for anything to bring me down. I hardly felt the cool air on my back, only the sweet, searing touch of her skin against mine. I did, I remember, have one passing thought, wondering whose garden we were in and what the consequences would be if we were discovered. But she kissed me as though drinking my soul, and thought fled away. I was just able to control myself enough to try to be gentle with her, but my need for her – and hers for me – impaled us on its imperative so it seemed we must do this or die.

I can remember it now in two ways, one as it must have seemed to an outsider, if any had been there, or to the sentinel in my brain if he had remained on duty: the cold and discomfort, the pain of my knees and elbows on the rough stone, a rustling of a breeze through the leaves that started a fear of discovery. Unmarried sex in those days (how the world has changed!) was always a thing of furtiveness and makeshift with a sweet taint of shame.

But that was not the reality. The reality was that entering her was a thing of mingled agony and relief; that joy and sensation leapt together like flame and salamander. We moved together, clinging and gasping like swimmers being dragged away by an undertow. She made a sound, a little shuddering 'Ah!' that might have served equally for pleasure or pain, and love pierced me through like a thin, hot rapier. It broke over us, that great breaker of the First Time, and I drowned, in a bliss so overwhelming it felt as though I might die of it.

Afterwards we were both silent, neither of us wishing to break a silence so precious and so fragile. I found that I was looking up at the sky, and that the clouds had parted again, so that I could see the distant, indifferent stars. She was resting with her head against my shoulder. I wanted to look at her, but it would have meant moving, and if I moved it would all be over. I never wanted to move again.

At last she stirred, and sighed, and muttered something.

'What is it?' I murmured. She didn't repeat it, and I asked with awkward tenderness, 'Are you all right?'

'All right,' she confirmed, her voice faint and far away. 'Only cold.'

It was cold. I noticed it only then, when she said it. I tried to feel around with my free hand for some clothes to pull over her, but I couldn't reach anything, and my movements broke the spell. She sat up. 'We'd better get dressed,' she said.

I couldn't tell from her tone what she was feeling. It seemed quite neutral – but wasn't that in itself a comment on what we had done? Shivering, I sat up too, and found my clothes, and we dressed in silence. For all that she wore so little, she took longer than me, fiddling about for some time with her back to me. Then at last she was still. We were sitting on her coat, so I put my jacket round her shoulders, and said, 'Give me your hand.'

Hers was icy cold, like a little corpse, and I chafed it between mine until it warmed. Now I wanted us to speak, but I couldn't think what to say. I wanted to know how she felt about it. In the face of her determined lack of comment, I began to feel a chill of self-reproach.

'Jo, I'm sorry,' I began.

That roused her. She swung towards me, gripping my hand so hard it hurt. 'Don't!' she said fiercely. 'Don't say sorry! If you apologise you'll make it all wrong – sordid and horrible. It wasn't! It was beautiful, and right, and I wanted you as much as you wanted me. I'm glad we did it. Say you're glad, George! Say "thank you", as if you meant it.'

'Thank you, Jo, my darling Jo,' I said. 'I do mean it.'

'Say you're glad. Say it!'

'I'm glad. Of course I'm glad. I've been wanting to make love to you since the first time I ever saw you. You don't know how much! I was only worried about you, that's all.'

'You needn't be,' she said. She seemed reassured now. She rubbed her face up and down my arm with catlike delight. 'It was all my idea. I knew you never would unless I made you. The perfect gentleman, dear George! And I had to know—'

'Know what?' I asked when it was clear she would not finish that sentence.

She still did not. 'I wanted you so.'

'I wanted you, too,' I said, and that seemed enough for now. There would be other things to worry about in due course, but I was still riding the zephyr of sexual contentment. The clouds overhead parted even more, and there was a luminosity in the sky that suggested the moon was rising somewhere behind them. The increase of light showed a massive tree, ragged against the stars – a cedar, I thought. I turned my head and saw another enormous tree – a yew, perhaps – on the other side, and behind it the loom of a tall building.

'What is this place?' I asked. 'Is it somebody's garden?'

Before she could answer, a clock struck the single note of the half hour – a very large clock, an outdoors clock, and shockingly near.

When she answered, I already knew. 'Not someone's garden. It's the churchyard.'

'My God,' I said, startled.

'Mine too,' she answered, calmly, and with a hint of laughter in her voice.

'Jo, the churchyard?' I protested. And then a horrid thought came to me. The stone we were lying on – I felt it. Its edges were unnaturally smooth, symmetrical. I got up hastily. 'My God!' I said again.

'What's the matter?' she asked.

'This thing we're lying on. Is it—? It's not—?'

'A tombstone. Yes,' she said. 'It's the topstone of a sunken vault.'

There was enough light to see now. An old part of the churchyard, with the stones worn, leaning, mossed over, some toppled, some sunk almost below ground. They were not rocks I had stubbed my toes on.

'My God, Jo. I don't know what to say.'

'It's all right,' she said, matter-of-factly. 'He died centuries ago. William Herring was his name. It's one of my favourite stones. I've often come and sat here, sat and read, or just thought. I've brought my sandwiches and eaten them here. He doesn't mind. He's an old friend.'

'But – a churchyard. It's a—' I was going to say, holy place, but it wasn't quite that. 'It's disrespectful,' I said, feebly.

The fierceness was back. 'It *isn't*!' She stared at me, defiant, at bay. 'You don't understand. I *wanted* it to be here. To make it – like a sacrament. So that you would know it meant something. So that you would never forget it. There was nothing disrespectful. There was nothing that wasn't beautiful and important, until you said that.'

She sounded close to tears. I said, 'I'm unsaying it. It was stupid of me. I do understand. It *was* beautiful.' I held my arms out to her, and after a moment she came to them, a little unwillingly. I held her close and quietly, and in the silence I could hear the wind in the yew tree. Though it was only a little breeze, it made a muffled roaring sound, like the sea.

'How could you think I would ever forget

this?' I said softly. And then, as I felt something more was needed. 'It was a wonderful idea of yours.'

She sighed and nudged a little closer, and I stroked her hair. Then she pulled reluctantly away from me and said, 'I should be going back.'

Back, I thought; back to Daddy, back to the colonel. She was the colonel's daughter, and I had just...The full import, in the real world, of what we had done, came home to me, from where it had been waiting in the corner of my mind, with the patience of the self-righteous, for me to notice it. I had allowed myself to be carried away by passion, and it had been wonderful, more wonderful than anything in my life until then. But now there was a responsibility to be shouldered. It had not been in my plans, but if it became necessary... At all events, she must not be allowed to be worried, or frightened, or think herself abandoned. She had to know I would do what was right.

She had begun to move away, and at her arm's stretch I stopped her and turned her back to me. 'Jo,' I began.

In the starlight I could see an expression of alarm cross her face. 'Don't say anything,' she said. 'Don't spoil it. Please George.'

The real world, where I lived, demanded it. 'I have to say this, Jo. I'm *not* sorry we did what we did. But if anything should happen

– you know what I mean—' I was not entirely sure she *did* know. She was so innocent and untouched in some ways, it was possible she had not taken in the fact that such actions could have consequences. She had made love with me as though they did not.

'Nothing will happen,' she said with quiet sureness.

'I don't know if you understand me,' I said helplessly. I felt I had to go on. 'What I'm trying to say is that if you should find, afterwards, that, well, that something had happened, I would—'

'George, stop it,' she commanded, almost sternly. 'I told you, nothing will happen. I promise you. It's all right.'

I gave her a troubled look, but she seemed calm and certain. I had little experience of women then, and women in those days, in any case, kept their mysteries. They always had an air about them, to us men, of being a little apart, a little *other*; of having secret rites we were not to know about. I thought perhaps there was some way she knew that for sure. Some half-heard, half-understood wisdom about dates tugged at memory. And so I left it.

She led me back, across the churchyard and through the hedge, down the shadowed lane to the road, and on to the crossroads. The clouds had almost gone now, and out here in the open the rising moon was pouring a steady stream of thin silver over the grey tarmac. We stopped there to look at each other. With enough light at last to see her properly, I searched her face, feeling that she must be different now, after what had passed. I felt I must look different. The moonlight across her face made its whiteness look blue, and her eyes were hidden in dark caverns, with only a glitter deep within. Her face was like a mask, and something cold touched the back of my neck with that old fieldmouse awe I had felt before. But then I saw her lower lip tremble, and she tucked it in under her teeth to stop it, a gesture so human, so *her*, it made my heart ache.

'Will you be here when I come back, George?' she asked, standing straight like a soldier called to discipline.

'Yes,' I said. In reality I had no idea, of course, but it was the answer she needed. And it seemed then as though I would be.

'Be safe,' she said, and turned away, straight and soldierly, and marched back into the darkness.

In watching her, I forgot to say goodbye. 'You too,' I said belatedly, but I don't think she could have heard me.

Chapter Ten: 1964

The summer was a glorious one, like all the summers of the world come at once in one great spendthrift burst; day followed day in the colours of the cornfield, gold and deep blue, rich with the smells and sounds of summer. There were little refreshing breezes just when they were needed, and sometimes in the night light fragrant rains to revive the fields and wash the dust off the hedges, just enough to stop the farmers complaining. The whole world seemed sweet-tempered. It could hardly have been better done if it had been designed.

Josy's knowledge of the twins' background sank swiftly into the depths of her mind and became old knowledge. Its only effect was of making her feel more than ever at home in this place. She became brown and hard with outdoor life and physical exertion, and peaceful with the lack of mental effort. Every day she spent on the beach, drawing the boats in and out of the water, taking money, passing the time of day with the holiday-makers. When there was nothing to be done for the boats, she stood ankle-deep in the water staring out at the horizon, or sat on the hot shingle with whichever of the twins happened to be about, talking or not talking as the spirit moved them.

And at night, when the blissful, stock-scented darkness drifted down, warm and caressing and a-glitter with great white stars, she sat on the windowsill of the cottage and chatted; or went to one of the pubs and played darts; or sometimes, when both twins were off somewhere doing something else, she walked along the cliffs and watched the great yellow moon ride clear of the eastern hills and float off like a luminous soap bubble out into the empty air. She forgot quite soon that there had been a time when she had not done these same things every day, and no-one reminded her. She felt herself a fixture. She felt as if there were tendrils growing out from her and sinking themselves into the light, chalky earth and taking root there.

Frank disappeared in the evenings quite often, and Josy spent many of them with Jim instead. She didn't mind – in fact, she was pleased, rather than otherwise, for Jim was more interesting to talk to, and she felt more at ease with him than with the twin who lusted after her so persistently. She still did not sleep with Jim, literally or metaphori-cally, but there seemed such easy warmth between them that summer that somewhere in the wordless depths of her mind she began to toy with the notion. *Why not?* was the only reason that presented itself as a counter argument, and that was in some ways the strongest argument of all.

One rare rainy evening in August she and Jim went to the Bull together, and a holiday-maker came in with a guitar, seeking relief from the tedium of his lodgings. He played and Josy sang with him, the poignant folk songs of England, the melancholy ones of Scotland, and the sentimental ones of Ireland. With the windows open and the soft pattering of rain on leaves coming from the darkness outside, there was a late-season nostalgia in the air, a kind of sweet digestive sadness after the long banquet of hot summer days. It persisted in Josy's mind as she walked home with Jim. The rain had stopped but the world was damp and dripping, the air warm and smelling deeply green, fertile, with a hint of black mould underneath and the faint spike of nettles coming up from the ditches. She was glad of Jim's comfortable silence; and glad, too, when they got home, that Frank was not back, to disturb her with his importunings. She wanted to enjoy the pleasant melancholy without having to think about it.

She went into the room she shared with Frank and took off her clothes and replaced them with a loose cotton frock that felt fresh and cool against her hot, brown limbs. Then she leaned against the cold stone of the windowsill and let the night come in to her. It was full of tiny, far-off sounds that told of people still up and doing in the village. Nearer there was the heavy, intermittent burring of a bee still stumbling about in the roses. Probably he had taken shelter there from the rain, and was just now emerging, deceived by the yellow lamp light from Jim's window. He was drugged from the day-long sweetness of their scent, a fat little winged bear after honey, careless of the approaching cold of the night that could easily kill him. She watched dreamily as he buzzed testily at the mouth of a white rose not opened wide enough for him, and hoped he would find somewhere to shelter until morning.

'Silly thing,' she said to him. 'You could have done that tomorrow. You should have gone home long ago.'

'They get drunk this time of year,' said a voice close to her. She was so relaxed it did not startle her, though she had not seen Jim in the garden, on the other side of the roses from her.

'I hope he won't get cold,' she said.

'He'll be all right,' Jim said. 'It's a warm night. Like to come for a walk?' he asked diffidently, not looking at her. 'Too hot to sleep yet.'

'All right,' she said. She climbed over the windowsill and fell in beside Jim's tall shadow. They walked in companionable silence down the narrow road to the beach, and then turned left towards the track that led up onto the cliffs. Josy felt happy, and because she was happy she attributed the same mood to everything around her, so that tonight the sea was sighing with pleasure, the soft airs rustling the sharp-edged sea-grass was a happy singing, and the crickets were chirruping their content in the grass. The green lights of glow-worms were strung all along the path in front of them so that it looked like an airport runway seen from a great height. In the west there was still a luminous turquoise strip of sky; the darkness had a tinge of green light to it. Josy was content just to walk and look and smell the earth; she was barely aware of Jim beside her.

At the top of the cliff they stopped and with silent accord sat on the highest rung of the wooden stile facing out to sea. Josy almost expected Jim to take her hand – it was that sort of night – but instead he lit up a cigarette. She heard the scratch of the match, saw the sudden yellow flare out of the corner of her eye. She smelt the first fragrant cloud of the smoke, and thought piercingly of her father, just for an instant, before she pushed the memory firmly away.

Then Jim said in his unemphatic way, 'D'you know where Frank is tonight?'

'No. He didn't say,' she replied, thinking he wanted to know.

'Where he was all them other nights, too,' Jim said.

'Oh,' she said; and then, feeling she was supposed to ask, obliged him. 'Where's that, then?'

'Out with a girl.'

There was quite a long pause as Josy slowly digested the news. Because it was Jim who was telling her, she felt there must be an underlying reason for it, for he would not be doing it just to cause trouble. That was not his way; and in any case, the twins never spoke against each other. She tried for some time to work out what she ought to under-stand – and also feel – from the words. Even-tually, tired of waiting for her, Jim went on unprompted.

'Frank's getting married,' he said.

Josy looked at him. He was slightly uphill of her, and so towered above her, framed against the sky like a Viking with his sharp nose and crest of blond, blown hair.

'To this girl?'

'Uh-huh. Local girl. Been going with her since last autumn.'

'I didn't know that.'

'Thought you ought to.' There was a pause. 'I dunno if she knows what she's taking on.

Maybe she does. She's a tough one, really. She'll make something of him.'

'Well, let's hope so,' Josy managed, bewildered.

Still without looking at her, he said, 'I'm going away too. Getting a job with a feller down Southampton way. Boat-builder. Real good job, too – taking me into the business. He's seen me work, reckons I've got a real gift. We're gonna sell out, Frank and me – the boats and that – and we'll split it half and half. Give us both a new start.'

'I see,' she said. She felt she ought to congratulate him, but she was too stunned by the suddenness of it all.

He looked towards her apologetically. 'The way we been living – it's no good for ever. Been fun while it lasted, but sooner or later, a man's got to settle down. Not so young as we were any more. Thirty-five come September.' He studied her mute face for a moment, and then felt he hadn't made himself quite clear. 'So we're both going away, you see. Frank's going away with his girl after they get married. Going to settle in Southampton, near me. Lot of boat work down that way.'

'It seems so sudden,' Josy said, humbly.

'Only 'cause you didn't know,' Jim said. 'Frank wouldn't have told you, either. Frank's a bad lot, like our mother. But I thought you ought to know.'

'I had hoped to stay here,' Josy said, rather ashamed now of owning it, since she was so clearly not wanted.

'Stay here? Where?'

'With you and Frank. Here in the cottage. I wanted to stay for good.'

'You, stay here?' Jim looked shocked. 'Oh no, that wouldn't do. You don't belong here, not the way we live.'

'I thought I did belong. I've been so happy here, I felt like one of you.'

'Well, we've liked having you here. But it was a holiday thing, not for permanent. It wouldn't do, permanent. You're not like us. You're different.'

'But why?' Josy protested. 'I come from round here – I'm a local girl, if you like.'

'But your mum and dad was high-ups. You've been to college and everything.' He scratched his head with the unfamiliar effort of finding the right words for this delicate situation. 'Me and Frank, all of us in the village, we're just ordinary folk. You're too good for the kind of life we have. You're different.'

It's funny, Josy thought, how everyone thinks he is the norm and someone else is the different one. But if there is a norm, Jim's as far from it as I am.

'You've got a future of your own,' Jim went on, still groping after clarity. 'Not like this here. Not hiring out boats. That's no good for someone educated.' Josy wanted to tell him she understood, to save him this painful effort of explanation. But before she could speak, he went on, 'Face it girl, if you hadn't been different you couldn't have come here in the first place. I mean, if a village girl did what you do – come and lived with us, worked on the boats – slept with Frank – well, folks'd think she was—' He didn't know the word déclassé. 'Well, they wouldn't like it. She'd be looked down on ever after. But when you do it it's sort of different. High-ups like you can do queer things, and nobody thinks anything of it. I dunno why,' he added at last, shaking his head a little with the mystery of it all.

'Yes, I understand,' Josy said quickly, to stop him blundering on any further.

A silence fell, and now, because he was afraid he had hurt her, he did what he had not done before – he took her hand. His was warm and hard, as she had imagined it would be. She thought of him and herself, tried to see herself through his eyes, but she couldn't. It was plain he didn't dislike her or condemn her, but that was hardly comforting. A girl of his own sort he would condemn, she thought, but not her. Because she wasn't real, and therefore what she did did not matter?

Jim looked at her sideways out of the corner of his eye and wished, not for the first time, that he was educated, and knew the proper words to tell her how he felt about her, how he had felt for all those years. She was familiar to him, as familiar as a favourite garment; and at the same time breathtakingly strange. What was she thinking now, for instance? He imagined her brain whirring away inside her head like a machine. What could people think about so much, hour after hour? He had hurt her feelings, he thought, telling her a village girl couldn't have done what she did. But he didn't mean it in a bad way. The way she came and went was part of her strangeness, but not a bad part. He didn't know why a person like her, with her brains and her accent and all the toff things of her background, should want to come and live with him and Frank in that cottage, no better than a hovel, and eat café food, and get dirty pulling boats about, and spoil her hands with blisters and calluses; but he had never expected to know why. Her sudden appearances and disappearances were like natural phenomena, like the migrations of birds, which he did not think to question.

But he loved it when she did come. When the time grew near that she might come, he would think about her and long for her to arrive. She was like a dream you had had often before, but could never quite remember. It was like that moment when you wake up and you know you've been dreaming something nice, and you want to go back to sleep so you can get back to it, and you try not to wake up properly so you can slide back under. That was the feeling she gave him, and he had always loved her that way, loved her hopelessly but not miserably, because she was part of another world, like the dream, and so not to be thought of as a real chance. If he married, it would be, like Frank, to an ordinary girl; but he would long for her always. He wished he could tell her all this as she sat there beside him in the gathering darkness, thinking away behind her silent face; but all he could do was to squeeze her hand.

'So this will be my last summer here,' she said at last. 'I wish I had known sooner, to make it last. But then,' she added honestly, 'I don't suppose I could have managed it any better than I did. I'm glad you told me now, anyway.'

'I had to,' he said. 'I was watching you when you were singing with that chap in the pub.' The thoughts burst out of him almost involuntarily. 'She had yellow hair, and she used to sing like that to our father.' It was years since he had mentioned his mother, and now he had spoken of her twice in a matter of minutes. 'I remember her sitting by the fire, drying her hair after she'd washed it, and singing to him.' He looked at Josy shyly, and saw that she was interested, and not looking mocking or superior. It reminded me, when you were singing.'

'Do you remember her clearly?' Josy asked, sensing that he would not mind talking about it now.

'A bit. She was very pretty. At least, before our dad died she was. After that she got tired and ill and she lost her looks. But she was a bad lot,' he said sadly. 'She – she had other men. Dad beat her once, gave her such a black eye she couldn't go out for three days. But she couldn't seem to help it. I think she loved our dad, but she couldn't stop herself. Frank's a bit like her. I'm – well, I take more after dad, I suppose.'

Josy nodded, just enough to keep him going. She didn't quite understand what he meant about Frank, but she didn't want to press him for explanations when he was opening up so much.

'See, Mum, a man'd look at her, because she was so pretty, and she'd sort of go to him, like a dog being called. Couldn't help it. And Frank's a bit that way with you. That's why he wouldn't tell you about this other girl.' He stopped abruptly and closed his mouth tight, as though he had said too much. After a minute he stood up, and Josy stood too and fell in beside him.

They walked along the cliff top, and watched the moon rising. How many times, Josy thought, have I done this? She had watched so many, the hot moons and the cold, with Rob, with George, with Frank, with Jim – alone. And this was the last, the last summer, the last visit. Tears came to her eyes. I can't stay here, she thought, and I can never come back. Her life seemed to be closing in on her, closing down this place and that, driving her towards – what? But this place was the most important, always had been. She felt the up-surge of a gnawing sadness, the particular sadness of the exile, who can never go home again.

'Remember when you first came here?' Jim asked her out of the darkness. His hand was still warm over hers, but she had not noticed it for some time past.

'Yes, I remember,' she said.

'I thought it was me, then. I thought it would be me you liked.'

The moon was pulling free of the earth now, and she was thinking of all the velvet evenings, walking along the cliffs with George. Such a long time ago it seemed now. Her thoughts turned longingly towards George; but he even more than this place was the home she could not go to. She drag-ged her mind away from him.

'I did like you,' she said. 'I do.'

'I loved you – in a kind of a way. But Frank had to have you. So it never happened.' A silence, and then, sadly. 'I just wanted to make sure you didn't mind.'

Didn't mind what? she wondered. But the thought was only vague and distant. Other things were more urgently occupying her mind. The fact that already the reality of this place seemed to be shredding away. She had to go; and so this was becoming part of her past, another inaccessible part. However much she loved it, she could not keep hold of it. It was always the way with the things she loved. They slipped through her fingers – and when they did, she mustn't grasp. It was the rule. The more she wanted them, the more she must let them go.

I'm lonely, she thought in faint surprise. I've been lonely all summer. I want to be with someone who knows what I'm thinking, someone who remembers the same things as me, someone I can talk to about them. She knew who that was. She knew where she wanted to be. But she must not.

Jim had stopped, had turned to face her; his hands on her shoulders, he was looking down into her face. 'It was hard to see you like Frank best,' he said, unaware that her thoughts weren't with him. 'He's my brother, but I know what he's like. None better. All these years, I've wondered what it would've been like if you'd liked me best.'

Her head moved sharply, her face turning up to him, focusing on him. 'What?' she said.

'But you do like me a bit, don't you?' he

asked gently, insistently. He was trembling a little with his own boldness, but he knew there might never be another chance like this – that there almost certainly would never be another chance at all.

'I've always liked you best,' she said, and her voice sounded faint, like something brought from a distance on the breeze. 'But Frank—'

'Yes,' he said. 'I know.' He understood. And he knew she did. It was all right. 'Shall we go back to the cottage?' he asked softly.

'All right,' she said, as if that was all there was to it. He led the way, but kept hold of her hand, leading her carefully down the crumbling path, across the still-warm pebbles of the beach, up the road under the high stone walls and the overhanging sea-pinks, through the tangled garden, in through his window, helping her courteously over the sill. He didn't light the lamp. He was shy and afraid; and there was just enough light from the village street to see the shape of each other, not enough for embarrassment.

His roomed smelled different from Frank's, and the surprise of it woke Josy from her half-dream. She had thought that they would smell the same, as they looked the same. Now she was properly aware of him, she realised his shyness, and knew he needed help to move on. So she began unbuttoning his shirt. He stood still, like a horse for grooming, while she took off his shirt and undid his trousers. Then he gently put her hands away and took them off himself. She quickly removed her two garments, and then stepped closer to him, and put her hands on his lean body. He felt unnervingly like Frank, and unnervingly different.

She was lonely, and she held on to Jim almost desperately as they made love, but it didn't help. It didn't touch anything in her except a sort of kindness, born of familiarity and common affection. It was Jim who was moved, having her at last, the longed-for goddess. He trembled at the wonder of it, the strangeness, the once-in-a-lifetime, never-to-be-repeatedness of it. There was no thought of wrong, or of consequences, in him. She lived by her own rules, different from anyone else's. If she chose at last to make love with him, it was not for him to question.

Afterwards he sat up and lit a cigarette, wondering if she would say anything about it. But she got up and went away from him, over to the window, where she leaned on the sill, listening to the faraway sound of the sea. It sounded autumnal, melancholy. The roses, too, smelt different now. And did she not detect a hint of the woody, leafy, sharp scent of September in the air? Everything was changing. Summer was dying.

'You'll catch cold,' Jim said at last, gently.

He wanted to hear her voice, to know whether it was all right.

It was not cold, the night was warm, but she understood that it was only a code phrase, and answered the underlying meaning by going back to where he sat on the bed. The moon had not swung round enough to penetrate the room, and she could only see his vague outline. She groped for his hand and squeezed it.

'I'm going tomorrow.'

He felt a pang of regret, that she'd said nothing about what they had just done.

'I thought you would,' he said after a pause. 'Will you be going home?'

'I haven't got a home,' she said automatically. It was what she always said, and it had always been a thing of pride to her. But now in her mind the words had an echo of wistfulness.

Jim wanted to say thank you to her, for what they had just done, but he didn't know what would be the right form of words. And so he said at last, 'I'll give you a lift to the station. Fred at the Bull'll lend me his van.'

'Thanks.'

There didn't seem to be anything else to say, and she let go of his hand, and wondered how to spend the rest of the night.

Chapter Eleven: 1954

I didn't really expect her to write. She hadn't promised to, and I remembered my own first days at university: the excitement, the novelty, the busyness; the strange new responsibility for one's own studies; the freedom; the wonderful accessibility of new friends and social activities. There was simply so much to fill one's mind that the last thing on it would be writing letters home.

But she did write. For the first three weeks I had a letter a week: letters like her conversation, full of incident and observation – I have them still. But she said nothing in them about herself, about whether she was happy or homesick. I took that to mean she was happy, and that the link between her and her home – between us – was weakened. A fortnight passed between her third letter and the fourth, and it was briefer, with the air of having been scribbled between dashing in from one engagement and dashing off to the next. A month passed before number five came, and it was very brief. I guessed from its tone that it would be the last.

After the dinner with the colonel that had been arranged on Jo's last night, I was sent on secondment for a month to another unit at Aldershot, where they were doing some building work. When I returned I hesitated about making any further contact with him. We were worlds apart, both in age and socially. He had been welcoming that evening at dinner, but I had found it a little awkward to be there without the impetus of Jo's presence. We had no common frame of reference but her, and he did not talk about her, so I had felt a little lost. So I did not contact the colonel to say I was back, and since he did not contact me, the relationship lapsed. It seemed that fate was drawing me away from the Graces, or them away from me.

I did miss Jo – that was only natural. At first I thought about her a great deal, and wondered with some urgency whether I would see her again. But I was a young man with a great many occupations: my army duties, my ongoing studies, and above all my plans for my career when I should finally be released. Without the constant reminder of her presence she gradually slipped into a backwater of my mind, a constant dull ache, as something loved and possibly lost, a dear memory and an unsubstantial hope. I did not go out with any other girls – to that extent she had changed my life. In my present circumstances I could not hope to meet anyone who came near to matching her. I did not want anyone else. In abstinence, I suppose, I kept her memory green.

My release would come the following July, the month that would mark the end of Jo's first year at university. Smart was getting out before me, and in celebration of his approaching freedom he drank more than ever, and managed to involve me in some pretty outrageous scrapes. He remains on record as the only soldier ever to have a girl in the marking pit of the firing range – though not, I should add, actually during a firing practice, as the legend has it. We both earned tremendous kudos among our fellow squaddies for managing to get in and out of the WRAC's dormitory undetected one night, though our purposes while in there were far more innocent than the reported ones. I was merely there to 'keep nick' for Smart and his female; and he and she did nothing but talk in urgent whispers until growing anxiety made me drag him away. Still, the fable was born, and did the circumstances more than justice.

However, what with one thing and another, I often found myself mired with Smart in his misdemeanours and suffering his punishments along with him. One freezing December day he managed to get us in bad odour with Sergeant 'Mad' Bull, and we were dragged back after a piece of tank drill to clean the blasted thing. It was one of the Mad Bull's favourite ways of punishing minor offences, and this was not our first stint. On a summer day it hardly impinged on us – something to be shrugged about and got on with; but on a day when your fingers froze blue and numb in the air alone, it was not pleasant to be mucking about with cold water and icy mud while your whole being cried out for hot tea.

'I just don't understand you, West,' said the Bull, shaking his head sadly. 'With your brains, you ought to know better. Look at yourself, lad – covered in shite from head to foot. I'd have thought you'd've learnt something, visiting up Colonel Grace's house, but you're just as big a military moron as Smart here.'

'Sarge!' Smart protested automatically in wounded tones.

'Get on with it,' said the Bull witheringly, and left us to it.

Later, when we had buffed the tank up to his requirements, Smart and I trotted back through the freezing mist and went straight to the showers, where we stood under the hot water until the feeling came back into our extremities and our skin burned and itched with reaction.

After that, there was nothing we wanted

more than a pint of bitter and the welcoming fug of a bar parlour, so we sneaked out through a gap in the fence we knew about and believed no-one else did. We thought it best to put some distance between ourselves and the camp – and in any case Smart could no longer use the nearest local, where he had got himself into an awkward situation with the barmaid – so we fetched my car and drove to Lulworth, to the Castle. The bus stop was just outside the pub, and as we walked up to it, the little single-decker bus from Wool came chugging and sneezing up, and stopped to let a few people off. We stood aside to let them go by. One of the winter-muffled figures had two shopping bags with her, bulging full and evidently heavy from the way she held them. She stopped and looked at me and said, 'Mr West?'

It was Jean, Colonel Grace's housekeeper. Her head was swathed in a woollen scarf with the end pulled over her mouth and chin, so I didn't recognise her until she pulled it away.

'Oh, hello,' I said. I felt a little awkward. It led me to babble. 'How are you? Just back from shopping?'

She brushed my waffle aside, looking me straight in the face with a reproachful sternness. 'You've not been near us all these weeks,' she said. 'And the colonel so lonely with Josella gone away. Shame on you, when he's been so kind to you.'

'I – I didn't think—' I began.

She didn't let me finish. 'I know very well you didn't. It's all the same with you young people. It's me, me, me. No gratitude. No proper feeling.'

'I didn't think he'd want to see me,' I said, determined to get my defence out. Smart had melted gracefully into the background at the first words, and out of the corner of my eye I saw him backing into the porch of the pub and then whisking in through the door.

'I thought he'd made it very clear he wanted to see you. Invited you to dinner, didn't he?'

'I'm sorry,' I said humbly. 'If you really think it would cheer him up – I mean, give him pleasure—' I didn't know what words to use. It all sounded too patronising from a nobody like me to a distinguished warrior like Colonel Grace.

She patted my hand to stop me. 'All right then. You come along and visit him. I'll tell him you're coming tomorrow.'

'Oh, but I—' I had plans already for Saturday night.

She gave me no room for manoeuvre. 'Tomorrow at seven. He dines earlier in winter. Don't be late. He hates unpunctuality.'

And so it was that my relationship with the Grace family was resumed.

I arrived punctually and was received by Jean with much better grace than I had expected. She smiled at me approvingly and showed me into the drawing room and announced me almost with a flourish. In winter the former garden room was made cosy by floor-to-ceiling curtains of a heavy burgundy-coloured material that covered the whole wall – an unusual arrangement, and having a rather theatrical appearance, but effective. Against the curtains the scene, lit by lamps in various corners, was almost like the set of a play. The furniture, arranged in conversation pieces, stood out darkly; and in a chair under a standard lamp the colonel sat reading some papers.

He stood up and came towards me, his hand extended, and as he came close enough for me to grasp it, I almost quailed. The change in him in those few months was ferocious. I had last seen him a retired but vigorous man; now age had sunk into him like winter cold. He seemed almost shrunken. His clothes hung on him, his face was deeply lined, his skin slack, his colour bad. He was a different man still wearing the remains of the colonel's outward appearance in a sort of mockery of life. He moved still with military uprightness, but the effort it took him was visible. As we shook hands he smiled a welcome, but mortality was in his eyes, a grim message that left no room for doubt or hope. I saw, as I automatically returned his greeting, the reflection of my own reaction in his eyes. He knew that I had seen, and it added to his burden. I tried to smile in a social way, but I'm afraid it must have been more of a grimace.

'It's pleasant to see you again,' he said. 'It has been a long time.'

'Yes. I'm sorry. I was away for a time,' I stammered. 'I was seconded. And then, when I came back—'

He pressed my hand briefly before releasing it and said, 'There's no need to explain. You are a young man at the time of life that holds many engagements. I did not mean to sound accusing. I'm grateful that you spare me the time.'

'It's an honour to visit you,' I said, and I think I sounded sincere.

'Please, won't you sit down?' He waved me to a chair, and then, with a gesture of exasperation, said, 'Oh, I meant to bring up a new bottle of sherry. I seem to forget so many things these days. Will you excuse me for a moment while I go down to the cellar?'

'Oh, please, don't trouble on my account,' I began bumblingly.

He cut me off with a smile. 'It's a particular sherry I would like you to try. Fine sherry should be drunk in company. I shan't be a moment. Please help yourself to a cigarette while I'm gone.'

I watched him leave the room by the door at the far end, still feeling cold with shock. To give myself something to do I got up and went to the cigarette box on the table, and as I took out a cigarette her movement towards me made me realise that Jean was still in the room. She came over and took up the cigarette lighter from the table and struck it for me.

'Thank you.' She replaced the lighter and as she straightened up she met my eyes. 'The colonel,' I began, hardly knowing what I was going to say. 'He looks—'

'I know how he looks,' she said in an undertone that was almost fierce with her protective feelings. 'He's dying. How should he look?'

Through my renewed shock at the bare words, I thought back to things he had said in the past, little hints I had not known I had picked up. 'He's known for some time?'

'All this year.'

'Does Jo – does Josella know?'

'She does not,' she said with a finality that told me her father had wanted to keep it from her, and that it was not for me to question that decision, or bypass it. But I couldn't help it.

'She would want to know. She would want to be with him.'

'That's not for you nor me to decide,' she

said, and turned away. There were things I wanted to ask her, but my mind felt thick and numb, like one's face after the dentist's novocaine.

At the door she paused and turned, fixed me again with that fierce eye, and said, 'Don't upset him.' And then she was gone.

I smoked nervously for a few minutes. Then the colonel returned, holding a dusty-looking bottle by the neck. 'This is something rather special,' he said.

'I hope it won't be wasted on me, sir,' I said, stupidly.

He paused in the action of applying the corkscrew. 'It would be foolish of me to hang onto it, would it not? Now, please, don't distress yourself. Let us, as men and soldiers, acknowledge the truth and be done with it. Otherwise conversation will be difficult, and I am looking forward to talking to you.'

'Just as you say, sir,' I managed to mumble.

'And as I said,' he went on cheerfully, 'fine sherry should be shared, and I'm grateful to you for providing an opportunity to open it.'

'In that case,' I said, summoning all my courage, 'I shall be most interested to taste it.'

It was, to my untutored palate, quite extraordinary, as different from family-funeral sherry as if it had been another drink altogether. It was pale golden, delicately scented to the nose, and smooth, nutty, and not at all sweet to the taste. While I sipped it, the colonel talked comfortably about wines, giving me, if I had had the wit to take it in, something of a tutoring which might have stood me in good stead later. But it was hard for me to concentrate on anything but the ruin of the man in front of me.

Soon Jean called us to dinner; afterwards we retired to the drawing room again. A fire was lit and we sat in chairs drawn up to it. With the soft lamp-light leaving much of the room almost in the dark, the leaping flames reflected off hidden things in distant corners, throwing little ovals and ripples and occasional sparks of light, as if they were joining in with the conversation. The colonel provided brandy, and though I had had more than my share of the wine at dinner, I did not refuse. I felt I needed it to get me through. My mind felt wide open to him, with all its nerve endings over-sensitive.

And yet throughout the evening he chatted pleasantly to me, covering a range of general topics, doing everything in his power to put me at ease. He had considerable charm, and I was now made the beneficiary of it, and saw how it would have been when he was a serving officer – how his men and his juniors would have loved him. But this very gallantry was what made my mind feel raw. I could only think of the wonder of the human spirit: it was the man facing the annihilation of his own precious self who was exerting himself to comfort *me*.

At last he offered me more brandy, and when I accepted and he began to rise, I said, 'No, sir, let me.' He sank again into his chair, and let me do it – the first crack in the armour. I picked up the decanter from the table and refilled his glass and then my own, and he watched my movements, his hands loose and folded in his lap. They looked – *he* looked as though he would never move again. But when I had resumed my seat, he sighed and drew himself a little up, reached for his glass and sipped, and then returned it to be cradled in his lap.

And he said, 'You see how it is with me.'

It did not sound like quite a question, and I had no idea how to answer it. But he met my eyes, and I could only nod. He nodded in reply, and looked into the fire – a more comfortable arrangement for me. Perhaps for him, too, because he began to speak. His voice was quiet, and sometimes a word would lose itself in the small, unimportant noises of the fire. The flames were lower now, and did not reach the dark corners of the room. We sat in a warm, glowing cave, and the reflections were tiny sparks thrown from the cut glass of decanter and tumblers, and a more uncertain shine from the curves of leather of the armchairs, where the fire-light rubbed itself like a friendly cat.

He said, 'We have not been acquainted very long, but I feel as though it has been much longer. Without precisely knowing very much about you, George, I feel I know you. I suppose that comes partly from the fact that Josella had spoken about you so much and so often. She has always been one to make up her mind quickly about people, and it was plain from the beginning that she had taken ... a liking to you.' The tiny pause showed that this was not quite the word he had wanted. 'In that respect she takes after me. As an officer, of course, one has to be able to exercise judgement about people, and to do it quickly. During the war, one's life, and those of many others, could sometimes depend on the ability to make such judgements instantaneously. I think – I like to think – I was a successful officer. But an officer is only as good as his men.'

'You are a legend in the regiment, sir,' I said.

Without looking at me, he smiled. 'How kind of you to say so. But I was not fishing for compliments. I only wished you to understand that I am not speaking carelessly to you, but out of a feeling I have, that in some way you and I understand each other.'

Nothing I could say that would not have sounded ingratiating. I could only nod, though he was not looking at me.

'Josella doesn't know that I am dying,' he

said, coming abruptly to the point. 'She has been uneasy about me all summer, but there was nothing she could put her finger on. It was the way I wanted it. I did not want to spoil her last summer of childhood. And I suspected – no, I knew, really – that if she had known how it was with me, she would not have gone away to university, however much I insisted.'

'I'm sure she wouldn't have,' I said. 'She'd have wanted to stay with you while she could.'

He looked up then, detecting a note of criticism I had not intended to make apparent. 'You think me unkind? But I should not have wanted her to witness my deterioration. That would have made it too hard to bear. And I had a very particular reason for wanting her to go to university. I have been living with this knowledge for a long time, and I have thought about the consequences in great depth.' He studied my face a moment. 'You are fond of her, are you not?'

'Yes,' I said awkwardly. 'I – yes, very fond.'

He did not follow this up, to my relief. He looked away, at the flames again, and said, 'When I am gone she will be very much alone. The only family she has is her brother, who is, of course, unable to be often with her. She will also be not very well off. This house, I'm afraid, is heavily mortgaged. We live comfortably enough on my army pension and some small investments I have, but the pension dies with me, and the investments will do little more than clear my debts.' He smiled ruefully, to take the sting out of the information, and said, 'The post-war economic situation has not been kind to people like me. So you see, I have been much exercised over how Josella will be placed when she is left alone.'

'I understand,' I said.

He nodded. 'She is an intelligent girl, and always did well at school. I decided some time ago that the best course would be for her to go to university and so qualify herself for a career that could support her in comfort. In the civil service, perhaps. I want her to be independent. Without a degree she would be much less likely to obtain a position of the sort I would like for her. I should hate to think of her having to find a *job*.' He spoke of it with a distaste that had me suppressing a smile. 'So for some time I have been putting aside what I could into a fund to pay for her university fees and expenses. I think – I hope – it will be enough.'

I nodded again. I wondered whether Jo had been as ignorant of his approaching end as he thought. I remembered that night on the moonlit cliff, her mourning over approaching loss, her fear of going away, how she had said that all we had was there and then. I understood, too, or I thought I understood now, something about the occasion when we had all gone riding and she had had the bad fall. I had been shocked that the colonel had not gone to her, had seemed to feel no concern over her hurts. But he loved her intensely, I knew that now. I think he had been remembering that soon he would not be there to pick her up and comfort her. He had been schooling himself to let her go.

Thinking of this, I said, 'I understand,' again, but with more warmth in my voice.

He looked at me. 'Do you, George? Do you? I hope so. Because, you see, I am very well aware that money isn't everything. It is the only thing I can arrange from this side of the grave that will carry on afterwards. For the rest, I can only hope. She needs friendship, too, you see.'

'Yes,' I said. I remembered Rob at the station, asking me to take care of her. Plainly he had known. 'Her brother—' I began.

'He is quite considerably older than her. Ten years. Of course, it would be different if he were settled, with a home and family of his own, but at present he cannot even be often in the country. I want to ask you – I hope you will not think it an imposition—'

'To look after her,' I said, remembering Rob's words.

He seemed to sink back a little in his chair, as though he had been braced for something and had now relaxed. But was it with relief or disappointment? With retrospect, my voice had revealed more than I meant it to. As when Rob had asked the same thing, I had felt a little dismayed, a little imposed upon for having been asked.

'No,' he said at last, and his voice was flat and black, like canal water. 'No, I couldn't ask that. That would not be proper. You are hardly older than her. And your life is just beginning. There is no knowing where your career will take you. No, what I wanted to ask you was to be her friend. She will need all the friends she can find. Her life has not been an easy one and it will – it has—' He lifted his glass to his lips still cradled in both hands, and sipped. A little shudder went through him, and he straightened his shoulders again. 'There are things about Josella that you do not know,' he said. 'Her mother – she perhaps told you her mother died some years ago, when she was eleven.'

'Yes,' I said.

He nodded. 'That was not quite true, or rather, not all the truth. Her mother – my wife – killed herself.'

The words fell into a little silence that seemed created to receive them. Perhaps such words always would, carrying their own silence with them. I didn't know what to say. I thought of my own mother with a quick, glancing touch, in the way a Catholic might cross himself to avert evil. How terrible, how terrible for the colonel. I looked at him with real pity. I remembered my own father's death, and my mother's agony. How much worse would it have been if he had taken his own life? I couldn't begin to think what a blow that would be, on top of the other.

'Does Jo know?' I asked at last.

'Oh yes,' he said, in the flat voice.

I was silent. What kind of a mother would do that to her child? My first thought was of how selfish she must have been.

'She – my wife – had been drinking a great deal. She had been unhappy for some time, and that was her way of coping with it. But in the end even the drink was not enough. Josella was profoundly shocked, of course. It is a thing hard enough for an adult to cope with. I suppose in many ways I have never come to terms with it myself. What it has meant to Josella one can only imagine.'

'Yes,' I said. I stared into the glowing heart of the fire, and thought of her, her brightness, her laughter, her occasional strangeness. She had never hinted at this particular tragedy. She had made light of her motherlessness. But I remembered how scathingly she had spoken of her mother. I tried to imagine, now, the colonel as I knew him marrying a 'flighty' actress, and could not. But what about the actress – as she had been painted for me, selfish, fun-loving – marrying a colonel? How unhappy must she have been, and for how long, to have killed herself?

The colonel sighed and stirred himself at the end of a long silence in which we both pursued our own thoughts. 'Well,' he said, and finished his brandy in a final sort of way, 'I hope I have not bored you with this recital of our family history. I hope you do not think it impertinent of me to burden you with it. But I have felt that you are fond of Josella, and she of you. I build nothing on that, I assure you. I only wanted to ask you to be her friend. Just that. She is not quite like other girls. And she will always go her own way, I know that very well.'

The words spoke themselves without my volition. Here in the magic circle of the firelight, in the strangeness of the company of a dying man, the air vibrated with secrets, and vows, mysteries and longings. I said, 'She can always count on me. Whatever happens, she can come to me for help or advice or—'

I hardly knew what else. I understood what he was asking, that I should always be available, at the end of a telephone or a letter, for a girl whose family had disintegrated and left her alone. It was a compliment to me, on the grounds of so short an acquaintance – though the sentinel in the back of my mind had an unworthy thought later, that perhaps there simply wasn't anyone else. But I would have promised a great deal more just then, had he asked me, and afterwards I appreciated his restraint.

'Thank you,' he said. And then he sighed and seemed to sink in his chair with the suddenness and hollow collapse of the fire falling in when it is at the end of its fuel. He looked quite suddenly tired to death. I thought I had better take my leave. I stood up. His eyes turned in my direction, but without lighting on me. 'Would you be so kind as to ask Jean to come in?' he said with remote politeness.

The train came in on time, and I was waiting on the platform by the exit, as I had been for half an hour past. It was deadly cold, and the sky was mute with impending snow, making an unnatural twilight of the early afternoon. Christmas was a week off. A sad homecoming for her, poor Jo. As the train sighed and shuddered to a halt, doors flapped back all along its side and a crowd of new recruits poured off, looking all ears with their brutally fresh haircuts. I guessed that she would be at the far end of the train, as distant from them as possible. As they poured towards the exit I worked my way through them, in time to see her slam the carriage door behind her and pick up her suitcase. She saw me straight away, and our eyes met through a gap in the bodies, but she made no gesture of greeting beyond a small nod of the head.

She looked both taller and older than when she had gone away, though perhaps that was the effect of having had her hair cut almost as short as the squaddies – an urchin cut, it was known as in those days, I believe. Her face was pale and there were dark shadows under her eyes, but her mouth was set firm, and there was no trace of tears as she walked towards me, her back straight and her shoulders back, as though she were under discipline. I took the case from her and fell in beside her, at a loss to know what to say, and we walked out of the station to the car. I didn't dare touch her, nor did she offer to touch me.

She said, 'Is Rob home?'

'Yes. He arrived this morning,' I said. 'He asked me to come and meet you.' She didn't answer, and I felt I ought to apologise for it. 'He thought it would be easier for you, to meet me first.'

'Yes,' she said. 'Thanks, George.'

We reached the car now, and while I put her case in the boot, she wandered round to the passenger side. The first tiny fragments of snow began to fall, too small to be called snowflakes, the merest flecks of white, disappearing as soon as they touched any surface. When I had shut the boot and looked up, she was still standing there beside the car, looking lost, so I went round to open the door for her. When I reached her she turned to me and scanned my face as if she wanted to say something. Indeed, her lips parted, and I saw her breath cloud small on the bitter air; but then her lower lip trembled, and she had to catch it under her teeth for control. I ached for her. I let her in, and went round to my own side. By the time I had settled in beside her, her lips were set firm again, and she stared away, ahead of her, resolutely.

We drove out of the village, past the Black Bear and up the hill. When we reached the great elm tree at the crest, she said, 'He knew. I know that now.'

'Yes,' I said.

'He knew,' she said. 'Why did he send me away?'

Nothing I could have said would not have sounded trite. I drove on in silence, into the gathering snow. I don't know if she cried at all; I only know I never saw her shed one tear for her father. I think perhaps she thought it would not be seemly to let anyone see her weep, though she had loved him so much. She was a soldier's daughter.

Chapter Twelve: 1964

Frank came in at about two in the morning. Josy, who had been asleep in his bed, was woken by the slight sound he made climbing in through the window. She sat up, and watched him as he began to undress. He didn't look at her or speak, and though that was perfectly normal in him – the enigmatic one – she found it now unnerving. When he had got down to his trousers, she felt that it was now or never, and forced the word out.

'Frank?'

'Uh-huh?'

'I'm leaving. Tomorrow. I mean today. In the morning.'

'Uh-huh.' His voice betrayed no particular interest. His hands worked mechanically at his belt buckle, and then stopped as the news made itself understood. He thought a moment, and said, 'Bit early, isn't it?'

Was that all? she thought, suddenly exasperated. Just for a moment she couldn't think what to say next in the face of such phlegm. And yet the fact that he had stopped undressing and was looking at her suggested he was waiting for an answer, rather than having made a finite comment. So she decided to broach the subject.

'Frank, why didn't you tell me?'

'Tell you what?'

'Oh don't be tiresome. You know what.' He made no answer, but still looked at her steadily, and in the end she said, with growing irritability, 'About your getting engaged, of course. You should have told me.'

'Engaged?' For a moment she thought he was going to deny it, but after a pause he said, 'But why should I?'

He sounded so genuinely puzzled that her irritation faded, and she thought instead, he really doesn't know what I was talking about. He really doesn't know why.

'We are friends,' she said. 'It's the kind of thing friends tell each other. We are friends, aren't we?'

He considered the proposition in apparent depth, and then said, 'You're a visitor.'

'You are typically cryptic. It's a division of humanity I only begin to understand. Well, I know that to all of you down here visitors are a separate species, hardly members of the human race. But surely I'm different. I was a native once too. And you and I have been close all these years. I must mean more to you than just a visitor?'

He looked at her blankly, the edges of his face limned with lamplight from the street, a handsome statue.

She felt the first flutterings of panic inside, and went on, 'Do you mean to tell me that I mean nothing more to you than any of the other holidaymakers that come down here?'

He regarded her without answering, and then, as she said no more, he turned his head a little away from her and lit a cigarette. Had he done this only a few minutes before, she would have translated it as a typical piece of his inscrutability, perhaps as an arrogant gesture that said, *cease your prattling, woman: I am a law unto myself.*

But now, with a great illuminating flash of understanding, she realised that it was simply the temporising action of a man completely out of his depth. He had not understood anything she had said. He was simply waiting for the conversation to come back within the range of his comprehension.

Suddenly she felt an insane desire to giggle. *How* long has she known him? And was she only now discovering a fundamental truth about him? His cryptic utterances that had so long intrigued her, his casual, indifferent gestures, his most piquing, enigmatic silences – all the things she had taken as the outward signs of a complex character, perhaps the hints of a natural genius locked behind an untutored tongue – all this, it was now clear, were merely the function of stupidity. He wasn't inscrutable, he was dumb.

In the same illuminating flash many things became clear to her. Jim Boda had said his brother was a bad lot, but he, who was intelligent enough to behave properly and understand social rules, had not the detached intellect to understand his brother. Frank was another such as his mother, that was probably true: but the famous Rose's bad behaviour had probably stemmed not from promiscuity, but stupidity. Frank was not wicked, not a bad lot, he simply did not connect any one thing with any other. She saw him now, tall, handsome, besieged by visiting females, all fermenting with holiday licence and much taken with his noble, silent, godlike mien. How should he refuse them? *Why* should he refuse them? Either question was probably as impossible for him to answer as the other. Rose quite literally couldn't help herself, and neither could Frank.

Busy reshuffling years of accumulated ideas about him, she had time to wonder whether his new fiancée understood all this too, or whether she had been as taken in as Josy had been. But Jim had said she was tough and would make something of Frank. Josy imagined a busy, managing sort of female, bustling the easily swayed Frank towards the altar. Who had proposed to whom? She could believe that having found himself in a position where it was clearly expected of him, Frank had obediently done it.

Josy was beginning to feel a blush of shame as she scrutinised some part of her behaviour by this new light. Had she not made an ass of herself? But then dear, thick Frank would never notice, that was the beauty of it. While Jim had accepted her actions as a natural phenomenon, stemming from her 'differentness', Frank had never even had to accept them. He would never have noticed she was not like everyone else.

Really, when you came to think of it, the whole thing was irresistibly funny. She couldn't wait to tell George – how he would laugh. A soft chuckle escaped her now, and Frank looked across at her under his eyelashes to see why she was laughing.

'Come on to bed,' she said. 'I must get some sleep if I'm going to make an early start.'

He gave a small sigh of relief, stubbed his cigarette out on the windowsill and pitched the end into the garden. He removed his remaining garments and draped them over the single, all-purpose wooden chair in the corner, and stepped across the room with his neat, graceful step – like an Arab horse, she had often thought. She shifted over for him and he slid in beside her, looking at her almost enquiringly with his large, expressionless eyes. He ran his hand tentatively over her bare side, to see if sex was required. If only I had known all along what I know now, Josy thought, remembering all the times that the gesture had aroused a thrilled response from her.

Repressing a smile, she said pleasantly, 'Good night, Frank.'

He gave a grunt of content in reply, and turning his big body over onto its side fell asleep with the ease of the righteous.

She woke early and, not wanting to disturb Jim to fulfil his promise of a lift to the station, she put her few belongings into her bag and slipped quietly out of the window. The world was still asleep, and the morning had the dewy perfection of an unused summer dawn. The air was vibrant with cool, vivid smells; birds were chirping and busying in the trees and creepers. The road, still in the shadow of its houses, lay empty and a little damp, beckoning the way out of the village. Away to her right the sea lay out of sight past a bend in the street, but she could hear the occasional mew of a gull, and could just catch a hint of its breath on the freshness of the air.

Once past the gate she stopped and looked back. The faint, early sun was lying in a diagonal across the end of the thatched roof, illuminating a spray of roses which had climbed up with fortitude towards the chimney and the best view. I don't suppose I shall ever see this cottage again, she thought. She wondered if she ought to write the twins a note, saying goodbye, but then dismissed the idea as silly. They had made it clear that, each in his own way, they wouldn't care anyway. And strangely enough, she thought, neither do I. A piece of her life had ended, a door had closed behind her, but she felt light and cheerful in this beautiful morning, with the road inviting before her.

She walked out of the sleeping village and away up the road towards Wool. Nothing passed her on the road, only, when she was about halfway, the first bus trundling in the other direction. It was empty, and the driver looked at her enquiringly as he passed. She smiled back. In the village he would turn and then wait outside the Castle for departure time. She would be in Wool before he passed her again.

Just beyond the railway station was the main crossroads, where the north–south road made a brief but necessary acquaintance with the east–west road. Josy stopped and put her bag down, flexing her hand. Where to go next? John in Gloucester? Paul in Bristol? Andy in Suffolk? Or perhaps a completely new stamping-ground? Suddenly the very range of choice – effectively limitless – disconcerted her. She felt dislocated by her premature departure from Bodaland, proving that even she, with her much-vaunted love of freedom, depended on a routine of sorts. For an instant she saw herself from the outside, as from a height looking down: a small figure at the crossroads, untidy, unbreakfasted, not even a young girl any more; surely too old still to be living this way?

She twitched the thought away as a horse shakes off a fly. None of that, now! This was the life she had chosen, and for very good reason. There could be no repining now. Where to go next? Let fate decide – her favourite method. Whatever lift came along first should have her, and that's the way she would go.

It was still so quiet that she had plenty of advance warning that a vehicle was coming, and was able to be on the right side of the road and facing in the right direction. A small lorry with a tarpaulined load and a faulty silencer clambered slowly into view, a young male driver alone in the cab. He looked pleasantly relaxed with his shirt sleeves rolled up, his bare, brown forearm resting on the frame of his open window, the other hand draped over the steering-wheel. Josy thumbed, and he slowed immediately and stopped directly opposite her with courteous skill.

'I'm going as far as Bournemouth,' he offered, without waiting for her to ask.

'That's where I'm going,' Josy said with perfect truth.

'Hop in, then.'

She climbed up into the cab and settled herself beside him, and he let out the clutch and drove on, bumping slowly over the railway lines at the level crossing and then speeding up to a riotous twenty-five. A mile further on he said, 'My name's Tony.'

'Josy,' she said. 'Thanks for picking me up.'

He grunted. Two miles more, and he said, 'On holiday?'

'Sort of.'

'You're very brown.'

'Working in the open air.' He nodded, and glanced towards her with such polite lack of interest that she warmed towards him, and added, free of charge, 'Boats.'

'Very nice,' he said, and turned his eyes forward again. After a while, he began to whistle softly. He had the intensely blue eyes of angels and Irishmen; and having decided that, she managed to recognise the soft, airless tune as *The Leaving of Liverpool.*

Oh lovely, lovely relationships, she thought: miles and long miles of silent, distant intimacy, going nowhere, asking and promising nothing!

Chapter Thirteen: 1955

We were sitting in the dining-room of the Red Lion, waiting for the second course to be served. The first course had been *pâté de foie*, an over-pink, rubbery slab with the refrigerator chill still on it – we were the first and only customers. It tasted not unlike Spam. Jo from the depths of her social nous said it was not proper *pâté de foie*, and I accepted her verdict. Such a thing had never come in my way; besides, I was pretty sure it would have cost a lot more than this if it had been. At that time I still had very little restaurant experience. How much she had had, I don't know, but her attitude gave me to understand it was adequate to choosing the meal and the wine, so I let her do it, happy to confine myself to the privilege of paying for it all at the end. I could hardly complain: our dates had cost me little enough so far. And I had wanted to take her away from our usual haunts, to give her a respite from the grief and cares that were making her look pale and drawn. Hence the heady sophistication of Dorchester and a meal in a proper hotel restaurant.

We didn't talk much at first. The emptiness of the dining room, in which every touch of cutlery echoed clashingly like an entire percussion section, inhibited us. Besides, Jo seemed, understandably, wrapped in her own thoughts; and I was content just to look at her. The room was rather dimly lit with lamps on sconces on the walls, each fitted with a pink lampshade; at the far end there was a large fireplace which sported only a small, disappointingly electric fire. But with the curtains drawn against the wet March night outside it was cosy enough; and pink light is flattering to everyone. It softened Jo's rather sharp, forceful features, which had been made to look sharper by her new haircut. Poised on the end of her long neck, her head was like something carved in alabaster; the muddled locks of hair could easily have belonged to a Greek youth. Below, her round-necked black jumper cutting off head and neck enhanced the look of statuary. I did not like her in black: it seemed to drain her of colour and animation – but that could equally have been the effect of her grieving. The colonel's death stood unspoken-of between us like a barrier, and I did not know how to breach it. I was afraid of asking her anything about it direct; yet to raise any other subject might have seemed frivolous and uncaring. So we sat in silence.

The waiter, an elderly man in a tailcoat much shiny at the seam, brought the fish, and served it laboriously from a platter, from which the silvering was wearing brassily, onto our plates, where it lay adorned only by a sprig of parsley. He poured some wine and shuffled off, leaving us to our revels.

Jo roused herself from her thoughts with a small sigh and looked up at me. I smiled tentatively, and she smiled back, which seemed a good start. What subject would she choose? Would she speak from the momentum of the thoughts she had been pursuing? I tried to look receptive of whatever she might want to say.

'I wonder why fish knives?' she said.

'Why fish knives what?' I replied, tacking hastily away from all my lines of thought.

'Not why anything. Just why are they? At home we always used two forks, but you could eat fish equally well with an ordinary knife, and from what I've seen most people do. So why did whoever it was first make one?'

'I expect they were invented for distant relatives to give sets of to brides who have everything else,' I said.

'Or to give people something to discuss at dinner when they can't think of anything to say.'

'Well, that has never applied in our case,' I said.

'Except that now most of the things we might discuss are too ... are off the agenda.'

'Are they?' I said. 'I thought we were friends. Can't friends discuss even painful things?'

She nodded, but looked down at her plate, pushing the sprig of parsley back and forth with her fork. 'But not yet,' she said. 'Please, George.'

I grabbed the first topic that offered itself instead. 'Tell me about Edinburgh,' I said. 'From your letters it sounded as if you were having a good time.'

'Did it? Duty, I suppose. One always put the best shine on things in letters. You're taught that from the nursery. "Dear Aunt, Thank you for your lovely present. It was so kind of you to think of me." You're not allowed to say you have three of them already and that what you really wanted was a junior conjurer's set.'

'I'm not your aunt.'

'It's not the aunt that's the point, it's the letter. They make one formal. Besides, I suppose I wanted to give you what you wanted. You were so keen to persuade me that university would be a wonderful opportunity, and such fun for a young gel.'

'I don't talk like that.'

'Not literally. But sometimes, George, there is that vast age difference between us in your tone.' Having pronounced, she broke off a piece of fish with her fork and put it in her mouth, as if the matter was concluded.

I was a little hurt. 'Very well,' I said. 'If it was not what I said it would be, tell me what it was like.'

She chewed and swallowed, and then put down her fork with an air of not knowing she had been holding it. 'What was it like?' she repeated with a bemused look. 'It was like a kind of dream – but not a nice one. Nearly a nightmare. It was like discovering that you're not real at all. I was a sort of figment of other people's imaginations.'

'That's not very helpful,' I observed. 'I take it you didn't enjoy it, then.'

'Oh, it wasn't a matter of enjoying,' she said, with slight impatience. 'Some things I suppose were pleasant. But mostly it was like groping through a fog. Everything I love, believe in, live by, everything I am used to, it was all alien to them. *I* was alien to them.'

'Who are "they"?'

She shook her head slightly at my slowness. 'There's a group, you see, the people who run the societies and stand for election to the Union, the people everybody knows. And they are all-important. Like a cross between politicians and film-stars. They decide the fashions, the ins and the outs, and you have to fall in with what they decide, or you're an outcast.'

'And you didn't fall in?'

She looked a little bewildered. 'I hardly had the chance. I was out before I was anywhere near the entrance. They hate everything they think I represent. They hate England, and the establishment, the countryside, the church, the army – oh, especially the army. They insult all those things as if they were loathsome. They're socialists, or communists – that's all the rage now: you can't admit to being anything else, or even to not having decided yet. They want to be rid of the Old Guard – which is you and me, George, in case you didn't know. They want *everything* to be different from the way it's always been. Even the good things. Well, to them there are no good things. Everything's bad and has to be changed.'

'Can't you just agree to disagree?'

'You don't understand. Being socialist isn't just having a point of view, it's being *right*. If you disagree with them, you're somehow evil.'

'Well, I suppose there are a lot of people who can't argue objectively. But one would hope there'd be more who could at university,' I said.

She shook her head impatiently, as if I were still missing the point. 'They hate me,' she said bluntly. 'There's a girl in my lodgings, Caroline Bray, for example. She's very popular, part of the inner circle. She's expected to be Union president one day. She never misses a chance to insult me. I'm decadent, upper class, elitist, fascist, capitalist – all the "ists" she can think of, every one of them non-u. She says I'm stand-offish and think too well of myself. And apparently I want to oppress the working classes.'

I suppressed a smile. 'And do you?'

'It isn't funny, George.'

'Well it is, a bit. Besides, I'm sure there are nice people there too. This inner circle – who cares about them?'

'Everybody.'

'Come on, you're exaggerating. There's always an elite at universities – there was at mine – but there are hundreds of perfectly nice, ordinary people that you only have to get to know—'

'And they would have to get to know me,' she added in a low voice, as though that were the problem.

'Why not?' I said. 'Once they do, they'll love you as much as—' I almost said 'I do,' but pulled back at the last moment, from some feeling that it would not be the right thing to say just then.

She didn't seem to notice the stop. 'I tried burying myself in the work, but there isn't such a great deal in the first term. Everybody's settling in. I went to all the lectures, and quite a few not on my course. You can go to any lecture you want up there. And after the beginning I avoided the common rooms.

But you have to be somewhere, and they'll always find you out. Asking questions, questions, questions – so that they can laugh at you, or hate you for the answers.'

'Not *hate*,' I began.

She looked up. 'Caroline Bray told everyone about my being a colonel's daughter, and they all laughed and called Daddy names. To them, the army is both ridiculous and loathsome. They talk about the war as if there was no need to fight it and *we* were in the wrong, not the Germans.' She looked down at her plate and went on in a low voice, 'When the message came about Daddy – about him dying, she even used that against me, made it somehow his own fault for being in the army, as if it served him right, and served me right, too, for being part of it all.'

'What a bitch!' I exclaimed, angry for her. 'But you can't pay attention to the opinions of people like that.'

She only shook her head again, and applied herself to her fish, finishing it off in a few mouthfuls. Then she sat back and took up her wine glass, and sat staring into it, turning the stem round and round in her fingers.

The waiter came and cleared, and we were silent. I watched her, thinking of how lonely she must have been up there, coming from her closed, safe world where she was adored – the army, Dorset and her own family had all conspired to keep her insulated from the world most people knew. The colonel, I thought, had been right but belated in wanting her to be independent and stand on her own two feet. But I thought of what he had told me about her mother, and forgave him. After that, of course you would try to protect your child.

Perhaps if his circumstances had been different, he could have kept her in the protective circle for ever. Married her to one of his own kind – an officer and a gentleman – so that she need never change worlds. But as it was, the chick had had to break out of the egg. Most young people leaving home for the first time and going to university find the adjustment a shock. London had seemed very different from Bournemouth to me, though the changes, in my case, had been all to the good. It was different for girls anyway, and for Jo it seemed to have been a greater shock than for most. Still, no doubt she would adapt, harden her skin, find her niche. I thought of the golden girl I had wandered the fields with and knew I would regret it when the bloom wore off and she became like other people. But I had no right to want to keep her unchanged and vulnerable.

The waiter served us with our roast chicken and vegetables and handed the bread sauce, and Jo seemed to cheer up, as straightforward people can always do in the presence of food.

'Roast chicken,' she said. 'Just like someone's birthday.'

'We only ever had it at Christmas, at home,' I said.

'We always had goose at Christmas. Sir Hugh always sent one, because Daddy let him hunt over our land. When we still had land. And when we didn't any more, he just kept sending it out of habit. Or kindness.'

'I've never had goose,' I said, to encourage this happier train of thought.

'The skin's lovely,' she said. 'And it makes tremendous amounts of fat. Jean loved it, the fat, because it was so good for making pastry. She used to hoard it. She nearly had a fit once when Rob took some of her precious goose-fat for Minstrel when he had a cough.'

'Did it work?'

'Goodness, no. I don't know what Rob was thinking. Treacle's the thing for that, spread on the bit, but it makes them salivate so much, and then they dribble dark brown foam all down their chests, and when they shake their heads they spatter you with it. I suppose he thought goose-fat wouldn't be so messy.'

I laughed at the story, and she smiled too, and then grew sad. It was like watching fast-moving clouds crossing the sun. 'Oh dear,' she said. 'And now it's all over. No more horses. Daddy sold them as soon as I left. And now no more house. Roselands has to be sold, you know.'

I nodded.

'And soon, no more Jean,' she went on. 'She's going back to Scotland, where her family is. Her sister and brother-in-law have a guest house at Braemar, and she's going to help them with it. Daddy left her something in his will, and she's going to put that into their business so they can expand. The tourist trade is picking up there, because of being near Balmoral, and everyone being so interested in the Queen.'

We talked a little then about the Queen and the royal children and tourism in general, and it tided us over nicely, through the remains of the main course and the frankly dull ice-cream-with-a-tinned-peach-on-top that followed. While we talked I thought of Jo's life and how it was changing, so violently and so completely. Her home and all her family gone at a stroke; she was cast out like a piece of flotsam on the tide. It was good that she had university to go back to, or she would have been quite lost. The colonel had at least foreseen that correctly. However little she had enjoyed her first term, it was a purpose, an occupation. Like a rudder it would keep her moving in a useful direction until the storm of loss subsided and she could decide what to do with the rest of her life.

Perhaps eventually Rob would come home, marry, make an anchor for her. For now, I appreciated fully – as I had not done before – why he had asked me not to keep an eye on her, but to be her friend. She might not want or need me, but the colonel had wanted to know I would be there.

I paid for the meal and we walked out to the car. The fine drizzling rain that had been going on all day had stopped, but it was a cold night, and the air smelled damp. The clouds were just beginning to break up, but as yet there was no moon, so it was very dark. Jo walked a little ahead of me, and I watched her, wondering with sudden nervousness what would happen next. I had seen her several times since she came back, though this was the first thing that might be classed a 'date'. On no occasion had I kissed her, nor so much as touched her hand. In the circumstances it had not seemed appropriate. Though I had more than once longed to offer her comfort, her bereavement, and her absence before it, had seemed to put a distance between us, and I was no longer sure where I stood with her, how she viewed me. I had never been sure whether that occasion in the churchyard had been meant to be a one-off affair or the setting of a precedent, a conclusion or a beginning. In the last half hour over dinner she had seemed so nearly back to normal that I wondered if she might now welcome a little physical attention – a reassurance, if nothing else, of my affection for her. I, quite frankly, wanted her, though part of me felt it was reprehensible to feel that way, given her circumstances. But perhaps warm manly arms around her and a not-too-passionate kiss might be just what she wanted.

I decided, weakly, to pass the buck. When I was settled into the car beside her, I said, 'What would you like to do now?'

'Let's just drive for a bit,' she said. 'I don't want to go back yet. Let's find a nice field to look at.'

'Anything you say,' I agreed, feeling my blood start to run faster. On this dark night there would not be much looking to be done. Down boy, I commanded myself. Of course she doesn't want to go back to that house of sorrow. It probably doesn't mean any more than that. But while my mind was quite rational about it, my body sang at the nearness of hers and the memories of the drives of the summer. I headed in the direction of the sea. I knew a turning that led off the main road into the densest part of nowhere. While I drove, Jo looked out of the window; at nothing, since it was dark. Now and then we passed a light which made a mirror of her side window, and allowed me to see her face. There was a strange little smile flickering round her lips – seraphic, perhaps, but definitely not angelic. Something was on her mind, some devilry. I was only glad she seemed for the moment lifted out of her sorrow.

I took my turning, and then drove more slowly, partly because the lane was narrow and unlit, and partly because I was looking for a suitable place to stop. But then she preempted me by saying out of the blue, 'Turn left here.'

It was an even narrower lane – hardly more than a farm track, really. I took the turn, and bumped slowly over the uneven surface between high hedges.

'I know this place,' she said, as if I had asked. 'I've ridden round here. There's a barn just round the next bend, on the right. You can stop there.'

Round the next bend I drove, and the barn loomed up, bulky in my headlamps against the featureless sky. I stopped by the gate that gave access to it, pulling the car just enough off the track to allow anyone else to go by – though who would be coming down here in the night I couldn't imagine. I turned off the engine, and the silence dropped instantly over us, like a booby-trap blanket.

We got out of the car, and stood a moment, listening. There was no sound of man anywhere near us: that wonderful, deep silence of undeveloped countryside that now is being eroded, year by year. There was plenty of it in those days, but even so I appreciated it, having been brought up a townie. The tiny, satisfying sounds of night were there, the shiver of the grass, a distant call of an owl, and tiny and far away, the bark of a farm dog. The smell of the damp earth was just discernible. A light breeze had got up, hardly more than a movement of air, and the cold of it lifted my hair, touched my scalp and made me shudder. Something ran scufflingly through the dead leaves along the bottom of the hedge, and left behind it a stillness the more profound for its small disturbance.

Jo looked around her with an air of satisfaction, and then held out a hand to me and walked to the gate. The hand was only a gesture meaning 'come on', and I did not take it, but stood back to watch her climb lightly over and jump down on the other side in a flurry of skirts. My mouth was dry with excitement as I followed her, climbing over less neatly than her because I was watching her and not what I was doing.

She walked ahead of me, going towards the barn as surely and calmly as a horse towards its stable. The door was propped a little open. It had several planks missing, and I guessed from the angle of it that it would no longer close properly, or not without considerable effort. Inside there was a dry smell of stale hay, and very little light, so that at first I could not see anything. She had gone forward, at once invisible in her black clothes on black; I heard a soft rustling of movement, and then she came back for me, her face suddenly swimming white in the darkness near me. 'Come on. It's all right,' she said. She touched my arm, and then felt down to my hand and took it to lead me. I could see a little better now. There were bits missing in the walls and the roof, and through them a very little light came, just enough for it not to be pitch black. I could see the shape of her, and a less-dark patch ahead which turned out to be a pile of loose hay. She folded down on it gracefully, drawing me down with her; and when I was sitting, lay back and put her arms out to me, inviting me in.

Darkness and soft sounds; no words for us, but soft breaths drawn and sighed, and the rustling of the hay; the barn moaned a little when the breeze moved it; outside, somewhere far away in another world, a vixen screamed. I kissed her, slowly and then deeply, tasting her, sinking into her as in a dream. Long kisses, with pauses in between only to sweeten the anticipation: we savoured each other. Our hands moved gently, enquiringly, found each other out. And when it came, the pleasure, the passion was fierce in our quietness, quiet in its profundity. In the churchyard we had been like careless children; I had made love to a girl. In that barn we were man and woman. Her sorrow had ripened us both. We made love, wordlessly in that small, dark safety away from the dangerous world, making something that could never be undone.

Afterwards it seemed like coming to, reviving from near unconsciousness. I felt as if hours had passed, though I suppose it could not have been more than minutes. How long does it take to make love? To change one's life, and another person's? Time out of time; no time and all of time. I was lying on my back in the hay, with her in my arms, her head on my shoulder. Slowly my diverted blood returned to its normal courses, and I felt beautifully exhausted, lungs and muscles that had been stretched to their limits relaxing into delicious limpness. Her body folded flexibly into the contours of mine, her breathing was shallow and regular now, though it had gasped and torn in passion. Soft, milk-white, my girl lay in my arms, and we drifted.

The wind got up a little, and the barn crooned to it, shuddered now and then. The wind must have blown the clouds away because through a hole in the roof above me, I could see a star, blue and bright. There was more light inside now, a greyish luminescence by which I could see her. I lifted myself a little on one elbow, carefully so as not to disturb her, so that I could look at her.

Her eyes were shut. She seemed asleep, breathing so easily she barely moved; her milkiness was cradled in shadows. I wanted to touch her now in coolness, smoothe my hand over her body with deliberation, to know it, but I was afraid to wake her. If she woke, she might move, speak, she might get up to go, and then the moment would be over.

The odd smile was gone now, and she looked only tranquil, or perhaps a little tired. It seemed right that she should be tired, like a soldier after a successful campaign. I felt as though there had been a battle, though not between us. We had brought about something decisive, fighting side by side. I felt for her not only the expected romantic love, but a sort of comradeliness. I hoped that she would feel it too, for me. She was a soldier's daughter: she ought to understand.

I shivered, suddenly aware of the cold air from the half-open door on the naked flesh of my side. I could not reach my discarded clothes without moving, and I didn't want to move; but I shivered again, and the shivering woke her.

She opened her eyes and sat up, and looked at me as if she had come back from a long way away – looked without smiling, her face numb, her expression without curiosity or fear or questioning. She looked at me as she might have looked at her own face in the

261

mirror, as something she knew so thoroughly there was no longer any need to see.

'I'm cold,' she said.

'We'd better get dressed,' I said.

'Not yet,' she said quickly, and put herself into my arms, and we hugged each other for a long time, until I felt her grow a little warmer. Then we separated and reached for our clothes, and dressed quickly.

I saw her shiver, and said, 'There's some whisky in the car. That'll help.'

She nodded and made for the door. Outside it was surprisingly light, as if dawn was coming. The clouds had blown away to the edges of the sky and the starlight was clear, but there was more light than the stars accounted for. The moon must have been about to rise. I looked round the horizon for its position, but everything seemed extra black against the starry canopy.

Jo looked heavy-eyed, as if she had been woken from a deep sleep. She combed her urchin cut with her fingers, straightening its designed roughness; brushed hay from her clothes. Every gesture of hers was now very dear to me. Just those small actions made me want to hold her close to me again. We climbed back over the gate and got in at opposite sides of the car, and its leathery smell seemed strong and alien after the pale dusty smell of the hay barn. But its shelter was welcome. I hauled the rug over from the

262

back seat and we put it round our shoulders while I felt in the dash compartment for the whisky bottle. We each took a drink, and I felt the pleasant shock of it as it hit my stomach and spread its little pool of warmth through me.

'More?' I said, handing the bottle back to Jo. She smiled as she took it, a tired but contented smile of someone who was grieving but had been comforted. I felt the love of her strong like pride in me. I had done that, I thought. I had done that for her.

I started the car, turned, and drove back towards civilisation.

When we were on the main road, she said, quite abruptly, 'I'm not going back.'

'Back?' Her thoughts had evidently been otherwhere than mine, and I did not understand.

'Back to university.'

She had been given a term's sabbatical to sort out her affairs. 'Not going back?' I said again, stupidly.

'After Easter. I know it's what Daddy wanted for me, but it's not what I want. I hate it there. And it's my life now.'

She looked at me a little defiantly, as though she thought I would argue. I *wanted* to argue, but I didn't see that I had the right. Instead, I said, 'What will you do, then?'

Perhaps she had wanted me to argue. She seemed faintly disappointed. She shook her head slightly, and then instead of answering my question, asked me, 'When do you finish here? It's not long now, is it?'

'In July,' I said.

'And what will you do then?'

'Pick up where I left off, I suppose.'

'Architecture?'

'Of course.'

'It's what you want to do?'

'It's always been what I wanted to do,' I said.

She sighed slightly. 'You're lucky to be so sure. Where will you go, then?'

'In July? Well, I've promised to go home and see my mother first, for the two weeks of demob leave, but then – London. That's where everything's happening, where the big firms are.'

'London,' she said. I couldn't fathom what the tone of her voice meant. She seemed to be tasting the word or the idea, but her thoughts were closed to me.

Did she think I was going away, abandoning her? It was the furthest thing from my thoughts. I thought about our lovemaking. I was the man, and responsible for her, no matter that the decision to do it had been joint and equal. We had 'got away with it' last time, but every new time was a new risk. She should know that what we had done was never to be undone; that she and I were together, partners in everything. I would much prefer to get my career under way before marrying, but if necessary we should marry right away. She was not to be afraid, or to have any finger pointed at her.

We drove in silence until I reached the turning for her house, when she said, 'Stop here. I'll walk up.'

I pulled in at the side of the road and switched off the engine, and turned to face her, the better to talk seriously.

She turned too, looking straight into my eyes now, and though she was not smiling, she seemed happy, or at least content. Some of the strain had gone from her face. I felt close to her, at ease, as if we had stepped onto a particular path together, hand in hand. I wasn't sure where the path was leading, but I knew it was somewhere I wanted to be. It seemed a propitious time to talk about things I had been thinking.

'Jo, what we did tonight – it was wonderful. More wonderful than I can tell you.'

Her eyes widened a little. 'You're going to say "but". Oh, don't say "but"!'

'No, no, there's no "but",' I said quickly, smiling a little at her reaction. 'It was perfect. *You* are perfect. But – no, no, not but, *and* – and I just want you to be sure that if anything should happen—'

'Oh George, don't talk like that,' she said. Her eyes moved away from mine. I saw that I had saddened her, and I didn't know why.

'In fact, don't talk at all. Give me some more whisky.'

We both had some, and then she shifted over along the seat and snuggled up to me, and raised her face to be kissed. Everything seemed quite ordinary, just like the ending of an ordinary 'date': we sat close together, kissing now and then, silent in between. But I felt lost, bereft. I could not think of any way to approach again what she had forbidden me; and even when we kissed, I felt she was kissing me to stop me talking. Though she was in my arms, I felt miles away from her, desolate at the turn things had taken, not understanding what I had done wrong.

A car went past us, momentarily bathing us with its headlights. She drew away from me and said she had better be going in, and I agreed. There was nothing here to prolong. We arranged to meet on my next night off, and she said goodnight in a normal tone and walked off up the lane. I drove back to camp feeling most unreal, tired, blunted with whisky, my mind a whirling mass of unsorted impressions dominated by two huge question marks: where had that path been leading to; and where had we missed the way?

Chapter Fourteen: 1964

Mrs West came back from her shopping expedition to find Jo sitting on her doorstep in the sunshine, her bag beside her, peacefully reading the newspaper.

'Hullo, love. Been here long?' she said.

She did not look particularly surprised to see her visitor, but then her well-worn face was not particularly adapted for displaying emotions. Its lines and tracks had been formed in old, happy days, and it was set now into a permanent expression of contentment. Her mouth seemed always on the brink of smiling: people passing her in the street often smiled at her, thinking they knew her. George had a little of that look, too, Jo thought: the look that good humour was built-in, and that anything negative would have been quite hard work and so probably not worth the effort. Mrs West's faded blue eyes and softly grey hair looked as though they had been bleached of colour by years of washing. Her unexpectedly smooth skin looked washed, too, as a river stone is smoothed by the passage of water. It was pale – she was always pale – but it was not the pallor of ill-health. Rather it just gave the impression of great cleanliness.

Jo adored her, had adored her ever since she first met her. To Jo, Mrs West was everything a mother should be: warm, kind, unflappable, understanding, always ready to listen. Most of all, she was always the same, and always to be found where she should be – at home. Since fate had seen fit to provide Jo with an unmotherly mother of her own, and then to take even that away, she had rectified the error by adopting Mrs West. Sometimes, in bed and on the edge of sleep, she would pretend that she really was her mother, and imagine how it would feel. But she told no-one that. Her passion for George's mother was her own secret.

'Not long. About half an hour,' Jo said, standing up.

'You must have only just missed me, then. I only popped out for one or two things.'

It had never occurred to Jo that anything else was the case, or that Mrs West might have been away for any longer or more permanent reason. She never did go anywhere. She never went on holiday. She had never even visited George in London, though he had offered to put her up in an hotel and take her to a show. She had not made a fuss about it, only thanked him and said it was not her sort of thing. Since her husband had died, she had not strayed far from the house. She was not sad or gloomy about it, and she never went to visit his grave. It just seemed that she had no ambitions or wants of her own to fulfil.

She stood now, faintly smiling at Jo, with her shabby old handbag over one arm and a string bag bulging with shopping in the other hand. She gestured slightly with the latter and said, 'Funny thing, I bought two doughnuts. As I walked out of the shop I realised, and thought it was absent-mindedness again. But now it looks as though it was second sight.' Jo took the bag out of her hand so that Mrs West could get her key out. 'Thank you, dear.'

Mrs West pushed the heavy door open, and Jo followed her into the cool, shadowy hallway. The house smelled, as it always smelled, of lavender wax, with a hint of soot and a hint of tea behind it, and another smell, very faint and slightly metallic, like knife-powder, that old houses like this always had. It was a smell of *small* old houses. Big old houses, like her childhood home, had a different characteristic odour, a mixture of damp, woodsmoke, pot-pourri, candlewax – rather churchy. Sweetish. It occurred to her now that the one was acid, the other alkaline. Like bees and wasps. Not sweet and sour, because both were good smells. Sweet and savoury, perhaps? Mrs West's house was alkaline and savoury.

They walked through the house into the kitchen, where the sun was shining at an angle through the window and making an asymmetrical rhomboid on the symmetrically tiled floor. Jo put the string bag on the table and watched it sag with relief, while Mrs West went straight across to open the kitchen door and let in Martha from the back garden.

The small cyprian cat, rescued years ago from drowning, walked in on tiptoe with her tail up and stood at Mrs West's feet, looking up at her like a furry croquet hoop. She chirruped, and Mrs West stooped to run a hand firmly over her from head to tail, while every part of Martha rose a fraction to the touch as it passed. As Mrs West straightened up, Martha tiptoed over to Jo, rubbed politely across her ankles and then, as Jo bent down to stroke her, expertly evaded the caress and walked with a more businesslike gait to her food bowl under the sink where she stood patiently, to see if the manna would descend as it sometimes did, and sometimes didn't. She was a cat: what did she know of mechanisms, or cause and effect? Jo thought it must be nice to live in such a state of primitive belief.

'I'll put the kettle on,' said Mrs West, shutting the kitchen door again to 'keep the flies out', as she would have said if anyone asked.

She never left doors or windows open. Apart from the eternal flies, and wasps in August, there was soot. No point dusting and polishing if you went and left windows open and let it all in.

'Could I have a quick wash?' Jo asked. 'I was up at dawn.'

'Of course, dear. You know where the clean towels are?'

'Yes, thanks. I won't be a sec.'

The house always struck her as being terribly lonely. Even in the midst of summer's heat, it was always cool – in winter it was cold. It was dark, and clean, with polished gleams reflecting here and there in corners. Above all it was empty, echoing like a boarding house at midday. The tall, Victorian bathroom with its original claw-footed bath and beautiful green tiles, and the anachronistic geyser, was somehow rather frightening, like a left-over presence from another age, the ghost of a mad old great-aunt locked up at the top of the house. Its cadaverous chilliness, its brooding silence were somehow emphasised by the presence on the shelf of Sam's shaving-gear, a personal, human touch that seemed out of place. To Jo it was as if a corpse had winked. But the whump and roar of the geyser dispelled the silence, and the comfort of hot water and the familiar smell of Palmolive soap made it just a bathroom again. She washed thoroughly at the basin, cleaned her teeth, combed her damp hair, and then went back down to the kitchen feeling refreshed; and renewed, as if she had washed off a piece of her past and could start again.

'I see Sam's home again,' she said as she went in. The fat brown earthenware teapot was breathing steam gently from under its knitted cosy, and the two doughnuts were now on a plate on the table, in the company of two home-made scones.

'How did you know that?' Mrs West said, and then, thinking, 'Oh yes, I guess – you saw his razor. Yes, he's been back now, let me see, nearly three months this time. I don't suppose he'll stay, though. He's another one like you, restless. But he's such a good boy, and he works so hard.'

'He's not married?' Jo asked, and then wondered why she did, for this was a subject she had always avoided as far as possible with Mrs West.

'No, he's not married. I often wish he would settle down, because that might keep him in one place. Though of course, if he did that, it might not be *this* place. But all the same, you can't help thinking he'd be happier. It's natural for a man to want to get married. Still, I don't think he ever will now, not Sam. I have to pin my hopes on George, though he doesn't show much sign that way either.' She sighed. 'Oh, I forgot the cups. I don't know what's the matter with me these days. Head like a sieve.'

'I'll get them.' Jo jumped up.

'Thanks, dear.'

'You know,' said Jo, when they were seated either side of the table with their cups before them, 'tea is a completely different thing when it comes out of a teapot like this. I hated it at home. Beastly, washy stuff. It was nearly always Earl Grey, which tastes like medicine anyway, and made too weak. And it was always nearly cold, because it came out of a silver pot and no teacosy. And of course there'd be Mother fussing about and saying "Cream or lemon?" and the teaspoons making an awful racket in the saucers. You had to have a spoon, even if you didn't take sugar – and of course Mother *knew* you didn't take sugar – and the spoon always managed to fall off the saucer and you got *looked* at. It was like a live thing, you had no chance of keeping it in its place.'

'I couldn't fancy cream in my tea,' Mrs West said peacefully. 'Though I like a drop of milk. We used to have evaporated sometimes, in the war, when you couldn't get fresh. I didn't like that, either, but in the war you had to make do. Have a doughnut, dear. Or a scone.'

'Thanks,' said Jo, taking a doughnut. It was still faintly warm. Fussell's Hygienic Bakery was only just down the road, and made the best doughnuts in Hampshire. She bit into it, and the raspberry jam flooded into her mouth. 'Mmm,' she said appreciatively, and then, 'You know, I think my whole childhood would have been different if only we'd had a brown teapot like this, with a cosy, instead of Georgian silver.'

Of course it would, Mrs West thought, because then you'd have been coming from a completely different sort of background. But then, perhaps that was what Jo meant. She settled herself comfortably to listen as Jo talked, and to try to fathom what was going on in her mind. It was all so foreign to her, the way Jo lived, wandering about the countryside with a bag of clothes, stopping here for a while and there for a while, like a gypsy. Of course, that wouldn't have been possible when Mrs West was young. Girls were much more closely kept. But even nowadays, most girls weren't like Jo. She was an odd creature, not like a female at all, in some ways. Jo, George called her: like a man. And there was something mannish about her, in a way, the way she thought and the way she talked and her not wanting to settle down and get married. Probably would have been better for her if she *had* been a boy. Then she could have joined the army like her brother and done her travelling that way. Still, with her background, she ought to have been able to get on even as a girl, and didn't that just go to show that money and education weren't everything? A bit of love and understanding were worth a lot more than a big house and new clothes. From the first time George had brought her home, Mrs West had thought Jo rather a sad creature – a kind of waif. She might talk like a man, boldly, even shockingly sometimes, but underneath she was just a lost girl. Mrs West knew a stray when she saw one. She'd taken in enough of them in her time.

After about a quarter of an hour, Jo found herself talking about the Boda twins, and Frank in particular. At first she tried to make it sound funny, in case Mrs West should be shocked: after all, sex outside marriage was not a done thing for her generation. But Mrs West's face never showed anything of what she was thinking, and it simply wasn't set for disapproval or condemnation. It was just a listening face, calm and sympathetic, and after a glance or two Jo was reassured, and let the flippancy drift out of the telling.

In this way George and his mother were alike: that when Jo told them things, it sorted out for her what she really felt about them. So when the story was done, she was able to say, 'I think what has shaken me is the realisation that all these years I've been thinking I was sharing a friendship, when in fact there was nothing there at all. Not even so much affection as you'd get from a budgie. How could I be so stupid? How could I have deluded myself so thoroughly and for so long?'

She didn't really mean it as a question, but her pause afterwards was long enough for Mrs West to think an answer was required. 'I expect it was because you wanted to.' But she spoke softly and Jo didn't seem to have heard her, lost in thought as she was. It was plain the poor child was lonely and wanted friendship, and so saw it where it didn't exist. *That* was simple enough to understand. The thing that puzzled Mrs West was why a nice, bright girl like her couldn't find the real thing. There was some kind of hurt deep inside Jo that stopped her, but what it was Mrs West didn't know, and had no way of finding out.

'I thought I knew them,' Jo said at last, sadly, 'and it turns out I didn't at all. So all that time was wasted.'

Mrs West lifted her hands absently from her lap so that Martha could jump up. The cat turned round twice and lay down, and she let her hands drop back into place. 'It happens all the time,' she said. Sometimes you couldn't help people or correct them or change them, you could only comfort them. 'It can happen with someone you've thought you were really close to – even a husband or wife. I suppose the thing is, you can never really know what another person is thinking.

Even if they tell you, you don't know if they mean it or not.'

'That sounds a bit depressing,' said Jo ruefully.

'You just have to trust that they do mean what they say,' said Mrs West. 'And I suppose mostly they do.'

'But if they didn't, as long as they never told you, it wouldn't matter. I mean, if they always pretended the same thing, and you didn't know it was pretence, it would be as near true as mattered.'

'I suppose so,' said Mrs West, not really following that bit. It didn't really matter whether she understood or not. The important thing was that she had got Jo talking, and there was nothing like talking about something for helping you to put it away in the past. She watched the animation return to Jo's face, pushing out the sadness and hurt, and she marvelled at how easily the young healed. Though, of course, Jo was not as young as she seemed. Her gypsy life always made Mrs West think of her as a girl, a teenager as they said these days, but she must be not far off thirty now.

And perhaps she was not really healing, only carrying on that same process of self-deception that had got her hurt in the first place. But – what was that queer twist she had spoken of? As long as she managed to believe her own story, it was as near the truth as made no difference.

So in another half hour Mrs West could see that Jo had talked herself back into her pose as the carefree, happy-go-lucky Queen of the Road, who travelled the world because of the gypsy in her blood and the wanderlust in her feet. Here today and gone tomorrow, always someone else's horizon. She watched Jo bring herself back to the point where she didn't know it was a pose, where she had convinced herself that she wandered because she wanted to, and it saddened her. But why spoil the girl's illusions? she thought. If you had anything to offer her in place of them, all well and good, but since you haven't, best to leave well alone. All she could do was to welcome the poor thing when she turned up, give her something to eat, and let her go. Some cats would come to your back door and let you feed them, but they would never come in the house, never stay.

Jo came to the end of her eulogium on her way of life and stopped, so Mrs West said, 'Are you staying to dinner?'

Social background made, unusually, a misunderstanding between them, for by 'dinner' Mrs West meant the midday meal that she was about to start preparing, while Jo thought she meant her evening meal. The latter implied a commitment of so many hours that Jo panicked. If Mrs West expected her to stay all day, she might want her to stay several days, and Jo had just talked herself up for the joys of departure. She said quickly, 'Oh, no, thanks all the same. I have to be moving on. I only dropped in on my way through. I have to go any minute now.'

Mrs West saw the panic and was sorry. If she hadn't asked, maybe Jo would have just not thought about going. 'Pity,' she said unemphatically. 'Still, can't be helped.'

'I think I need to change my clothes. I wonder, could I borrow your bathroom again?'

'Of course.'

Upstairs, Jo took off her jeans and tee-shirt, and put on a skirt and blouse. The blouse was rather crumpled, but the heat of her body would make enough of the creases drop out. She changed her sandals for her good shoes – her legs were brown enough not to need stockings. And then she hauled out her coat. It was of good wool, so it didn't crease, in a herringbone pattern of two shades of blue, and with it she wore a velvet beret of the darker shade. Dressed, she glanced at herself in the mirror and saw herself transformed from an anonymous hitchhiker to an obvious member of her class. It was an almost complete disguise. She pushed her discarded things into the bag – without the coat it was suddenly light and roomy – and went back down.

At the sight of her, Mrs West had an odd,

fleeting wish that George had married Jo years ago when she had really been what she now appeared to be. But that was all folly. George and Jo, she had always thought, were more like brother and sister, and it was impossible to think of them marrying. George had never spoken about marriage, not even back then, when he had first brought her to visit.

'You look very smart, dear,' she said. 'I hope you have a good trip.'

Just as if I was going on holiday, Jo thought. 'I shall, don't worry,' she said gaily. It was an effort. Now the moment had come, she didn't want to go. But at least this part of her life was not likely to fold up and close down. This was one place, like George, she could always come back to, though it could not be often.

As if the thought of George had communicated itself to Mrs West, she said, 'Will you be seeing George at all in the near future?'

'I don't know. I'll be seeing him again, of course, but I don't know exactly when. Why? Did you want something taken for him?'

'No, it's nothing really. It's just that he hasn't written for a while, and I was hoping he'd come down for a few days in the summer. He usually comes in August or September.'

'Well, when I see him, I'll tell him,' Jo said. 'If it's not too late.' She meant, of course, if it wasn't already past September, but the words came out rather ominously, and they looked at each other awkwardly.

'It doesn't matter, dear. I can write to him,' Mrs West said faintly.

'I'll tell him if I see him,' Jo replied.

There was a pause, and they seemed stranded in the moment, like actors who had forgotten their lines. Then Mrs West roused herself and said, 'Well, goodbye, then. Take care of yourself.'

'You too. Thanks for the tea and everything.' On an impulse, Jo leaned forward and kissed Mrs West's smooth cheek. It was warm and very soft, softer than a child's because it was without resilience, with the slackness of age. It felt very odd, because it was not what she had expected, not thinking of Mrs West as old; but the lips that kissed her cheek in return were firm enough, and restored the ordinary so that she was able to withdraw in good order.

Sustained, fortified, re-equipped to meet fate's hazards, she thought facetiously as she walked briskly down the road, past houses identical to the West house, but containing no comfort for her, now or ever. Her feet in their hand-made, brown, low-heeled shoes set themselves down with military precision. This outfit was all she had left from home, which was why it looked so different from the cheap clothing she had bought since, why it made her look so different. She looked like Miss Grace again. *Again?* Had Miss Grace ever existed? If so, she had never been what she seemed; she had always been a cheat of the eye. But the outer shell was nice, she thought wistfully, *felt* nice. Suddenly the thought of the journey wearied her. She didn't want the dirt and the makeshift, the suitcase and the strange bed. She wanted to go to a bed she knew, and stay clean and smart and nice-looking. Oh suburban capitulation! But the longing was there. Suppose she went to London?

No, she mustn't go back so soon. She mustn't let herself go to George, not yet, not yet. Besides, she must keep London for the winter when she couldn't go anywhere else. Perhaps she ought to have stayed with Mrs West, just for a few days – putting off the evil moment. But that wouldn't be fair to George's mother. No, she must move on.

But where to? What was it she wanted? There was a restless longing inside her for – what? A succession of houses flitted through her mind, her father's, Mrs West's, the twins' cottage, all the others in between. There was a place she wanted to be, but it was none of them. That was the trouble. What she really wanted was something she couldn't even visualise, because she had never experienced it. You've got problems, she told herself with a grim kind of smile.

Chapter Fifteen: 1955

The last weeks of my National Service passed quietly. With Smart gone, and Horrocks soon after, I was without bad influences. A great many of those I had served with had gone, in fact, and I was surrounded by a new intake who were five years younger than me, and seemed almost like schoolboys, with pink cheeks and outstanding ears, smoking their cigarettes with an air that suggested they might easily turn green and run behind a hedge any moment. I left it to others of the last few veterans to torment and initiate them. I was happier lying on my bed with a book, or boning up on architecture and dreaming of my future.

I continued to see Jo, though not regularly. It was hard to tell how I stood with her. Sometimes she was her old self, natural and talkative and warm, and I felt very close to her. On other occasions she would seem withdrawn and silent, and I could not get near her. We did not make love again, but when she was herself we kissed, often passionately, and spent much time wrapped in each other's arms, just like any other young couple, in my car or, as the weather improved, on our favourite clifftop walks.

I was not surprised at her changeable mood. Everything was happening to her very quickly; the dismantling of her whole life could not have been easy for her. Roselands, the colonel's house, was sold. I heard through the grapevine that it had been bought by some government department to be turned into laboratories, or else into a cottage hospital – the sources varied. Private people were not buying large country houses any more, and when they were sold they nearly always became schools or mental homes or other such public places. Jo did not tell me anything about the sale and I did not ask her, feeling it would be too painful for her to discuss. I heard that the whole contents of the house were taken to be sold by an auction house – that, too, must have been hard to bear, to see the furniture and ornaments and books she had had around her all her life packed up and taken away.

Jean had left and gone back to Scotland – I didn't see Jo for a fortnight after that parting – and Jo herself went into lodgings. She might have taken a room quite economically in one of the village pubs, which was what I half expected her to do, so as to be at the heart of things, but in fact she went to lodge with an old lady who lived in an isolated cottage up a lane about a mile and a half outside the village, involving an inconvenient and often muddy walk whenever she wanted to get anywhere. I never saw the cottage, but was told it was without modern conveniences, damp and comfortless. Why did she choose it? I did think at first it might be a form of self-flagellation, understandable in the suddenly bereaved. But I learned later that she had gone there because the old lady was very hard up and needed the money.

It was not Jo who told me that, of course. Because of my association with her, and the length of time I had now been around, I was quite well known in the area, and when I passed through the village people stopped me and told me things: I was included in the gossip circuit. Her choice of lodging was not her only piece of kindness. As the weeks passed, I came across her spoor in many places, in little gifts and actions I heard of by accident or by other people's design. They liked to tell me what a nice girl she was. The colonel had been held in respect and affection, and they honoured him by talking about her. They pitied her for her loss and her situation, and I think, knowing she and I had been 'walking out', that they were looking to me to see she came to no harm.

I only once made the mistake of talking to Jo about it. I had heard that she had been visiting an old man up School Lane and reading to him, because his sight was failing, and I mentioned it. She shrugged if off and would not discuss it; but when I said that the village people thought her very kind, and that I agreed, she became angry.

'People think they know you, but they know nothing about you. Nothing! They don't know you, and they don't own you.'

'No-one's trying to own you,' I said, surprised at her reaction.

'That's what comes next,' she said. 'They probe and pry – but they couldn't cope with the truth, if they knew it.'

'What truth? Jo, what's the matter? Why are you so upset?'

'Oh, leave me alone, George. Just leave me alone!'

We had been walking on Chaldon Down, and she dragged her arm free from mine and ran away. It took me a time to catch up with her, for she was fleeter over the rough grass than me and was soon out of sight. When I found her again she was leaning on the top bar of the stile, where the footpath joined the road to West Chaldon, her face a mask of misery. I gathered her into my arms, and asked her no more questions. After that I tried to avoid delicate subjects, though it was difficult sometimes to know where unexploded shells might be lying buried. I comforted myself that she was still seeing me, so I must not have done too badly. But loving her so much, I worried about her. I could not ask her how she was managing financially. The colonel had told me that he had made arrangements for her, and I hoped he had put something into trust for her, for I knew how long probate could take. The local solicitor was handling things, but naturally he did not discuss his client's affairs, though that did not stop the speculation that I caught the edges of in many a village conversation. I supposed she must have been all right because she paid the old woman rent, and did not starve, but I wished I could have asked her outright and relieved my mind.

Another thing I could not discuss was what her plans were for the future. I wished – unselfishly, for it would have taken her away from me – that she had gone back to university. It seemed to me that to be taken away from things that reminded her daily, hourly, of her loss would have been beneficial. But she seemed just then only to want to stay near home. I could not discuss marriage with her, either – that was the most explosive subject of all. But I hoped that, discussed or not, it was something that had taken root in her mind, and would happen quite naturally one day.

I took her one Saturday to Bournemouth to meet my mother, and was happy to see how they took to each other at once. Mum had always been one for taking in waifs and strays, and I think she saw, without any hint from me, that Jo was suffering. And Jo responded to Mum's quiet motherliness, and seemed calmer and happier and more like her old self than she had for weeks. They had a long talk together while they did the washing-up after lunch. I was banished to the sitting room with the paper, as Dad had always been, menial tasks being in my mother's view very much a woman's province. I don't know what they talked about, but Mum obviously crossed the minefield with great nimbleness, for when they came into the sitting room afterwards with the tea-tray, Jo was smiling. We left before Sam got back from work, and she expressed regret at not having had the chance to meet him, which I thought a very good sign.

I had planned to spend a fortnight with my mother and Sam when I was finally discharged, a time to get used to the new clothes, write letters, sort out my affairs. I had also looked on it as a means to stay near to Jo a little longer, and perhaps to find out what her plans were and whether, crucially, I figured in them after all. I even thought she might come to Mum's with me – there were three bedrooms and I could share with Sam. But only a week before my release she told me that she was going abroad to stay with Rob for a while.

'He's just been transferred to Cyprus, and

he's got a house on the base there, at Akrotiri, so there'll be plenty of room for me to stay.'

'Cyprus,' I said. 'Lucky you! I hear it's really lovely there.'

'Well, it's safe at all events,' she said.

Safe from what? I wondered, but there was something else I wanted to know more, so I asked, 'How long will you be staying?'

'I don't know,' she said. 'I thought I might keep house for Rob for a bit. We haven't spent any time together really in years, just a few days here and there. I might stay a month, or two, or three. He's going to be there at least a year, he says.'

A year! I thought, but I didn't say anything. Of course she would want to be with her brother at a time like this. He had been home for three days' compassionate leave for the funeral, but that was a drop in the ocean compared with the time they must need to talk things out. I could not begrudge her her visit, but I was afraid if she got settled in there she might simply stay for his whole tour – perhaps even, when Rob moved, move with him. She might never come back to England. She might fall in love and marry a serviceman – really, nothing could have been more natural for a soldier's daughter. What had I to offer her, beside that great centripetal pull of the army?

I said, 'I hope you won't forget me while

you're away.'

She looked surprised. 'Forget you? How could I forget you?'

'Not literally,' I said, slightly impatient. 'You know what I mean.'

'You might forget me,' she said. 'That's far more likely. And probably the best thing for you. London's a big place, and there are a lot of people there.' She looked at me as she said it, her eyes wide and blank, and for the life of me I couldn't fathom what she was thinking.

'I don't have so many friends I'm likely to mislay one of them,' I said. 'Not through carelessness.'

'Perhaps you don't now, but you will,' she said sadly. 'You're going to have a real life, full of normal people.'

'Aren't you "normal people"?'

She laughed. 'Oh George!' And she sounded suddenly lighter, almost merry. 'But I shan't mislay you, at any rate,' she concluded, and I had to be satisfied with that.

In a couple of days she was gone, and in a couple more I left the army and Bovvy Camp for ever. And so for a while I lost contact with her. She said she would write from Cyprus and give me her address to write back to, but she didn't. One postcard came, two weeks after she left, sent to my mother's house, but there was no address on it. I waited for more, a letter, reasoning that she would be much occupied at first, too busy and happy to write; but nothing came, and a dull ache of doubt settled into my bones, that she did not care for me in the way I cared for her, that the army had reclaimed her and I had lost. I treasured the postcard, though the writing had got wet somehow and smeared, so I could not make out what it said. They remained tantalisingly unintelligible, her last – perhaps her last ever – words to me.

My interest in architecture had first been aroused by a schoolbook about Isambard Kingdom Brunel, whose bridges struck me as things of such power and beauty I went on to seek out other books about bridges. The Blitz interested me in buildings, but after a long detour through the Georgians, Palladio, Ancient Greek temples, and English cathedrals of all ages, my interest returned to its first inspiration, and for my future employment I settled with a sense of coming home on that fault line where architecture meets engineering.

My qualifications were good, and my experience in the army had done me no harm. Without much difficulty I got myself a good position with Avery Harrup, the construction company, at their office in Piccadilly, at a salary that seemed to me enormous after my army pay; and after only a few days in lodgings I found a small but very pleasant flat in Queen Anne's Terrace, in a house that was rather shabby and in need of paint, but whose architecture delighted me. There were sixty-foot-high ancient plane trees all along the road, beautiful in all seasons, and a tiny railinged garden opposite, overgrown and neglected because there was no gardener since the war and, in any case, the key to the gate was long lost. My little flat was at the top of the house, and unfurnished, which made it rather Spartan at first, but at least saved me from the horrors of other people's taste. I had fun painting it, and finding second-hand things, bit by bit, over a long period, to furnish and embellish it.

My salary continued to seem comfortable, perhaps because I spent most of my spare time exploring London, which cost nothing. The greatest city on earth was at that time full of bomb sites, damaged buildings, the crash of demolitions and the racket of erections. There had been talk straight after the war, as there had been after the Great Fire, of using the opportunity to realise Wren's dream of a planned and elegant London of piazzas and palazzos, but of course it never happened. Building went on piecemeal, as money was found piecemeal, and a great deal of what went up was, sadly, hideous. But it was all fascinating to an architect; and for a young man just out of the restrictions of the army, even the drab and rationed

London of the fifties seemed to throb with excitement and possibility.

Once I had got used to living and working in London, I settled down to make money. Everyone needs some tangible goal to aim for, and I made mine the purchase of some kind of property, a flat or house of my own. It seemed to me at the time very important: everywhere I looked in London the old and graceful was being pulled down wastefully for the new and ugly to go up. People who had lived through the war, its squalor, destruction and make-do, had no time any more for the antique: they thought anything old was ugly, dirty, undesirable. They wanted new things – shiny, sparkling, unused, brightly coloured things – no matter in how dubious a taste. Modernism was all; America the model. The style called Contemporary sang to them; glass and steel had the right 'clean' look; anything made of plastic was the last word in luxury. In the midst of this iconoclasm I wanted to be sure of saving at least one small piece of Georgian elegance; which meant buying it; which meant saving.

My other preoccupation was in learning to cook. My little flat had a tiny kitchen, and since eating out was expensive – and dull when one was on one's own – I got hold of some of the new cookery books that were just coming out then, and began experimenting with food. My early failures were extensive, but there was no-one to know about them but me, so at least I was saved embarrassment; and soon I was secure in the basics and learning to improvise. A man who can cook, as I've learnt since, is an object of fascination to women, and the ability to knock up a delicious dish in a short time is a great advantage in the mating game. But at that time no females tasted any of my dishes, or got to admire the interior decorations of my flat. I had no vacancy in my heart for another woman.

I worked hard, saved, and lived simply and delightfully, with little leisure to think about anything but architecture and food. I did find time, especially just before falling asleep, to think about Jo; but I had not heard from her since that one postcard, and as summer turned to autumn I began to believe that I would not see her again, that she had drifted deliberately out of my life. It was a matter of infinite regret to me. She was my first love, and I mourned her; but there seemed nothing I could do about it.

By the beginning of November, the weather had turned wintry. 'My' plane trees were bare and black, tossing their arms against the sky; their leaves, which had carpeted the railed garden with gold for weeks, had darkened and rotted to invisibility almost overnight. When I came out of the office at lunchtime one day, it was definitely cold, spitting rain from a solid yellowish-grey sky which made twilight of noon, and too uninviting to want to do anything with my lunch break but get something to eat. Usually I liked to walk in St James's Park, or down to Trafalgar Square to feed the pigeons; or sometimes I would wander round one of the galleries. But today I decided I would just buy a sandwich – there was a salt beef place just off Shaftesbury Avenue – and take it back to my desk to eat.

While I was in Shaftesbury Avenue I bethought myself of a play I wanted to see, and went into the theatre to buy a ticket. There was rather a queue at the box office. At the sandwich shop they took an age, too, so by the time I was walking back along Piccadilly there was not a great deal of my lunch hour left. And then as I got opposite Fortnum's I thought about dinner that night, and decided to buy a bottle of wine to go with it, to cheer the dreary day. I popped in, chose a bottle of Burgundy, had it wrapped, and headed back to the door, noticing that it had got even darker outside. Looking outwards, I did not notice someone approaching the door from another direction until I almost ran into him.

We uttered a flurry of I'm-sorrys and beg-your-pardons, and then at the same moment

looked at each other properly and stopped
dead.

'Well I'm dashed!' I said.

'George West!' he exclaimed. 'What a coincidence. I came to London to see you.'

It was Rob Grace. He had grown a small
moustache – a mistake, I thought, since it
was so fair it hardly showed, and did nothing
for him. But he still looked young for his age,
with that smooth, light gold skin, the pale
hair and level grey eyes, and the odd look of
fragility he carried about him. Most of all,
hauntingly and painfully, he had a look of Jo,
which brought all my feelings for her suddenly awake out of their hibernation. I felt a
sharp pang of longing in my vitals, which
told me I hadn't got over her at all.

An elderly man, blocked from the door by
our immobility, began tutting, and we stepped aside out of the flow of traffic to stare at
each other some more.

My first question, of course, was 'How is
Jo? Is she here with you?'

He stared at me searchingly. 'You haven't
seen her, then?' he asked.

'Seen her? No. I haven't heard a word since
she went off to Cyprus to stay with you.'
Now I stared. 'Why are you asking me?
Don't you know where she is?'

He gave a slight shake of his head. 'Look,
we can't talk here. Can we go somewhere?'

I glanced at my watch. 'I haven't long. I

have to be back in the office in five minutes. What's happened? Where is she?'

'It's a long story,' he said. 'There's a lot I want to tell you. What about tonight? Are you free?'

'Yes, I'm free,' I said. 'Come to dinner at my flat. We can be private there.' It seemed to me from his expression that he would want to be private.

'Thanks,' he said.

I gave him the address, and we settled on seven thirty, and then, thinking of the hours that lay between now and then, I asked, 'Is she all right? Can you tell me that, at least?'

'She hasn't been all right for a long time,' he said. 'But if you mean is she in any immediate danger, I don't think so. She's not ill or in trouble. That's all I can tell you now.'

So with that I had to make do.

I learned, when I got back to my desk, that a tall, fair stranger had been there asking for me while I was out, and said he would return later. That explained, I thought, why he was hanging about in Fortnum's – a good place to kill time on a grey and spitty day in Piccadilly. How he had known where I worked was another matter.

I modified my dinner plans to something that could cook itself unattended – a casserole out of my Elizabeth David book – and knocked up a quick fruit salad for a pudding.

I lit the fire as soon as I got home, and by the time Rob Grace arrived, with military punctuality, my small flat was warm and welcoming against the wet and gusty evening outside. The flat had one living room, large enough to serve as a sitting room at one end and dining room at the other, which meant a minimum of moving about on an occasion such as this. The fireplace was at the sitting room end. The kitchen led off the dining room end, and the bedroom and bathroom led off the landing to the stairs. I had managed to get some very good pieces of furniture – everyone was throwing away antiques those days – and a fine Turkish carpet in that sublime state of wear that takes generations to achieve.

Rob cast an eye around it as I relieved him of his overcoat and said, 'You seem very cosy here.'

'As the great Duke of Wellington said, any fool can be uncomfortable,' I replied. He smiled, a tired, worn-looking smile. 'Drink? Sherry or cocktail?'

He accepted a sherry, so I joined him in one and we sat by the fire, he on the chesterfield and I in an armchair catty-corner to him.

I did not wait for any more pleasantries. 'Tell me about Jo,' I said. 'Where is she?'

'She is in London,' he said, 'but she didn't come with me. I'd better tell you the story from the beginning. She came out to me in Cyprus in July. I think you knew that?'

'Yes. She left Dorset a few days before I did.'

He nodded. 'I was glad to have her. I haven't often been in a position where I could have her to stay, and so I haven't seen as much of her over the years as I would have liked. And after my father died, I worried about her a lot. We hadn't had a chance to talk things out properly, just those few wretched days after the funeral. So I was delighted when she said she'd come.

'It's a nice base at Akrotiri. Very pleasant grounds, its own beach, sports facilities – there's even a riding school. She found plenty to do while I was on duty. She rode a lot, swam, sunbathed, helped out at the summer school for the base children. She even helped at the riding school, taking beginners' lessons for some disabled Greek children – it's a charitable thing they do. And she seemed happy. I was glad to see it. She'd had to bear the brunt of Father's death, and I thought she'd be affected by it. But she seemed to have got over it very well. In the evenings we were able to spend time together. There was some socialising with other families on the base – everyone always wants to dine a newcomer – and sometimes we went out to a native restaurant, just for fun. But often it was just the two of us, alone, and that was very satisfying.'

'I imagine so,' I said. It sounded like heaven to me – alone with Jo on the isle of Cyprus in summer.

'The weeks passed pleasantly,' he resumed, 'and at the end of the first week of September she said she had to go back to England. I assumed it was because the new university term was going to start. I *think*,' he said with a small frown, 'that I asked her something along those lines but I can't now for the life of me remember how she answered.'

I smiled grimly. I had been on the other end of that evasiveness myself, more than once.

'Anyway,' he said, 'she left, as far as I was aware, to go back to university, and that was that.'

'But she didn't go to Edinburgh,' I said.

He raised an eyebrow. 'You knew?'

'She told me back in the spring that she wasn't going back after Easter.'

'I didn't know that!'

'She didn't tell you? What about her letters?'

'There weren't any for a couple of months. I was in a state of transition until I got to Cyprus. That's partly why I invited her to stay for the summer, so that we could catch up.'

'I half thought she was going to make a new life with you.'

'Well, she didn't. She went home. I was pretty busy over there, and I didn't notice that I hadn't heard from her in a while until a letter arrived a week ago. It was from an address in London, telling me that she had hated university and that it wasn't for her. I suppose her conscience had pricked her at last and she was telling me some part of the truth, at least. She said she had got herself a job and somewhere to live and that I wasn't to worry about her. Naturally I couldn't leave it at that. I managed to get a forty-eight and cadged a flight from the RAF base and flew over. I saw her this morning. I went first to the address – a place in Earl's Court. She has a bedsitting room in one of those tall terraced houses.'

'I know the sort.'

'It seems a clean and respectable sort of house, thank God,' he said. 'There's a housekeeper who lives in the basement and keeps an eye on things. She was able to tell me where Josella was.'

'At work?'

'Yes. She's got herself a job as a reception-ist in a hotel.' He accepted more sherry absently, rubbing his forehead with a fore-finger. 'She seemed happy enough there. We couldn't talk much while she was on duty but I hung around and took her out to lunch, and she told me emphatically that she would not go back to university. She said there's so much of England she hasn't seen yet, and she wants to travel round and see the country. She has enough money from my father's trust to keep her for several years, especially if she ekes it out with casual employment. She spent September in Torquay and October in Bath, and now she's settled in London for the winter.'

'That at least shows good sense,' I said.

He looked at me sharply. 'Good sense? My father wanted her to have a decent career, so as to be able to support herself in comfort, not this, this—'

I nodded sympathetically. 'But it may be something she has to get out of her system, before she settles down.' I searched for words to comfort him. 'I imagine sheer discomfort will make it a short experiment. She's used to a nice home and regular meals and so on.'

He nodded, but gloomily, as though he was not convinced. He said, 'The thing is that, while Josella is technically a minor, she *is* nineteen, and in practice there's nothing I can do to force her to go back to Edinburgh. And I can't make a home for her myself. I shan't be in Cyprus for much longer, and the places I shall be sent to after that are unlikely to be suitable. England is the best place for her; and she seems well, and she says she's content, so I shouldn't worry. But—'

'But you still do.'

He looked up. 'There are things about Josella that you don't know. A very particular reason why I do worry. It's what I've come here tonight to tell you.'

I guessed from his expression it was going to be a long story. 'Shall we continue over dinner?' I said.

So we moved the conversation to the table, and with the intimacy generated by candle-light, the comfort of food and the lubricant of a not-half-bad Burgundy, he told me.

'My father was away from home for most of the war,' he began. 'In 1945 he hoped to catch up with family life. But the army need-ed him, and asked him to stay on for two more years. At that time his private income was declining, and the pay and the defer-ment of his pension were important financial considerations, so he accepted. But the tour was in Kenya, and as he did not want to be separated all over again, he insisted that my mother and Josella go with him.'

'I see,' I said. I had heard some of this from Jo, of course. 'Jo said your mother was not happy about that.'

'She was furious,' Rob said. 'She had never wanted to live anywhere but London, and she'd been hoping, with the war over, to be able to go back. It was penance enough to her to live in the country, but to live outside of England was a thousand times worse. She hated everything about it – the heat, the rain, the insects, the natives, the food. She raged, she sulked, she grew depressed, and she drank. She had always been fond of a drink, but now she became a heavy drinker.'

In the quiet room, within the quiet circle of candlelight, his quiet voice was precise and without emotion, yet I could see the emotions under the surface in the small muscle that ticked in his jaw. It shamed him to have to tell me these things about his own mother; but like a soldier he would not shrink from what had to be done.

'And she took lovers,' he concluded.

I remembered how Jo had said the same thing, used the same word. Had they talked about it together? Had the colonel known at the time? Did he turn a blind eye, for the sake of peace and quiet? Or had there been rows about it, that the child Jo heard going on in the background, like a low mutter of thunder from behind the closed door of the marital bedroom?

Rob ate a few mouthfuls, perhaps to give himself time to assemble his words. Then he put down his knife and fork and took up his wine glass; but he didn't drink. He held it before him, looking, it appeared, at the candleflame through the red heart of the wine.

'They had a large house,' he resumed, 'a little out of the way, up a country road. A little isolated, perhaps, but this was before the Mau Mau, and it wasn't considered dangerous. Father's job was liaising between the military authorities and the police. He was well liked by the African leaders. Already, in those days, we were beginning to ease the country towards self-government. Of course, there were always bad hats, unemployables who lived by theft, and who were generally out of their senses from smoking bhang, but Father had good, loyal houseboys, so he wasn't worried when he was away all day.'

I was beginning to see where this might be tending, and I didn't like it. I refilled both our glasses. I don't think Rob even noticed, though his glass was held before his face.

'My mother had a lover who came to see her, always in the afternoon. She used to send the houseboys away, because she wasn't sure they would be loyal to her rather than to my father. She'd give them money and tell them to have the afternoon off. One day, when she was expecting her paramour, Josella happened to be home from school, in bed with some mild ailment. But she didn't cancel the assignation. The house was a large one, and I suppose she trusted that Josella would stay in her bed, and would not hear anything.' He sighed. 'If she hadn't been drinking steadily all day, I don't think even she would have been so thoughtless. When her lover arrived, he was horrified at the suggestion of making love – or whatever it was they made – with a sick child in the house. He and my mother quarrelled and he left, or she threw him out.

'So she and Josella were alone in the house, Josella in bed and my mother sitting on the verandah drinking gin. Shortly after the man had left, two natives broke in. They must have been watching for his car to leave.'

He stopped, took a sip of wine, and then resumed his staring at the candle through the glass, turning the stem round and round slowly in his fingers. My ears were on stalks, my nerves standing out from my skin with horror at what might be coming. Part of me hoped he would not continue, that he would never speak the words I felt hanging over me like doom. When I knew what he knew, it would be the end of something, of an innocence or happiness or both in combination. I wanted to cry out to him, 'No more!' but my mouth was too dry to speak; and besides, I could see he needed to tell me, to get rid of part of what must have been sickening him for years, and I could not have been so cruel as to deny him what comfort it might give him.

He spoke, in a voice dry and quiet and dead as an empty stream bed. 'They raped them both.'

He stopped again after that one sentence. I could not speak, my mind stretched with horror.

At last he drew a great, shaking breath, and put down his wine glass. Now he looked at me, and I met his eyes reluctantly, afraid of what I might see there; but he looked only tired. In the closeness of the candlelight I could see the lines around his eyes and across his forehead that went unnoticed in daylight. He did not look a young man any more; perhaps, carrying this poisoned knowledge, he had never been one.

'I don't know what would have happened if the houseboys had not come back. Probably they would have killed them both. But the houseboys had felt uneasy about taking the afternoon off when Josella was sick in bed. Perhaps they felt guilty about the other times, too, aware that my father didn't know about them. Perhaps they had heard or seen something that alarmed them. I don't know. But they came back, and frightened the intruders away. If they had arrived a little sooner... But I dare say that thought occurred to them, too, and haunted them afterwards. They had been very fond of Josella.'

He took up his glass and drained it. There was no more wine. I said, 'I think I could do with a brandy. You?'

'Yes,' he said. 'I need one.'

I found my hands were shaking when I tried to pour from the decanter, and I had to take several deep breaths to steady myself.

My mind was raw with what he had told me; my lungs felt scraped out as if I had been running hard. There were images in my mind, running through it like a loop of film repeated and repeated. I didn't want to look, but there seemed nowhere else to go.

'Thanks,' he said, when I put the brandy glass in his hand. He studied me a moment. 'I'm sorry to burden you with this. But I think it is something you ought to know about.'

I wasn't sure yet that I agreed with him, but I nodded acknowledgement, if not agreement, and said, 'Go on.'

'Well,' he said, 'after that my father got himself transferred home on compassionate grounds. Mother drank more heavily. The relationship between them was bitter. He blamed her for taking a lover and sending the boys away. She blamed him for making them go to Kenya in the first place. Probably,' he added thoughtfully, looking at the candle again, 'he blamed himself, too, for the same reason. I don't know. He never spoke about that side of it, or not to me, at any rate. But Mother drank, and then she committed suicide. She had sleeping pills in plenty since the incident, so the means were to hand.'

'But Jo – what about Jo?'

He looked at me. 'This is the thing – Josella has no memory of the incident. None at all.

I think it's called traumatic amnesia, or something of the sort. She and my mother were both in hospital immediately after the incident, to attend to their physical condition. And the doctors there discovered she did not know why she was there, did not remember what had happened to her. So when they came back to England, my father called in Sir Archie Benfield – you've heard of him?'

I shook my head.

'He's an eminent psychiatrist, and also a friend of the family. He was in Intelligence during the war and he and my father were friends. So Father was able to have him come down to Roselands for a weekend visit and talk to Josella without alarming her. They had several long talks over the two days, and he said it was definitely amnesia, that she had no memory of the incident at all.'

'What an extraordinary thing,' I said.

'It's a miracle,' he said seriously. 'I don't know how she could have faced life otherwise.'

'And you're convinced she still doesn't remember?'

'Of course. It's not something that would go unnoticed. Since coming home she has been to all intents and purposes a normal, happy girl, living a normal, happy life.'

'Except,' I said, thinking of that something

I had always sensed inside her, a place of hurt never spoken of, perhaps that she was not even fully aware of.

'Except, of course, for our mother's suicide. That was a terrible shock to all of us, but particularly to Josella because she was the one who found her.'

I was thrown again. 'I didn't know that. How did that happen?'

'My mother didn't come down to breakfast one morning. My parents had had separate rooms for some time, you understand. My father was always annoyed by unpunctuality. It was the maid's day off, so he sent Josella up to tell her to come down.' He sighed. 'I think he always blamed himself for that. Josella found her dead, her eyes fixed, a greenish foam dried on her mouth and chin. Horrible.'

It was enough and more, I thought, to account for that well of reserve and sadness I had sensed in Jo. Such a thing could affect a person's whole life. It was a wonder, perhaps, that she could be as happy and merry as I had seen her so often.

Rob regarded me gravely for a while, and then said, 'I thought very carefully before telling you about what happened in Kenya. I had some doubts – I was afraid it might change your attitude to Josella, that you might feel you didn't want to have anything more to do with her.'

I looked up, startled. 'Good God, no! Quite the opposite. What sort of swine would want to abandon her because of something that was so much not her fault?'

He smiled faintly. 'I'm so glad you feel that way. You see, I'd heard quite a bit about you before I ever met you. Josella wrote to me about you. And when I did meet you, I saw at once you were a decent chap. Since then, it has become clear that you are very important to her. She talked about you a lot when she was in Cyprus; and she told me you had taken her to see your mother, and she talked a lot about her, too. That's how I found out where you were. Josella and your mother have been corresponding.'

The pain of all these revelations lifted just a little at the discovery that Jo cared for me enough to keep track of me through Mum – though it would have been nice if she had made use of the information more directly.

'I have no right to place this burden on you,' he went on, 'but I believe you are fond of her, and she certainly is very attached to you. Now our father is dead, she has only me, and I am out of the country. She needs someone she can come to if things go badly.'

'Your father said almost the same thing to me before he died. He didn't tell me this story, though.'

'It would have been too painful for him to tell anyone, however much he liked you. The

311

thing is, George—'

The first use of my name, and the way he met my eyes levelly and insistently told me we were coming to the point – or at least *a* point. There had been points enough already this evening, and all of them sharp enough to run a person through.

'The thing is, George, that while Benfield is quite convinced that Josella remembers nothing of the incident, he also says that it's possible that the memory could come back.'

'My God,' I breathed. What a time bomb to be sitting on top of! What a sword of Damocles. I felt rather sick.

'He said another great shock could trigger the memory, and we were afraid that my mother's death might do it. Since she has weathered both that and my father's death, it seems not too likely now, after all this time, that she ever will remember, but it's still possible. It could come in a sudden flash, or gradually, bit by bit, over a time. If it did – if it should come back to her – she would need someone to turn to.'

I nodded painfully. 'Yes, I see.'

'And I need to know that there is someone who will keep an eye on her for me.'

I nodded again. 'I'll do that. If she'll let me.'

'I think she will,' he said. He stared at his hands. 'Did I do right in telling you?'

No! I cried inwardly. The scenery in my

head would never be the same again. I knew things I would far rather not know. My feelings for Jo were now churned and painful and half-frightened as well as all the disturbing things they had already been. I felt bitter towards Rob, though I understood completely. *Take this cup from me!* I might have cried. But, good Lord, we are Englishmen, and Englishmen don't make exhibitions of themselves. And so I answered, as calmly as he had asked, 'Of course. I'm glad you did.'

The following day was Friday. Rob had given me Jo's address before he went, and I was planning to go over there on Saturday morning and make contact. There was no telephone in the house, so I would have to take my chance.

The wind had dropped in the night and the day was still and foggy, very cold, with that yellow tinge to the grey of everything, and the bitter smell of sulphur in the air that was so very London. The bare black trees dripped condensation; in the murky half-dusk offices and shops had their lights on and glowed temptingly; buses rolled by silently like illuminated fish-tanks, the passengers goggling against the glass; wraiths of fog streamed around every headlamp.

At my desk all day I found it hard to concentrate, my thoughts going back again and again to that nightmare conversation; poring over things Jo had said and done in the context of this new information. *But she didn't know.* That meant, as far as she was concerned, it had never happened. Nothing had changed. She was the same Jo I had known before, all the way up to yesterday. But I knew. When I saw her, would she look different to me? Would I treat her differently? How do you treat someone about whom you know a terrible secret they don't, and mustn't, know? The dichotomy was likely to drive me distracted. She had always been the one to have power over me; she still did, but now, as well, I felt protective towards her. The mixture was richer. I found that I loved and longed for her more than ever. If she would let me, I would dedicate my life to making her happy.

Trying to catch up with my work I stayed at my desk all through lunchtime and left the office at six, after all the shops had shut – which meant I would be thrown for supper very much on what I had in the cupboard at home. I seemed to remember, on the bus home, that it was not very much. I was not in the mood to eat in a restaurant. Perhaps I might go out later and get some fish and chips somewhere. That seemed to touch the spot.

At home I changed out of my work suit and dithered over lighting the fire – not worth it if I was going out, but nice to come back to later. And then the doorbell rang.

It was a long way down, and as I ran down the stairs I thought it would be an idea to have some sort of 'intercom' fitted, like they had in offices. I flung open the door, and there was Jo, standing hunched against the chill like a bird, hands in pockets, fog jewels clinging to her hair, her pale face turned up to me, faintly smiling. My heart lurched with love, compassion, longing to gather her up and hold her. Everything Rob had said fled away before the natural impulse to be with her. She looked exactly as she had always looked; she was the same Jo.

'Hello, George,' she said. 'Surprised to see me?'

'A little bird told me you might be coming,' I said.

'A great big bird, more like,' she corrected. 'Can you come out to play?'

'Now?' I said.

'What I wanted to do, you see, was to go down to Pimlico, where I know a really good fish-and-chip shop, get four penn'orth of cod and two of chips, smother them with salt and vinegar, and eat them out of the paper walking along by the river. What do you think?'

The coincidence seemed like divine intervention. 'I think it's the best idea I've heard this week,' I said.

Chapter Sixteen: 1964

Just outside Bournemouth she got a lift that was going all the way to Reading, and she counted herself lucky, so lucky she was ready to indulge the curiosity of the driver, who was fooled by the coat and beret.

'Running away from home?' he asked her jocularly.

'Do I look as though I was?'

'You don't look like the usual run of hitchers,' he said, steadying the wheel with his elbows as he opened a packet of Players. 'Fag?'

'No thanks.' She watched, fascinated, the delicate manoeuvre of extracting and lighting the cigarette. 'What does the usual run of hitchers look like?'

'Beatniks.' He exhaled the word with the first smoke so it sounded like a sigh. 'Long hair and jeans. Duffel bags. Know what I mean?'

'Are they all like that?' She wasn't committing herself to any shared ground of knowledge.

'More or less.' He looked at her sideways

and tried again. 'Student?'

'I'm going on holiday,' she said, knowing the lift had to be paid for, one way or another. 'I haven't got much money so I thought I'd try and save the train fare.'

He smiled disbelievingly at this. He knew posh clothes when he saw them. 'Live in Bournemouth?'

'Uh-huh,' she said, which could have been yes or no.

He looked triumphant. 'I knew that. Tell by your accent. Know what I mean?' He gave her another sideways look, to make sure she was ready for the thunderbolt, and then loosed it. 'You're a writer. "Gathering material" – is that how you say it?'

'How did you guess?' she exclaimed in wonder and admiration.

He looked like a man who deserves all the praise he gets, took a suck at his cigarette, and said, lordly-wise, 'You get to spot people, this job. Got time to think about 'em. Sherlock Holmes stuff – know what I mean? See, I knew you wasn't a student, or any of the usual run. Tell you why?'

'Why?' she asked, waiting for the coat.

'The way you look at things. Ninety-nine out of a hundred, they watch the road, just wanting to get on. You, you look at things going by. Artists, they look at things properly so they can remember what they look like later. Well, you don't look like an artist to me, so I reckon you've got to be a writer, gathering material.'

Which just goes to show, she told herself severely, that you should never think you know what anyone's going to say next.

The driver went on to ask what her writing name was, and she made one up for him, and smiled gently, sadly, when he apologised for not having heard of her. He asked her what sort of things she wrote. 'I expect it's women's kind of stuff, is it?' he excused himself in advance. 'So what're you working on, that you're doing this journey for?'

So she told him it was a story about a hitchhiker, and he seemed satisfied with that, and began a string of stories about hitchhikers he had picked up, interspersing them with comments such as, 'Here, you can use this one. Free and gratis,' and 'Truth is stranger than fiction, isn't that what they say?' He was proud of himself for helping her so much, but the stories were all monumentally dull and quite pointless, and for a moment she felt as indignant as if she really had been a writer. What does he think I can do with all that rubbish? But it passed the time fairly painlessly, and at least when he was talking he wasn't asking her questions. She didn't want questions.

The sky over Bournemouth had been blue, but ahead of them, in the east, it was grey. They seemed to be driving away from summer. A few miles more, and a spattering of silver pinpoints appeared on the windscreen. They were driving into autumn, and just as spring made her feel restless, autumn made her feel sad. Normally it was a rich, warm sort of nostalgia that she felt, tinged with the excitement that belongs to winter, a noble sort of feeling one could enjoy having; but this time it was only a heavy melancholy. It seemed as though her world was closing in on her. The trouble had started in Edinburgh. No, that was wrong: the trouble had started on that last evening with George when he had broken the ritual and said he would go with her to the station; when he had almost asked her not to go. Her world was narrowing, and she was being hounded in a certain direction – towards what, she did not know, any more than the driven deer knows, though it fears it just the same. She felt a cold touch of it on the back of her neck, and shivered involuntarily. The driver glanced at her, wound up his window, and gestured to her to do the same.

Reading was ugly with greyness and rain, and to get out of it she took the first lift that came her way from a farmer in a Landrover that reeked of dogs. He set her down on the main road just before Abingdon, and she walked through it and started hitching on the other side. After a while a young man stopped and offered her a lift to Banbury, but she didn't like the look of him and accepted it only as far as Oxford, despite the fact that it was a Triumph sports car. When he dropped her in Oxford, it had grown dark.

She was lucky again, and was picked up almost at once by two students in a rickety fawn Morris. 'I'm Simon,' said the driver, 'and this is Mike.'

'I'm Jay.' They were so friendly she felt the need for some distance between them, and chose the most remote of the names she used.

'What's that short for?'

'It's a nickname.'

They said they were going to Cambridge for a party given by some other students, one of whom was Mike's brother.

'It's a long way to go for a party, isn't it?' she asked, privately doubting if the car, which sounded bronchial, would make it.

'It'll be a terrific bash, honestly. And anyway, we've promised. Mike plays the guitar, you see,' said Simon.

'Not very well,' Mike said, looking suitably modest. He was tall and dark and thin, Simon was stocky and fair and ruddy, and they both had clean pink faces of candid innocence, which surprised her, for she had thought that all students were world-weary and blasé, or else fierce communists with dirty fingernails. These two might have belonged to any of the families she had known in her far childhood. They seemed anachronistic in the slick new age of the sixties; delicately and, for her, heart-rendingly part of an old, superseded order. Why hadn't she known anyone like them when she was at university? It might all have been different.

'What are you reading?' she asked them.

'Law,' said Simon. 'We're at Balliol. Which college are you at?'

She was pleased that they thought she was a student too. 'I'm not at Oxford,' she said, and then, a little stiffly, as though using an unaccustomed muscle, gave them a little more. 'I was at Edinburgh, but I didn't finish.'

'Let me guess,' said Simon in delight. 'You got sent down for some fearfully naughty prank. Hanging a pair of knickers from the chapel spire?'

'Painting the Chancellor's dog purple?' Mike hazarded.

'Turning up at the Memorial Lecture dressed in a gorilla skin?' Simon tried.

'No,' said Jay, laughing now. 'I'm sorry to disappoint you, but I wasn't sent down at all. I came down of my own choice. I didn't like it.'

'Didn't like it?' Mike asked, wide-eyed. 'Why ever not?'

Jay looked at him helplessly. She had never tried to tell anyone about university – not even Rob – since that time George had asked, and even then she felt that she had by no means made herself understood. How could she explain to two strangers that terrible feeling of alienation, of being both different and horrible, of being out of her place, unplugged from anything that gave her solidity? More than that, why should she care whether they understood or not? Perhaps because they were not like the students she had hated; because they reminded her, in some faint, undisciplined way, of home.

'I couldn't make myself care who got elected to the Union,' she said.

Mike looked at Simon, and Simon looked at Mike, and they both laughed. 'I know what you mean!' Mike said, and she knew that he didn't really. They were just being polite; or perhaps, as they were very young, trying not to look stupid.

When they finally got to Cambridge it was quite late, and knowing that she would not have much chance of a lift in the right direction now, she accepted the two young men's invitation to go to the party with them. It was that, or find a hedge to sleep under. Luckily there was food at the party as well as drink, for she had not eaten since the doughnut and scone with Mrs West that morning.

It was the usual type of student party: the

stripped room, red cellophane over the light-bulb, boys in jeans and cable-knit sweaters, girls in tight skirts and tight jumpers and hooped earrings. There was a record-player and some people were dancing; others were kissing in corners; while in the kitchen the intellectual, or at least the unpaired, were hogging the beer and arguing about politics. Jay made for the food and ate steadily, standing up, like a horse. Someone gave her some beer in a jam-jar and someone else gave her a cigarette, and she listened half-heartedly to the chatter. A painfully young boy with acne asked her to dance, and she refused, knowing that 'to dance' was only a euphemism. His spots flamed at her refusal and he wandered away and picked up a newspaper and began to read it to show that he had not really wanted to dance anyway.

After a while Mike was handed a guitar which he tuned laboriously, and then someone gave him one of the new style of high kitchen stools that you saw in American films to perch on. Someone else shut the kitchen door on the smooching couples – if you had Sex you couldn't expect also to have Culture – and he strummed his way on three chords through an American folk-ballad. His audience listened seriously, like the disciples of a philosopher, heads bent, arms folded, lips pursed judiciously. He was not bad, really – his voice was weak but he sang in tune. She applauded with the rest. He sang another song, on the same three chords, and the others joined in the choruses. Simon came up beside Jay, and halfway through the second song dropped his arm over her shoulder with elaborate carelessness, like someone trapping, with infinite precautions, a tame rabbit.

She began to wish desperately that she had not come. It was a long time since she had submitted to being bored, and the idea made her panic. And the old sense of alienation was coming back in waves. She had liked Mike and Simon in the car because they were like the country boys of her childhood, but it came to her clearly, for the first time, that she was too old for them, too old for this. Though she had left off being a student she had remained at student age ever since; but now, looking around at them, listening to them, she felt her extra years. She was not like them any more. What was happening to her? Her life, carefully arranged never to make her feel like this, was closing down on her.

In the middle of the third song Simon pulled her against him and kissed her. The smell of him made her want to retch. It wasn't that he smelled bad – he was as clean as a whistle, she could tell – but that he smelled like any other young man of the same age, and it was a smell you had to be used to, or the same age, to like. His mouth was soft and inexpert, and he was trembling with nervousness and excitement. She endured it for a moment, in payment for the lift. His eyes were screwed shut, and at such close range she could see the soft pinkness of his skin and the delicate, downy hairs on his cheeks that didn't need to be shaved yet. He must be eighteen if he was at university, but he looked younger.

But then, encouraged by her quiescence, he pushed his tongue into her mouth. This she could not bear. She wrenched herself away. 'Excuse me a minute,' she mumbled, not looking at him, but seeing the surprise on his face as he opened his eyes and tried to regain his balance. She dashed for the door, and out, closing it behind her. She found the bathroom, locked herself in, turned on the cold tap and rinsed the taste of his saliva out of her mouth. She rinsed and spat, rinsed and spat; then she dashed water over her hot face. Looking up, she caught sight of herself in the mirror, flushed as if she had been drinking, water running off her chin. She hardly ever looked in mirrors, and her attention was unwelcomely caught now. In this downward light from the bulb over the basin, she could see there were lines around her eyes. She could still pass for nineteen in a less uncompromising light *but she was not nineteen*. What was she doing here? Ah, but that was the question she must never ask.

There was a bang on the door, and Simon's voice, concerned. 'Are you all right?'

Someone else, a female voice, said knowingly, 'She's being sick.'

There must have been quite a few out there, because she could hear the murmur of conversation. Go away, blast you! she thought.

'I say, are you all right?' Simon called again.

She had to answer, or they might think of breaking the door down. The latch didn't look all that strong.

'I'm fine,' she called gaily. 'I'll be out in a minute.'

She pulled the lavatory chain, and the sound of flushing must have embarrassed them away, for when she pressed her ear to the door afterwards she could not hear anyone talking close by. Cautiously she opened it. Only one person in the passage, and he was at the other end, with his back to her. She slipped into the bedroom where she had left her coat, dragged it out from under a fumbling couple who were half undressed on the bed, grabbed her bag, and made her escape. Well, at least I got something to eat, she thought as she gently closed the door behind her.

The air was chilly and damp, though it was not raining, and after the noise and crowd in the flat the night seemed hollow, dark and unwelcoming. She felt suddenly at a loss. The street was empty, but there were lights in most of the windows around. Why did she have to be the only person outside in the darkness, the only person with nowhere to go? She shook the thoughts away impatiently and stepped out briskly, looking for a road sign that would tell her which direction to take.

Here was a main road. Now, which way? Newmarket, that was about right. Newmarket and then Bury. She set out, the rhythm of her walk so steady that she quickly became unaware of the action or the pavement under her feet. Her thoughts wandered. D'you know what I'd really like now? A cup of cocoa. Frothy on the top, the way Jean used to make it on hunting days. Coming in cold and muddy and dog-tired, but in that lovely stretched way of after-exertion; frothy cocoa, and boiled eggs for tea, and hot buttered crumpets. She jerked back from the vision. Now that really was a sign of getting old – not wanting cocoa, of course, because love of cocoa was a constant in the well-balanced life, but thinking about old times. She had never used to do that – wallow in the past. Time she got her mind right and paid attention to what she was doing.

The houses had thinned out, and now were no more. There were open fields on either side of her. She turned her collar up and pulled her beret down more firmly on her head. Farm land was good, because farm land meant barns, and a barn was a much better prospect for spending the night than a hedge or even a country bus shelter. A barn could be very nice, like that time with George – no, no: no more nostalgia. That dark shape over there – was that a barn? Yes, good, it was. Now as long as it wasn't a) locked or b) full of machinery or c) guarded by half a dozen alsatians, she was all right. Only just in time, too. It had started spitting.

It turned out to be full of sacks of cattle cake. Not as good as hay or straw, but better than potatoes. There had been a girl at school, Sally Walsh, who used to eat cattle cake. Said it tasted like liquorice allsorts. She wished she'd thought to bring some food away from the party with her. There had been quite a lot of the sausage rolls left. A sausage roll would go down very well just now, along with the cocoa she wasn't having. She made herself as comfortable as she could, and listened to the rain pattering on the roof for a while, and then she fell asleep.

When you sleep in a barn, you wake early; and when you wake in a barn, you wake hungry. She was stiff, and it took a few minutes of staggering around, rubbing various bits of herself, before everything was functioning. It was not light yet, but dawn was coming. Better to be on the move. She must find a town, where there would be work and the possibility of food. She loved the country, yes, but that was for the times when you had somewhere to belong. In the machine age the country rejected the vagrant.

Outside the air was cold, with the kind of clearness that heralds a fine day. Jay brushed herself down, and shivered. Hunger was beginning to make her feel underprivileged. Her body felt thin under her coat, like an aged horse, not rubbery enough to keep out the cold. She put her hands nervously to her face and felt it for signs of deterioration. No, nonsense! She would never be old, she was eternally nineteen. Even those boys yesterday had assumed she was of an age with them. She started down the road, soon finding her pace and settling into her swinging walk, the cold leaving her and her interest in the surroundings sharpening as her blood got moving.

The morning was dim and milk grey, shadowless and holding its breath. Then from the darker half of the world on her left a blackbird spoke, not loud but brilliantly clear in the silence, defined like a cut diamond, a sharp, clean sound set on the newness and making it seem newer. Holy and new, perhaps like the first morning of creation, before anyone knew what the sun was like, but all waited for it. She turned her head away from the bird to watch what he was watching. The light was increasing and intensifying. It seemed to grow deeper, as if it were liquid being poured in, milk into water. You could see now where the source would be, and she stopped without noticing and fixed her eyes on that point.

Now colour was beginning to leak in, seeping through the porous walls of the sky: a dusty pink round the edges, a running gold near the centre. The flatness was going out of things: objects began to take their true shape, expanding into three dimensions; the sky, pulled down close for the night, drew back and assumed its proper distance. All the birds were singing now – she had not noticed them begin – and their racket would have been deafening if there hadn't been so much room for them, a whole world's worth. Their excitement grew to maddened pitch, and she held her breath as slowly the earth rolled forward under her feet and revealed the pale, brilliant gold of the sun hanging just beyond the horizon. The thing was accomplished. She let her breath out and turned to go on. The perilous magic was gone now; the birds got on with their business. The sun was up, it was fully daylight, and the world was prosaic and sensible again.

There were daytime pleasures to be had still: the smell of the earth beginning to warm, and of the dew and the rain drying off the grass. The hedges and trees smelled of autumn, and their hairstyles had a temporary look about them, though they hadn't begun to shed yet: it was fruiting time, not dying time. The birds were still trilling and jabbering and squeaking, but there was a domestic friendliness about it now. There had been no volition about their dawn song: it had been drawn out of them. This was what her wandering was all for, she thought vehemently, as though arguing with somebody. How could she live and never witness the singing-magic draw up the sun, as the moon draws up the sea? How could she live in a town and work in an office and lose contact with the earth? And yet, it would happen. In moments of honesty she knew that she could not live like this for ever, but would have to go back, as she already did for winter. How would she bear it? Being in one place, she would be vulnerable. People would ask questions, and would persist, wanting answers. The thought of those probing words and pointed looks filled her with craven fear.

Not yet, she said to herself. Not quite yet. The season was not over, and there would still be work by the sea. She walked on, briskly. The world immediately around her was waking up now, so that every individual noise was no longer distinguishable against the background. In a little while a milk lorry came along and stopped beside her, not even waiting for her to thumb – at that time of day and in that part of the world she could only be wanting a lift – and she begged a ride to Newmarket. On the other side of New-market she was picked up by a holidaymaker in a station wagon with his wife and two children and an awful lot of luggage and was driven slowly and noisily to Yarmouth. She sat between the children in the back and entertained them with songs and stories, and the mother and father warmed to her with gratitude. When during a pause her belly rumbled loudly enough to be heard, the woman asked her if she was hungry, and offered her sandwiches and chocolate.

I've become a professional beggar, Jay thought, and accepted gratefully.

'Didn't you have any breakfast this morning?' the woman asked.

'No,' Jay said simply.

'Nor any dinner last night either, by the way you're wolfing down that sandwich,' the man said jocularly.

'No,' Jay admitted. The children stared at her round-eyed, and demanded chocolate and potato-crisps.

'Do you live alone?' the woman asked, fishing.

'I suppose so,' said Jay, and then, taking pity on her, 'I slept in a barn last night. I work at seaside resorts in the summer. I was in Bournemouth last.'

The woman looked at her with slight disbelief, thrown by the coat and hat. 'And then you go home in the winter?'

'To London,' Jay amended, but it was taken for confirmation.

The children looked at her with envy. 'Are you a gypsy?' the elder one asked.

'Now, Robby,' the woman said in automatic reproof.

Jay felt a pang at the sound of the name and the instant memory it conjured. 'Is your name Robby?' she asked. 'I've got a brother called Rob.'

The woman nodded to herself, as if reassured by this mention of family.

'Tell us another story,' the younger boy demanded.

The family set her down in the main street, and she thanked them warmly, and then headed straight for the public lavatories to change her clothes. It was no good, she thought, looking for a job wearing her best coat and hat. The sandwiches had done little to appease her hunger, which craved hot food. As she dragged on her jeans and a clean shirt she tortured herself with visions of egg-and-chips, crisply frying bacon (oh the very smell of it!), thick steak oozing blood to the pressure of teeth, macaroni cheese topped with real, tangy English cheddar and a grating of nutmeg. She imagined lamb hot-pot with herbed dumplings floating on the top; she thought of bludwurst, sauerkraut and bradkartoffeln; she even attainted to a plate of chicken curry, the smell of which would make your jaws water weakly. I've missed my vocation, she thought caustically: I should have been in advertising.

A job in a café was her first thought, for there she could get food straight away as part of her wages. She tried some of the most likely ones, but had no luck: the season was almost over and trade was shrinking. They were laying off, not taking on. The first two she tried sent her away coldly; the third, more kindly, suggested she tried the funfair, where they often took on people for short periods. The idea had its merits. She had worked in funfairs before, knew some of the names to know, and some of the esoteric language. She thanked the café owner and turned to go, but he called her back.

'Wait a minute.' She turned, and he looked at her shrewdly. 'Hungry?' She nodded. 'Hang on.' He went through to his kitchen and came back out with a paper bag. 'In case you don't get took on,' he said, and thrust it at her.

'Thanks,' Jay said, smiling at him, and

thinking, this is getting positively Dickensian. Outside in the street she opened the bag and peered in. There were two cold sausages, a stub end of cheese, a heap of sandwich crusts, and two of those miniature fairy cakes with currants like fly-corpses scattered over the top. The crusts, she saw, had been cut from generously buttered sandwiches. A few doors along she found a shut shop, and sat down in the doorway to eat.

The town had a weary air, like a tired hostess whose husband will insist on offering the guests one more drink. Even the visitors seemed affected by it. They paused tentatively before the Hall of Fun, the ice-cream shops, the displays of rock and postcards, embarrassed by their numerical weakness, unable to plunge in unselfconsciously like the height-of-season holidaymakers. Only the brash youths with girlfriends to impress could take their pleasure without guilt: a Puritan lurks, tight-lipped, in almost every English soul. The sun was shining brightly and it was as warm as it ever was in summer, and people were being drawn inexorably towards the beach; but here and there a shop hadn't opened, here and there a kiosk was boarded up; the litter looked like yesterday's, and the smell of seaweed, tar and frying fish seemed melancholy instead of invigorating. As she walked along Jay noticed that most people kept moving instead of lying on the beach, nervous of being caught between the rising of the waves and the falling of the leaves.

The fair was just flexing its muscles when she arrived, getting ready for the early darkness, when it would take all the money the visitors were too embarrassed to spend in the daylight. Jay found the fairground boss and tried to chat him, while he looked at her with flat eyes, ostentatiously uninterested in her. But at last he said she could go and see Alfie on the Tote Wheel stall, and see if he needed a hand, and she knew she was in. Not the rides, of course, for that was where the big money was, and the jobs there were reserved for families, favourites and, of casuals, men. Girls never got to work the rides. But on the stalls she could earn her keep. She managed to avoid smiling her thanks, and slipped away to find Alfie.

He turned out to be a tiny, slightly bow-legged gypsy of indeterminate age. His body was thin and knotted, like an ancient whip, but his hair was still thick and black, worn long and swept back with a liberal application of oil to keep it in place. He wore a white shirt, open at the neck to show his vest and rolled up at the sleeves to show his beautiful tattooed forearms. His apparent major dread in life was of losing his trousers, for they were held up by red braces, two belts – one leather and one snake – and numerous pieces of string.

Jay introduced herself, and he smiled largely and lovingly at her, revealing horribly broken and browning teeth. It startled Jay, for he was otherwise rather handsome, with a big, straight nose, a full, beautifully sculptured mouth, and a firm chin, so that with his hollow cheeks and eyes he looked like a debauched Adonis.

Alfie owned several of the sideshows – the Tote Wheel, the Hoopla, the Roll-a-Penny, the hooking-plastic-ducks-off-the-imitation-river, the throwing-darts-at-playing-cards – and ran them with his wife, an enormous, harmonious woman behind whose opinions and say-so he sheltered, quoting them quite dishonestly, since she was never known to verse them.

This was not a travelling fair, and many things about it were different to Jay. The fair was permanently sited on this ground, and the big rides stayed put, along with the arcade, all year, while the smaller stalls were dismantled and stored during the winter. The owners and their families ran the fair during the summer, with the help of a shifting population of casuals, and lived nearby. In the winter they lived off the summer's fat, while their older sons and daughters got jobs as garage attendants or cinema usherettes, or sometimes went to bigger towns to live for a few months.

Alfie and his wife had no children, and lived well off their stalls, and they had an unusually open and frank attitude towards their casual helpers. They were born and bred to the fair life, and told her that in the old days – that is, before the war – they had belonged to a 'real, proper fair', a travelling fair with all the old sideshows that were no longer fashionable: the boxing booth, the two-headed calf, the fortune teller. Alfie himself had been the Tattooed Man – he promised to take off his shirt and vest one day and show Jay the full glory of his hieroglyphic torso – and his wife had been the Bearded Lady. Later on, as nature took its course, she had become the Fat Lady, though he admitted in a hushed tone of shame that she had always had to use padding, fatness not coming so natural to her as to make her a real Freak.

Jay helped him to get the stalls ready, and then he gave her half-a-crown, describing it with a wink as an advance against wages, and told her to go off and get something to eat, but to be back in half an hour for the opening. Pleased with this unexpected generosity she hurried along the front to buy fish and chips, and then ducked under the pier to eat them out of the paper. Fragrant, slippery and greasy they were, heaven to her empty belly. When she had nearly finished a dog sidled up to her from nowhere and stood before her, his nose quivering in an agonised way.

'Hello, dog,' she said. He wagged his tail tentatively and came forward a step, and sat down before her with the air of one who will do anything to oblige.

'You're a plain-looking animal,' she said conversationally, and the dog wagged his tail more definitely, this time in agreement. He certainly was a mixture, a black and white mongrel with collie and labrador prominent in his ancestry. There might even have been a trace of alsatian in the ears. She pulled off a piece of batter and threw it to his feet, and he snaffled it up with the speed of true hunger. In fellow feeling, when she got to the bottom of the bag she shook out the batter crumbs and the last few chips onto her palm and offered them to him. He stood up and licked them off daintily, and then sat down again with his tail neatly curled round his feet like a cat, and smiled at her.

'That's all. I have to go,' she said, and climbed back to the road, leaving him still sitting there.

Most of that evening Jay ran the Tote Wheel. It used to be the Film Star Wheel, Alfie told her, but film stars came and went so quick these days it was more than you could do to keep up with them, and it was a nuisance to keep changing the pictures, so they'd changed it to horse-racing. When she looked closely she could just discern under the new paint the ghostly images of former heart-throbs smiling toothily, Ginger Rogers and Clark Gable, Veronica Lake and Rock Hudson.

It was a popular stall and she was kept busy, checking tickets and spinning the wheel, taking money and handing over prizes. Standing on the other side of the painted wooden barrier, smelling the crushed grass and the oil reek of the generator, she felt safe and superior, as she did behind a bar, or working a switchboard, or tending the boats. She was the one they looked at but couldn't reach, the one with the knowledge, the one on the inside. She liked the familiar feeling of ministering to holidaymakers, safe from their uncertainties. Not for her the striving to enjoy oneself; no agony of weighing one pleasure against another, with the fear of missing out on something better; no disappointment when one got it wrong, no guilt over having wasted any of one's precious time. Why, she wondered, did anyone ever go on holiday? It seemed more of a toil than a pleasure.

The stalls closed first, and after they had been shuttered she was sent off to the Dodgems to help them to close up. Here was the other breed, the professional fairground casuals, the youths in tight jeans, with long sideburns and greased hair and black fingernails, who perpetually chewed on an untipped cigarette. They ordered her around in a lordly way, but tolerantly, for she was one of them now in her minor way. One of them even asked if she wanted to come afterwards for a quick one with him, but she thanked him and shook her head, knowing that even a pint of beer had to be paid for, and he laughed, thinking she was shy.

She slept that night on a piece of tarpaulin underneath the steps of the Merry-Go-Round, where it was dry, and warm with the residual heat of the engine. When she had settled down, the dog from the beach appeared from nowhere and sat near her to see whether she would accept him or send him away. She was surprised, not having seen him since she left him under the pier; but he must have followed her and been hanging around on the fringes all evening, waiting for everyone else to go.

'Persistent, aren't you?' she said. He thumped his tail softly on the ground at the sound of her voice. 'All right,' she said and flipped her fingers at him. 'Come on.'

He dropped flat and crawled up close to her on his belly, ears flattened in placation; and when she smiled at him, he sighed, and settled down against her legs.

There was not much to do during the days, and she just wandered around the town and looked at things. After a summer away, shops looked strange to her, filled with clothes and furniture and consumer desirables that she had nothing to do with. The dog stayed with her most of the time, though he had a knack for melting into invisibility if there were too many people around. When the fair re-opened he disappeared, to return later when it closed again, and when she settled under one of the rides he crept up close to sleep with her. The fair usually closed in time for the youths to get down to the nearest pub for a quick one before the bell, and several times she was asked along by one or another of them. She would have liked to go, to be in the warmth and light, to share the anonymous friendliness of the bar; but the idea of being groped up against a wall afterwards by any of them made her refuse every time.

Sleeping out, she was always hungry. She found which baker shops had stale cakes – or rather, which shops gave them away rather than selling them cut-price. Once when she was walking along the beach she saw a nicely dressed woman and her little girl feeding the gulls with perfectly good slices and crusts of bread, and asked if she could have some.

The woman looked surprised, and examined Jay carefully, before saying, 'Yes, of course, if you really want them. The gulls don't need them.' She handed over all she was holding. 'I have a boarding house,' she explained. 'I put bread out for the guests, but if they don't eat it, it doesn't go back. Either I throw it away, or if I have time we come and feed the gulls with it.'

'It's quite fresh,' the little girl added. 'It's this morning's.' She was staring at Jay with admiration and awe, rapt at the thought of meeting a real live beggar-woman. 'Is that your dog?'

'Sort of. He comes with me,' Jay said.

'What are you doing here? Where do you live?'

'I work at the fair.' It seemed to cover both questions.

'Where are your mother and father?'

'They're dead.'

The little girl looked even more thrilled – a real orphan, too! – but her mother was embarrassed by the words. 'That's enough questions, Beverley,' she said quickly.

'Can I give the lady my bread, too?'

Jay received it with grave thanks, thinking there would be enough now to give Dog half. There was almost a loaf's worth. The mother nodded uneasily to Jay and led the child away along the beach by the hand, and Jay turned the other way, to save her worry. Later she saw them coming back, but along the promenade. The little girl waved gaily to her, and she waved back.

On the third day she felt abominably grubby. She washed every day in the public conveniences, but there was a limit to how much she could do in such a place, and where people might come in at any moment. So in the late afternoon, when the visitors retired to their boarding houses for 'tea', she went down to the beach, stripped to her underwear and waded into the sea to get a bit cleaner. Dog came to the edge of the water, and sat down to watch her. She eyed him thoughtfully.

'You could do with a wash, too,' she said. 'Come on, Dog. Here, Dog.' He stood up and walked forwards, and then backwards as a wave flopped over and ran towards his paws. He shuffled forward and backward at the surf's edge, wagging his tail and smiling at her, but not seeing the point of doing more. She waded out, found a piece of driftwood of suitable size, and threw it along the beach for him. He barked and fetched it, wagging more enthusiastically. The third time she threw it out to sea, and he got knee deep before balking again. 'Enough dithering,' she said, picked him up round the middle and threw him in. He was thin under his coat, and not so very heavy. By the time he had stopped spluttering and got his bearings, she was out with him, and he seemed not to mind the water now that he was in. He paddled round her in circles, nose carefully above the waves, and when she threw the stick again he fetched it, as long as she didn't throw it too far. After five minutes she started to feel cold and turned for the shore. Dog paddled past her, found his footing and raced the last few yards. He shook himself vigorously, and stood swinging his tail to encourage her, as though the whole thing had been his idea.

One day the rain started. The town was emptying, though the fair was still doing all right: along with the cinema it was the cheeriest thing to do on a damp evening. Once she had got wet through, Jay stayed that way, and noticed it no more than a boatman; but Dog had a way of looking at her pathetically from places of inadequate shelter and shivering, which made her realise that it was nearly time to move on.

He was looking at her that way now, from under the lip of the Hoopla stall's counter: as the days had passed he had become less wary of the fairground after hours, and once the visitors had gone would come out of hiding to be near her, keeping just out of reach of any of the other fair people. He had his head stuck out from under the stall so that he could see her, and he flinched every time a drop of rain struck his head, which was about every ten seconds, rhythmically. Emotional blackmail, Jay thought. She was helping Alfie put up the shutters, he holding them in place while she slipped the bolts, for she was taller than he and could reach the top ones better. His wife brought out two enamel mugs of tea, carrying them hissing through the rain. She looked imperturbable under a huge sou'wester, which matched her gum-boots but went oddly with the cotton dress and cardigan in between.

'Season must be over soon,' Jay said, wrapping her numb fingers gratefully round the hot metal.

Alfie pulled his cap a fraction lower down his brow and sipped his tea. 'Katy says a couple more days'll do it,' he said, jerking his head towards his wife as he usually did when quoting his oracle. 'Pier show shuts up Sat'd'y. Boss'll prob'ly close up too.'

'I was thinking of going tomorrow,' Jay said. 'If you don't mind. Rain's getting me down a bit.'

'Suit yourself,' Alfie said pleasantly. 'Been a pleasure having you, ain't it, Katy?'

Katy smiled serenely, patient under her dripping canopy, waiting for the empty mugs.

'I never did see your tattoos,' Jay said regretfully.

'Next time,' Alfie promised.

At the edge of town Dog sat down at the side of the road. Sunk in thought, she had forgotten about him, and now did not notice that he had stopped; but when he whined at her she heard him, paused and turned. For a moment they sat looking at each other, she questioningly, the dog thumping his tail apologetically and looking back over his shoulder at the town they were about to leave.

'You're sorry, but you just can't come?' she translated. 'As you will. So long, Dog.' She raised a hand in farewell and walked on. The rain had settled into a steady drizzle, but she didn't really notice it. She felt dull and lethargic. The rain, sleeping rough and being dirty had blunted any exhilaration she would normally have felt at moving on, any anticipation she might have enjoyed at the thought of a new horizon. Lowestoft would be her likely next stop, a halfway town to ease herself into the winter and London. She hadn't much money, but she would need to get a room so that she could clean up before she could get a job; and getting a room when you looked dirty and scruffy could be difficult. Suddenly it all seemed burdensome to her, her way of life presenting problems to be overcome, rather than the absolute freedom she was accustomed to. She trudged along the country road in the rain, rather than striding it lightly, and when a car zipped past her, the water hissing out from under its tyres, she didn't even bother to thumb it.

This was no way to carry on, she told herself sternly, and tried to shake some spirit back into herself. A small van came up behind her. She held out her thumb, but the driver passed her, and his passenger leaned out to shout something, gesturing back with one hand, while the driver accelerated away.

She hadn't caught what it was, but it sounded angry. She glanced back and saw the dog trotting along behind her about twenty yards back, head down in the rain. She stopped and held out her hand to him, and he hurried to catch her up, and looked up at her, smiling, and licked the hand.

'Come on, then,' she said, starting off again. The dog fell in on the safe side of her and they walked on together. It occurred to her almost at once that it was going to cut down on lifts. Few people would pick you up with a dog, especially when it was raining and they might get muddy paw marks on their upholstery. But it couldn't be helped. He was there now, and she couldn't abandon him.

She had to walk quite a lot of the way to Ipswich. There was not much traffic on the road and what there was seemed to be private cars – and once a small rackety van that she had hopes of, but which did not stop. She guessed most of the traffic was local, using the main road to pootle between one village and another. At last a small builder's lorry came along and stopped for her, whose driver said he was going to

Felixstowe and would drop her in Ipswich on the way. He was cheerfully dirty from his work, and the cab was already daubed with clay, plaster dust and paint splashes, had a litter of empty cigarette packets and sweet wrappers on the floor.

'No, I don't mind a dog,' he said. 'Got a dog myself. Have a fruit gum. What is he? Good old Heinz Fifty-seven, eh? Best dogs in the world, mongrels. What's your name, love?'

'Jo,' she said. She was too tired to be anyone else.

'Mine's Arthur. What you going to Ipswich for?'

His curiosity was so open and honest she could not resent it, but for a moment she felt too tired to think up a good lie. 'Looking for work,' she said at last, feebly.

'What, you? Get on!' He eyed her sideways, dividing his attention between a thorough examination and the demands of the road. 'No, I can't make you out,' he said at last. 'You talk posh, you look posh, but...'

He waited to let her supply the answer but she remained heavily silent, wishing he would just drive and let her be.

'Cigarette?' he said when it was obvious she wouldn't answer.

'Thanks.'

He handed her the matches and she lit hers and then held the flame for him. He drove in silence for a while, but he hadn't dropped the subject, for after a few miles he said, 'You in trouble?'

'Trouble?'

'Police looking for you?'

'No,' she said, startled into enough vehemence to satisfy him on that point.

'A man, then?' She shook her head. 'You can tell me. Some man got you into trouble and your parents've thrown you out?'

She shook her head again, but he kept looking at her, and she felt obliged to tell him at least part of the truth, to shut him up. 'I do seasonal work. Seasides. Winter I work in a town. I don't have much money so I hitch, save the fare.'

Now he shook his head, still looking back and forth between her and the road. At last he said, 'I can't make you out. But it's none of my business if you don't want to tell me. Free world, isn't it?'

'I always thought so,' she said. It seemed to be getting less free all the time.

'I was just interested, that's all,' he went on. 'Asked too many questions. No offence.'

'No offence,' she said, and managed a faint smile. His open, weather-worn face was honest and kindly, and for the fraction of an instant she wanted to throw herself into his manly arms, pour out her story and have him take care of her. It didn't mean anything – it was like dreaming about what you would do if you won the pools. You knew it would never happen, and that life wasn't like that. There were no manly arms for her, no handing over of responsibility. When you were alone in the world you had to make your own way, and, that given, the less you told anyone about yourself the better.

Because she had had to walk so long, it was getting dark when they reached Ipswich. The driver pulled up and turned to face her. 'Look,' he said, 'my advice to you: if you're in trouble, go home. Your parents might shout a bit but they'll forgive you in the end. They'll sort things out for you. Running away never works.'

'I can't go home,' she said.

He sighed, shook his head, looked as though he was going to argue some more, and then smiled. 'Not my business,' he said. 'You got somewhere to stay in Ipswich?'

She barely shook her head. 'I'll find somewhere.'

'Here,' he said. He fumbled in his pocket and pulled out a pound note. 'That'll get you a bed and breakfast. Go on, take it. That dog's too tired to walk any further.'

She took it, rather than argue. 'Thanks,' she said. 'You're a nice man.'

'Try to be. So long, then. Take care of yourself.'

She watched him drive away with a feeling of having parted with her last friend in the world. Night was falling, as was the rain, and she didn't want to be in Ipswich. She didn't want to be on the road, she didn't want to be free – she wanted to be home. But she had no home.

She found a bed and breakfast place, one of many on the ring-road, and got herself taken in by putting on her coat and beret before she knocked on the door. Even so, the proprietress insisted on payment in advance.

'And no dogs,' she said firmly, staring at the shadowy shape hanging back near the gate. 'You can put him in the shed for the night, but if he makes a mess, you clean it up.' Jo nodded. It was as good as she could have hoped for. 'Are you wanting the evening meal?'

'How much?'

The woman eyed her. 'Three and six.'

She could get something cheaper in the town, but the thought of having to walk any more decided her. 'Yes please.'

'Seven o'clock, sharp. I'll show you your room.'

It was small but clean and perfectly adequate, and the narrow bed, covered in a faded candlewick counterpane, looked like the downiest feathered nest to Jo. 'Can I have a bath?'

'Bath's a shilling extra. For the gas,' said the woman. Jo nodded, but she held out her hand. 'That's one pound altogether.'

Worth every penny, Jo told herself later when she eased herself into the hot water. The bathroom was spartan and the towel was only a hand-towel, but the geyser was man enough for its task and she ran enough to cover herself to the neck and soaked blissfully until the water began to cool. Later she had her meal in solitary splendour in a small room furnished with three tables covered in plastic tablecloths, each bearing a cruet and a sauce bottle shaped like a tomato. No other guests came in, so either it was a quiet night or the season was ending for this house too. The food was adequate – brown soup followed by neck-of-lamb stew with potatoes followed by a rather hard piece of cold apple pie with evaporated milk – and Jo ate it to the last crumb, and felt very sleepy afterwards. She bethought herself of Dog, waiting patiently, trustingly in the shed. But if she went to say goodnight to him, he might think he was being released, that they were moving on, and wouldn't it be more unkind to him to raise and then dash his hopes?

While she was hesitating, a man came in, in shirtsleeves and braces, thin strands of hair slicked over his bald top, glasses not concealing his kind eyes. 'I took your dog a bowl of water and a few scraps,' he said, and laid a finger alongside his nose. 'Don't tell the wife.' He winked, smiled, and tiptoed out with elaborate caution.

The kindness of men, she thought as she hauled herself up to her room. Like their cruelty, it is often beyond expectation. Although it was only eight o'clock, she undressed and got into bed, and was soon asleep.

In the morning she washed and dressed and went down at the earliest time the land-lady had indicated she might be served breakfast. There was porridge or cornflakes – she chose porridge as being the more sus-taining – followed by eggs, bacon, sausage and fried bread. There was toast and mar-malade on the table, as well as a plate of bread. In between the woman's appearances, Jo managed to secrete quite a bit of the bread, along with her bacon rinds, while eating the toast herself. When there was nothing more to eat, she went upstairs for her bag, and left the house. There was no-one to say goodbye to. She let Dog out of the shed, and he bounded past her joyfully to relieve himself against the nearest privet hedge, and then bounded back to tell her how glad he was she had come. As she turned to go, she saw the man looking out of the kitchen window, and waved to him, and he waved back and then disappeared as though pulled by a string.

When she got out on the road she stopped and gave Dog the bread and bacon rinds.

Despite her long sleep, she felt very tired, and she had started a troublesome cough. The sky was heavy and threatening rain some time soon. She didn't want to stay in Ipswich and there seemed now no point in messing about with smaller towns. It was early for it, but she would go to London. Better jobs, more accommodation, and more, much more, anonymity.

Dog would pretty well rule out private cars. She would have to get a lorry lift. She knew a café on the A12 about ten minutes from here where the lorry drivers pulled in for breakfast. She'd get a lift there, for sure. She hitched her bag more comfortably and set off, Dog padding beside her. Yes, that was the best thing. Go to London. She could always lose herself in London.

Chapter Seventeen: 1964

She arrived on my doorstep one rainy evening in late September. I don't think I had ever seen anyone so wet. Her hair was flat to her skull, wet ends like jagged dark teeth against her white forehead tipped with glass drops; rain dripped from the points of her nose and chin. She looked up at me with an expression I could not interpret, for it looked almost apologetic, and that was something she had never been.

'I've come, George,' she said. 'I know it's not the right time—'

'There's no right time or wrong time,' I said. I noticed she was shivering. 'For God's sake, come in. How did you get so wet?'

'Walking,' she said. 'I've run out of money.'

'Come in,' I said again, for she was still hesitating, not even up under the porch but out in the weather like a penitent.

'Well,' she said, 'there's this, you see...'

Then I saw the dog, just about as wet as she was, drooping miserably a few paces to the rear. 'You've got a dog?'

'It's really more that he's got me.' It was the first evidence of her old spirit, but it quickly faltered. 'He's a very good dog.'

'Come in,' I said. 'Both of you. I can't stand watching any more water falling on you.'

It was fortunate that by now I had moved from my flat, where animals were forbidden by the lease, to a house: a tall slice of Georgian terrace in an unfashionable street in Islington, where there were all too many such buildings going to rot, or being turned into bedsits by ripping out everything lovely inside them. I had bought mine cheaply because of its condition, and had been restoring it for the last four years, but since

I was a) doing everything myself and b) extremely particular, it was still a work in progress. The benefit now was that there was still not much a wet dog could spoil – and of course as the owner and sole householder the decision was all mine to let it in.

Last winter, when Jo had been working in London, I had offered her her own room at the top of the house, but she had preferred to rent a cramped bedsit in Earl's Court, shying away, as always, from anything that looked like a tie, though I had been at pains to have her know she would be private up there and could come and go as she pleased. I wondered what had now brought her to my doorstep, with the apparent intention of staying at least for the night. It couldn't be simply the lack of money. I had known her sleep out under a bridge or on a park bench rather than accept anything from my hand.

She stepped over the threshold now and I said, 'Kitchen – both of you. It's warm down there.'

She walked ahead of me, showing no interest in what I had done to the house since she was last there – an ominous sign. The dog needed coaxing to come in, and went past me ears and tail down, eyes cast up and sideways pleadingly, begging not to be kicked. The kitchen was in the basement, and I had early decided to abandon architectural probity in this one case by knocking the

357

two small dark rooms into one long, light one. I had restored the old-fashioned range that still stood under the kitchen chimney, and I was glad now because it furnished constant warmth, and also provided clothes-drying facilities. As it happened I had been working at the kitchen table so I had also lit the fire down that end of the room (which had been the servants' sitting-room) and the whole basement was very cosy. Jo and the dog stood dripping on the stone flags of the floor while I ran upstairs for towels, my own dressing gown and slippers, and, as a last thought, the ironing blanket for the dog to lie on. Then while she stripped and towelled in front of the fire, I put cocoa on on the range and thought about what food I had in to offer the two waifs. She spoke only once, to say, 'Can I use this other towel to dry Dog? He's awfully wet.'

'That's what I brought it down for,' I said, without turning.

When the cocoa was ready I poured it into the biggest mug I had and carried it down to her. She was wrapped in my far-too-large dressing gown, sitting on a kitchen chair before the fire, her feet in my slippers resting on the chair rung. The dog was sitting before the fire staring at the flames with what I chose to interpret as disbelief, while steam rose gently from its coat.

As I proffered the mug Jo looked up and

her nostrils twitched. 'Cocoa,' she said. 'I dreamed of cocoa. Lovely, lovely.'

'It's hot,' I warned.

She sipped cautiously, and closed her eyes. 'Bliss. I never thought I'd taste it again.'

'Why didn't you make yourself some, instead of just dreaming?'

'I was sleeping in a barn.'

'Oh Jo!'

'Don't "Oh Jo" me – please. I'm not up to fighting you.'

She wasn't, I could see. Her face looked flushed – though that could have been the effects of getting warm – but now she coughed, a tight, uncomfortable cough.

'I don't want to fight,' I said.

'You never do. Poor George. Why did they ever make you a soldier?' It was an effort to replicate her old spirit, but it was unconvincing, and it made her cough again.

'How long have you had that cough?'

'Oh, not long. George, don't ask me any questions now. Please not now. I came to you because you're the only person who wouldn't.'

'I'm glad you did,' I said. 'Drink your cocoa and I'll see what I've got to feed you with. I've had mine.'

'Have you got anything for Dog to eat, first? He must be terribly hungry, poor beast.'

'Is that what you call him, Dog?'

'Imaginative, wasn't it?'

I had a tin of Fray Bentos stewing steak in the cupboard, which I sacrificed in the cause. I cut a couple of slices of bread and broke them up in the meat and gravy, scraped the whole mess into a soup plate and put it on the floor. The sorry animal cleared the lot in a frighteningly short time, and then looked up at me and wagged his tail tentatively. I stroked his head and the wagging picked up speed, and he even attempted to lick my hand. Evidently I met with approval. I showed him the bit of ironing blanket to the side of the fire and he seemed content to lie on it.

'Thanks,' Jo said, with a little sigh.

'Now can I attend to your needs?' I asked her, a little sarcastically.

She put down the empty cocoa mug. 'I don't want anything to eat just now, but I'd really like a bath, if the water's hot.'

I ran the bath for her, provided her with another towel and a pair of my pyjamas, and attended her upstairs. The dog, to my surprise, lay down again obediently when she told it to stay. I had thought it would not allow itself to be parted from her – perhaps it would not be such a troublesome guest after all. She had said it was a good dog. While she was bathing I took the things out of her bag. They were all wet, though the least wet thing was her 'good' coat, and remembering how she had arrived, I was angry with her for not wearing it and saving herself something of the soaking. The things were all dirty, too, and I mentally charted a visit to the launderette the next day.

When I heard the bath water gurgling down the outlet pipe, I went back upstairs to check on her progress and was in time to hear the tumbling thud of a falling body. I thanked God I had not got around to mending the bathroom door lock – low priority in a one-person household – and found her on the floor, struggling groggily to get up.

'What happened?' I grabbed the towel and gathered her wet, naked body in it. 'Did you slip?'

'I went dizzy,' she muttered.

It was more than that, I guessed. She must have fainted dead away to fall so heavily. 'You hit your head on something,' I said, brushing her hair away from the red mark on her forehead. A bump was already rising. It must have been the pedestal of the lavatory, from her position. As I rubbed her with the towel, I could feel she was shivering; yet her forehead where my fingers brushed it was scorching. 'I think you've got a temperature,' I said.

'No. I'm never ill.'

'There's always a first time.'

'I have to go,' she said.

'Go where?'

'Have to get on the road. Time to go. Spring's coming.'

'It's autumn. You haven't had winter yet.' Now I knew she was feverish. Her eyes were shiny with it, and she spoke in that confused, muttery way. 'Anyway, it's bedtime. Let's get you into these pyjamas and into bed.'

I was afraid she might resist me, but she sighed and yielded, allowing me to finish drying her and dress her in the pyjamas. It allowed me to see how thin she was, her ribs and hip-bones prominent, her breasts smaller than my hands had known them last winter. When she was pyjama-ed, I got up and lifted her into my arms, and she seemed insubstantial. I had planned to make up a bed for her in one of the upstairs bedrooms, but now for quickness' sake, and to save carrying her upstairs, I put her in my own bed. In my arms she had seemed drowsy; now as soon as I pulled the blankets and quilt over her, she began shivering violently.

I found another two blankets to put over the top of the quilt; found the hot water bottle and filled it, for convenience, from the bathroom hot tap. I untucked the bedclothes to push it in at her feet, and then tucked them in again.

Jo's eyes met mine, apprehensive, troubled.

'You've got a temperature,' I said. 'Don't worry. It'll pass.'

I sat on the edge of the bed and passed a

hand over her forehead. It was scorching. I thought about the places she might have been recently and hoped it was nothing worse than a feverish cold. After a few minutes the shivering fit passed and she began to look a little more comfortable, though her cheeks were still flushed and her eyes shiny. Then she coughed rackingly, and when it stopped she seemed flattened against the pillow, as though it had taken the last of her strength.

'I'm sorry, George. I'm so sorry,' she said.

'Sorry for what?' She didn't answer, but she gazed at me with that same troubled look. 'It's no trouble to look after you,' I said, in case it was that. 'I like looking after you. I'm glad you came here. Where else would you go?'

'Nowhere,' she said, which might have been confirmation of what I wanted to believe, that I was her first and proper port-of-call in an emergency; but it didn't sound like that. It sounded desolate.

'Don't worry about anything,' I said, stroking the hair off her forehead again. 'Just rest, go to sleep. I'll look after you. You're safe here.' She sighed a little and closed her eyes, and I took advantage of her quiescence to lay my lips a moment to her cheek. 'I love you,' I said, very softly, and I think the small sigh that followed was an acknowledgement.

I thought she had drifted off to sleep, but

when I stood up a while later her eyes opened. 'Dog?' she whispered.

'He's downstairs in the kitchen, warm and fed. Don't worry about him. He's all right.'

Her eyes closed again. I watched a moment, and when I was sure she was asleep, I left her.

I slept in the room with her that night, wrapped in blankets and with the spare-room quilt under me. I placed this makeshift bed across the door, so that she would have to step over me to get out, which I thought would wake me even if I was asleep. I was afraid that she might try to slip away – either in a feverish delusion that it was spring and 'time to go', or, worse, in her right mind, feeling she had accepted too much help from me, allowed me to get too close to her. That would have been disastrous, for it might stop her coming to me again for a long time in the future.

She had a restless night, sometimes shivering and coughing, at other times tossing feverishly, trying to rid herself of the blankets. I got up to replace them, refill the hot water bottle, give her a sip of water, but there was not much I could do for her otherwise. Once she did get out of bed, but it was only to go to the lavatory. I escorted her there, and waited outside to see her back to bed. I had thought she was almost sleep walking, but when she came out and saw me there she gave me a faint smile and said, 'Is this your usual beat, constable?' Towards morning she slept more quietly, giving me the chance to; but perversely I was wide awake, and lay thinking about her, her life, and what I was to do about it.

I finally got up at half past six and, seeing that she was asleep, went downstairs to rake and stoke the range and make myself some tea. I had forgotten the dog until he rose from his blanket at my entrance and waved his tail in cautious greeting. I thought about dogs' needs and let him out into the back garden while the kettle boiled. When I let him in again he went straight to his blanket, but sat looking at me hopefully as I drank my tea.

'I've nothing else remotely resembling dog food in the house,' I told him. He beat his tail softly on the floor and smiled at me. I cut him another slice of bread, which he wolfed down with the air of recognising it as his usual commons, and then I thought of a bowl of water, which he sloshed up thirstily. Then I went upstairs and, finding Jo still asleep, took the opportunity of washing and dressing and tidying away my bedclothes.

When she woke, it was obvious that she was ill, weak and feverish, and with the painful restlessness of a high temperature. When I asked her how she felt she said that her head and her back hurt, and then turned her face away from me, her expression remote. I thought she felt too ill now to try to run away, which was a relief to my mind; on the other hand I didn't like the sound of that cough, which was hard and dry and seemed to exhaust her. I was afraid that pneumonia might be setting in. I rang my own doctor, then called in to work to say I would not be coming in, and sat down to wait.

The doctor came and spent a long time examining Jo, which raised my anxiety, but when he left her at last he diagnosed influenza.

'Just influenza? Thank God for that.'

'Influenza is a serious matter,' he said sternly, looking at me as if I had been dancing on graves.

'I was afraid it might be pneumonia,' I said apologetically.

'Her lungs are clear – at present,' he said, as though afraid of being too generous.

'What can I do for her?'

'Much what you are already doing,' he said grudgingly. 'Keep her warm. Plenty of liquids. Clear soup and hot milk if she'll take it. You can give her aspirin for the fever, and this syrup for the cough.' He produced a bottle of cherry linctus which I supposed was his own make. 'She's likely to be worse before she's better. She'll probably be feverish for two or three days – that's normal –

but you can call me again after that if the fever doesn't break, or at any time if she seems to be having difficulty breathing.'

I walked him downstairs, and at the door he turned to survey me curiously. 'What is your relationship to that young woman? Are you a relative? I have it on my records that you are unmarried.'

I had only been on his list since moving to Islington, and during that time, being a normally healthy soul, I had only had to visit him once, for a vaccination when my job had sent me to South Africa. So we were almost perfect strangers.

'I'm not married,' I said. 'But I hope to be.'

I thought that about covered it, without actually having to tell a lie. He looked at me long and seriously – cohabitation of any sort was frowned upon in those days – but in the end I suppose he concluded that it was not his business, and he said only, 'Call me if she gets noticeably worse. I'll try and call in again at the end of the week.'

When I went upstairs she was awake and sensible. 'I'm sorry I'm being a nuisance to you,' she said.

'You're not. How are you feeling?'

'Hot,' she said. 'And sore all over. What time is it?'

'Nearly ten o'clock.'

'Shouldn't you be at work?'

'I've told them I'm not coming in.'

'Oh dear.'

'I'd sooner be with you. And I've got some work here to be getting on with. Do you want anything? A drink of water? A cup of tea.'

'Tea,' she said eagerly. I nodded and headed for the door. As I reached it she said, 'Is Dog all right?'

'He's fine.' I went down and made the tea, and then invited the mutt to come upstairs with me. He looked as though he couldn't believe his luck. The reunion between them was rather touching, though I looked forward to the time when I could give him a proper bath. 'He can stay here with you if you like,' I said.

'Thanks.' She was looking sleepy now, her eyes heavy, lying back in that flattened way, though one hand hung over the side of the bed to keep in touch with Dog's head.

'I have to go out and do some shopping. I wasn't expecting guests. Will you promise to stay put while I'm out? Promise you won't run away again.'

'I'm too ill to run away.'

'Promise all the same,' I insisted. 'I know you always keep your promises. Say you won't try to go away.'

'I promise,' she said, with a faint smile. 'I like it here with you, George.'

My heart jumped at that. It was the most she had given me for a long time.

I shopped for milk, bread, eggs, tea – the basics – and meat and vegetables. At the butcher I got some dog's meat, and some shin bones for stock to make soup (and I thought the dog could have them afterwards); and then I called at the pet shop for a large bag of dog biscuit. When I got back she was asleep, though moving restlessly. The dog was lying quietly beside the bed, and seemed to be no trouble. I straightened the bedclothes and left them.

Downstairs I put the dog's meat on to cook, then started making the soup. It was a long process, but I enjoyed cooking, and it was nice to have the time to do it. I found myself singing under my breath as I chopped and stirred. What was this strange happiness? Jo was ill, but she had come to me; she was upstairs and had promised not to run away. Perhaps now I might have the chance to talk to her seriously, to do something about the kind of life she insisted on living. It might be my best chance. But whatever came of it, I was glad she was here.

Chapter Eighteen: 1964

The doctor had said she would be worse before she was better, and she was. For two days she was too ill to know how ill she was. To her there seemed no difference between being awake and being asleep, for both states were stiff and hot with fever. There were occasional clear moments when she was aware of time passing, of it being daylight or dark outside the window; when George held her head for her to sip water; when she found Dog gazing into her face and felt him lick her hand hopefully. But for most of the time she lived in a timeless confusion of heat and discomfort, her bones aching, a headache gripping her skull like a vice so that it hurt to open her eyes.

Sometimes when she woke she didn't know where she was: there had been so many rooms, and when she could not immediately place this one, she panicked. Once she thought she must be in a boarding house, tried to get up to leave and found herself too weak to move. Sometimes when the fever mounted she saw people in the room, slightly distorted people with flushed, fire-rosy, devil faces, who goggled at her and touched her with huge, heavy fingers that made her ring like a gong inside her head. She couldn't remember how far through the year it was, whether she would see summer or winter outside the window if she looked. Sometimes she didn't know how far through her life she was, whether she was a child, an adult or an old woman. She felt a great sorrow at the thought that perhaps she was at the end of it all now, and it was time to go. She was not ready. She had not appreciated everything enough. She wept, and felt someone wipe the wetness from her face, and smelled Imperial Leather. George's soap. She had not appreciated George enough, and now it was too late. She tried to say, 'I don't want to die,' but no words came out. She struggled in red darkness, too weak to make her struggles felt.

Though it felt like an eternity, the high fever only lasted for two days. On the third day her temperature came down to below hallucination level, and she knew where she was, and felt only ill, hot, uncomfortable and weak.

George was there, wiping her face and neck and hands with a cool flannel (Imperial Leather, she remembered), making her pillows more comfortable, giving her orangeade with ice cubes in it (such luxury!) and linctus to soothe her cough. She knew she ought not to let him care for her, ought to get up and get out, but she was too weak and tired to give it more than a fleeting thought. When she was well she would go, take herself right away, but for the moment...

'Is this your bedroom?'

'Yes. Don't you recognise it?'

'I do now. The previous times I've been in it, I haven't been looking at the furniture.'

'When you arrived soaking wet, I didn't have time to make up a bed for you, so I put you in mine.'

'Kind, George. Why are you so kind to me?'

'You know why.'

She hadn't meant him to answer, and the answer made her turn her face away, reminding her of her duty when she didn't want to be reminded, when the last thing she wanted was to leave here.

'Is Dog all right?' she asked to get away from the subject.

'He's out in the garden. I thought he needed fresh air.'

'You could take him for a walk. I expect you need fresh air as well.'

He looked at her as though he suspected a trick, and in her illness it irritated her. She had promised, she remembered now, not to go. The memory eased her, for it meant she need not worry about her duty. She could rest on that, and not think about running away – not yet.

'If you don't mind being left for an hour,' George said, 'I could take him with me and do a trip to the launderette. All your things need washing, and I used a lot of towels on you two.'

'Yes, go,' she said. 'I'll be fine.'

The house seemed suddenly empty after she had heard the front door shut below. How long would he be? He said an hour, but if he was putting the things through the dryer, it would be longer, an hour and a half, three quarters even, allowing for time to walk there and back. It wasn't very far – she had been there once last winter, when she had come over and spent the weekend with him. It had felt funny to be doing something so domestic with George. They had put the washing in and then sat on the bench and tried to do *The Times* crossword together while his clothes revolved in stately manner, first this way, then that. She had thought about her own underwear and shirts being in with his, as he would have liked it, and laughed at herself for this sentimental nonsense. Hers was a life of excitement, movement and freedom – no domestic slavery for her! And yet, it had been nice, sitting in the launderette with him. Too nice. She must never think like that again.

But the house without him felt lonely. Even

when he had not been in the room with her, she had known he was there. It came to her that there was no-one in the world to whom she had the right to say, I'm lonely. That was something you had to work at to deserve. Since she left home she had led a selfish life, she had never given anything to anyone, and if it wasn't that George was a person of stupendous generosity she wouldn't even be here now. Well, be grateful for what you have; and she was. She would do all she still could for George by leaving him alone. But not now. When she was better.

Her head ached, and she closed her eyes, and drifted a little. She remembered the summer just past. All in all, it had been a glorious summer. She remembered the long days on the beach, the unutterable peace of it, of never having to look further forward than the next meal. She thought of the brief, perfect acquaintances with people who never tried really to know you, who passed you like trains speeding along parallel tracks, waving as they drew level, then pulling ahead and out of sight. She thought about the people like Alfie who employed her, all those who gave her lifts, the lady on the beach who gave her bread – casual acts of kindness, kindness that was the more pure because it might have been directed towards anyone, had nothing to do with her possible worthiness to receive it. She thought of the sunrises and sunsets, the smell of clean air, the road reeling out before and behind, the safety of being on the move, not quite sure of where you would fetch up but not minding wherever it was.

She drifted, and thought of the other side of the coin, the loneliness of not belonging anywhere, of being homeless; the great weight of communication that built up in her mind, waiting for someone who could take it from her, who could understand what she wanted to say. Most of her life was silent, whatever conversations were going on. That was the thing about being with people who did not know you, and never would – like Guy, the Boda twins, Alfie, all the rest – you could never talk to them. It seemed that for most of her life she had been talking inside her head, with no hope of letting any of it out. She thought of the people who had cared about her: Daddy, and Jean, and dear Mrs West. She could never talk to them either, not really. There had been Rob once – oh Rob! – but he had been home so seldom, though when he was it had seemed like a perfect communion. And yet, looking back, what had she ever told Rob about what was inside her?

And then there was George, who had known her for such a long time, who had been her friend from the beginning, stepping into her life almost as a known person, without the need for finding out; George who was always her friend, who never asked questions, never tried to hold her down or shut her in. She longed for him as an exile longs for home. Year after year she had thought she would come back and find him gone, or married and out of her life. Finding him still there, still her friend, she had allowed herself only a little time with him, exerting a discipline over herself that strained her almost to breaking, to keep away from him when everything in her called for him, miserably and insistently, like a dog shut out of the house.

Her temperature was rising again, and she drifted into the other place, the swollen, hot place of fretful thoughts and distorted images. She dreamed she was at home again, at Roselands. She saw her father with his reading glasses on, looking strangely vulnerable: he was sitting in the big wing-back chair, but he seemed smaller, shrunken. He looked at her but did not speak; and she heard Jean say, 'You'll have to look after him. He can't look after himself.' She felt the weight of responsibility settle on her, knowing it was impossible to fulfil. However hard she tried, she would not be able to save him, and the guilt would be on her soul, the guilt of failure and the disappointment of sin.

And then Rob came in from the garden, and her heart leapt with love – Rob, tall and young again, the way he had been that time he had come home for his birthday, laughing and holding out his arms to her, showing off his new suit.

'Well, Josella, what do you think of your boy?'

He stood there in the french windows, cut out against the light. She could not see his face; it was in shadow. She tried to go to him, but she could not move. She tried to speak to him, knowing that if she did not answer he would go away and leave her. Oh Rob, Rob! Then he turned to go, and as the light struck his face she saw it at last, and remembered he was dead. Died all those years ago, far away in Aden. He was going now, walking out through the french windows, into the garden where the light was so pure and strong it blotted out everything, so that she could not see beyond the path.

She tried to call him back. She struggled up onto one elbow, and in the halfway place between waking and sleeping she saw him still, and felt her heart beating fast with panic. Something dark had come between her and him, something more solid than his fading image, and she cried out at last in fear as well as longing. And then she was enveloped in strong arms, held tightly against a big, male body. Her face was against a man's cheek, cool and damp from outdoors, smelling familiar, so lovely, familiar and good. And then she cried easily, clinging where she was held. 'Oh Rob. Oh Rob. Oh George.'

Chapter Nineteen: 1964

She was crying easily; not the racking sobs of a grown-up, painful to cry, but the free tears of a child that seemed to pass out of the body without effort and almost without hurt. After a while they slowed down, and I loosened her hold, kissed her wet cheeks and restrained myself from kissing her mouth; and I found my handkerchief and dried her face and gave it to her to blow her nose.

'What was all that about?' I asked. I felt her forehead but though hot it was not burning. I settled her back on her pillows and brushed her hair off her face. It was almost white at the front where the sun had bleached it; white-gold on the top.

'I must have been dreaming,' she said in a subdued, post-tears voice. 'I can't remember it now. Something about Rob.'

'Yes. You said his name.'

She shook her head, frowning. 'I can't remember it now.'

It had seemed to me an unnecessarily harsh blow of fate when he had been killed, though all of a piece with whatever fate was dogging her. I heard all about it afterwards, not so much from her, but from other army men with whom I had kept lightly in touch. As Colonel Grace's son he had a certain fame; and he was loved for himself. He had gone to Aden from Cyprus, at a time when there was a lot of trouble from dissidents. One day he had gone out, travelling with a supply convoy for safety, heading for one of the up-country forts garrisoned by the British Army, where repair and improvement works were needed. The convoy had come under fire from ridges on both sides of the road. The dissidents were hidden in crevices in the rocks. It was their habit to have themselves sealed in, with food and water, leaving only a loophole to fire through, so they were impossible to spot and very hard to winkle out. The accompanying infantry attachment had been ordered up the ridges to sort them out; Rob had stayed with the convoy and the drivers. When the troops were far enough up the hillsides, a small band armed with machine guns and grenades had broken out of hiding to seize the supplies, killing every-one.

Rob had been buried over there. There had been no-one to pay for repatriation – and reading between the lines, I had gathered that there was not much left to bury. I had never discussed that with Jo, of course. To her it did not matter where he was buried. He had gone away and not come back, and was as lost to her wherever his mortal remains lay.

She had taken it very calmly at the time, with a kind of heavy resignation I had been sorry to see. Wild grief, I thought, would have been better, to 'get it out of her system' as they say; but she had suffered so many blows. I watched her nervously for any sign that this new one had triggered memory of the oldest one, but for the little time she was under my eye, there was nothing to suggest it. Soon, however, she was on the road again, and everything was as it had been. She pursued her gypsy life; and when I next saw her she seemed just like before, happy, amused and amusing, determined on maintaining her freedom, with the unspoken shadow I had sensed in her from the beginning no larger or darker than at any other time. She spoke of Rob naturally when his name occurred in conversation, but only in the context of live memories of him. She never mentioned his death; and I was glad enough not to bring it up.

I wanted to ask her now if she had dreamed about him before, but remembering she was ill refrained. Besides, there was always that fear of the amnesia reversing itself. But,

I thought, lost memories or no lost memories, when she was well again she and I would have to talk. Things could not go on as they were. It was time to sort them out.

When she recovered enough for me to be able to go back to work, I worried that I would come home and find her gone. She had promised me, but I was not sure she remembered that, and was afraid to remind her in case it provoked the very thing I feared. But even after her temperature came down and the symptoms were no more than those of a heavy cold, a terrible lassitude seemed to hold her. This, the doctor told me on his second visit, was a normal feature of influenza, which demanded a long convalescence. Four, even six weeks might pass before the patient felt fully well, and regained previous levels of energy. As the days passed and she did not disappear, I began to relax, and to enjoy the comfort of having her always about the house, going home to her at the end of the day, almost like a normal person.

At the end of the third week she was up and about, going out in the middle of the day to walk the dog, though an hour outside was enough to tire her and she spent the rest of the day on the sofa in the drawing room reading. During our evenings together we did not talk a great deal, and never about anything of importance. She was quiet – too quiet. The effort of talking seemed beyond her; I hoped the effort of thinking was, too.

During the fourth week she began to perk up a little, took over some of the household jobs from me – though I still did the cooking. Her way of life had never taught her anything about that most ephemeral of the arts. I watched anxiously for her to become restless, but there seemed still a heaviness about her: if she had not had influenza, I'd have called it depression. On Saturday at the end of that week the weather was fine and warm, and I suggested we take a run out into the country. Her face lit up at the suggestion, and I was glad I'd thought of it. The fresh air would do her good; and perhaps she needed a change of scene. My house, being tall and narrow, tended to be rather dark; and with the kitchen, drawing room, and bedroom-and-bathroom on three separate floors it necessitated a great many trudges up and down stairs, not ideal for an invalid.

I drove out on the A1 and the A41 towards Hemel, and then turned off into the maze of narrow country lanes that criss-cross the Chilterns, joining the small villages. We had a bread-and-cheese-and-beer lunch in a tiny pub in one of them, then got back in the car and climbed higher, parked almost at random, and went for a walk in the woods. The great beech trees lifted their smooth boles to a canopy that had turned vivid gold in the past week, and now shone in the pleasant sunshine like an anthem. The fallen leaves spread a carpet that crackled like toast underfoot, and the air was rich with the smell of them, of warm autumn loam and the faint distant tang of woodsmoke. We walked slowly, Jo's hand linked companionably through my arm. Dog went almost mad at first, racing back and forth, shoving his nose under heaps of leaves and blowing them upwards with great snorting breaths, scrabbling at interesting holes, barking at us when we did not move fast enough for him. But he settled down at last, simply coursing about with his nose down, coming back to check on our progress every few minutes.

'He's a different dog,' I said. 'Regular grooming and decent food have made quite a smart beast of him.'

'He's been so good, cooped up in the house all this time,' she said.

This was perilously close to the idea I didn't want to surface, so I said, 'I was surprised, really, at your taking on a dog. How did it happen?'

'He just came to me, one day when I was sitting under the pier in Yarmouth, and he stayed with me. I couldn't give him anything. I couldn't even feed him. He just seemed to want to be with me.'

'Sensible dog,' I said.

She frowned. 'When I went away, when I left Yarmouth to head for London, I didn't even think about him. He followed me anyway, but when we got to the edge of town he sat down and cried, tried to get me to turn back. I suppose it was the only place he knew and he was afraid.'

'Natural.'

'But, you see, I didn't help him.' She looked up at me a moment, a glance of shame. 'I just said, "So long, Dog," and walked on. He had to sit there with his heart breaking and decide for himself.'

'And he chose you.'

'I gave him nothing, and that meant he had to give even more. More out of nothing. That was his love.'

She stopped, and I waited, feeling there was something more she wanted to say, but she did not go on. We came out of the woods suddenly to find ourselves on the edge of a massive escarpment, with the whole of the Vale of Aylesbury spread out below us, washed with a smoky blue tint like a watercolourist's impression. We sat down on the grass to gaze, and Dog came and flopped down beside us, worn out at last. The long sunshine threw shadows of smudged indigo across the gilded grass; the air came clean to us above the valley, ruffling our hair softly. It was warm with that sweet, sorrowful warmth of autumn that says *the year is almost gone;*

enjoy this while you can.

'All this year,' she said quietly, out of nothing. 'I've felt something was changing; but I don't know what. Things closing down. As if I was being subtly driven in a certain direction.'

'Which direction?'

'I don't know. That's the trouble. I don't know, and it frightens me.'

I reached for her hand, and took it back to my lap, to hold it in both mine. This was not the moment to speak, I knew instinctively.

After a moment she said, 'Warm hands. Thank you. Dear George, always so wise.'

'Am I? Perhaps not always wise to myself.'

'Is any of us?' she said.

She was tired when we got home, but it was a better tiredness, the natural tiredness of the open air. I made Welsh rarebit for supper, and cocoa, and we played cards for a little while down in the warm kitchen, while Dog slept and twitched beside the stove, reliving the day in his dreams. Then I said she should not overdo it on her first real day up, and suggested she had a bath and went to bed. She got up meekly to obey me, but at the door asked if I would come up and tuck her in. I agreed, though with slight misgivings. I did not want to stand in the relationship of parent to her. That was not how I wanted her at all.

When I heard the bath water gurgle away,

I gave it another five minutes, and then went up. She was in my bed (I had not moved her all this time, but made up a spare bedroom for myself). Only the bedside light was on, and she was lying not in the middle, but to one side – the side that had been 'hers' on the occasions we had slept together here.

'Come to bed, George,' she said. 'I know it's early, but come to bed.'

She reached out her arms for me, and I could see she was not wearing my pyjamas any more.

I sat on the edge of the bed, looking down at her seriously. Her face was still thin, but there was a brightness to her eyes again, at last. Her hair had grown, I could see, to a less boyish length, and she had brushed it, so it shone softly gold, a little darker in the lamplight than it was in the day. I touched it with my fingertips – I couldn't help it – and she caught my hand and put it to her lips. 'You don't have to do this, you know,' I said.

'I didn't want you thinking I was looking on you as a father figure.' Strange how often she seemed to be able to hear my thoughts.

I smiled. 'You still don't have to do it.'

'Come to bed, George,' she said insistently.

I was undressed in moments, and under the covers, gathering her against me. She came yieldingly, fitting into my contours so naturally, as she always had. I wanted her desperately, and yet I felt something was wrong. I sensed not laughter but tears in her. It was like a spring day that's just too bright, with that uncertain sunshine that gives way in an instant to rain. I kissed the crown of her head, and then her brow and cheek, and she nuzzled round to give me her mouth, her hands clinging to me. I tried to draw back, afraid for her, but she held me. 'Don't stop,' she whispered. 'Let me give you this.'

And so we made love. I tried to be gentle and to go slowly, but it wasn't what she wanted. We met in flame and passion, and underneath it a tenderness so deep it was like a great stillness, a heart of silence at the centre of a storm.

Afterwards I was afraid she would cry, but she didn't. She lay quietly in my arms, and in a little while I knew she was asleep. I could not move to turn off the lamp without waking her, so I lay wakeful a long time, watching her sleep, wondering when and how I might talk to her about the future.

It came sooner than I expected. Sunday dawned wet: a storm was brewing up, and the rain hit the windowpanes in little gusts, whipping the trees back and forth and then dropping them, as a terrier shakes and drops a rat. The remaining leaves were being stripped off rapidly; sometimes they were whirled by the wind to stick a moment to the glass, before being peeled away.

I heard the rain pattering on the windows and the wind hooning softly in the chimney a few moments before I was fully awake, and became aware that Jo was not there beside me. I was up on the instant, afraid that she might have run, frightened off, as so often before, by the expression of love between us. But a quick scan of the room found her things still lying about. I got up and went to find her.

She was in the drawing room, sitting on the sofa, her legs tucked under her, her chin resting in her hand, looking out at the rain. Dog was sitting on the floor beside her, looking up appealingly, but she did not seem to be noticing him. She did not react to my coming in either, though I knew she must have heard me. When I came close, I saw her face a moment before she turned towards me, and was chilled by the misery of her expression. But she masked it smoothly and said, 'One day of sunshine is all we're allowed.'

'One at a time, perhaps,' I said. 'There will be others.'

She didn't answer, only looked at me long and carefully, as if to remember me. She *was* planning to go, I thought. I wondered how to stop her. I had hoped for longer to work up to it. Now I had to plunge in.

'It isn't necessary, you know.'

I saw her eyes flinch at my coming so

quickly to the subject. She knew what I meant, of course. The thing stood there like a third person in the room, always between us and keeping us apart.

'You don't understand,' she said sadly.

'Not if you don't explain.'

'I can't. That's the point, George, I can't. I never could. That's why I have to go. Believe me, it's better.'

'I don't believe that. But leave that aside for the moment. Where do you think you will go? It's October, nearly November. In the normal course of events you'd be coming to London now. Well, here you are.'

She got up from the sofa in one fluid movement and began walking around the room. I thought she was looking for something, but then I saw that she was merely beginning the journey. I saw it ahead of her as she must have, and it looked exhausting. *She* looked exhausted.

'I have to go. I have to keep moving,' she said.

'You don't have any money.'

'I'll get a job. There's always temp work.'

'In London.'

'Other places too. There's Birmingham, or Glasgow, or ... or—'

'Jo, *why*? Please, I want to understand. Just tell me.'

She stopped in her walking and looked at me in desperation, like something at bay. 'I can't let people know me. I have to keep moving, or people may find out about me.'

'What's so wrong with that?' I said. 'I know you, and I love you. So would other people.' She shook her head, too close to tears to speak. 'Look at all the kindness you meet with, all the time – you've told me yourself. People always like you.'

She cried aloud. 'You don't understand!' It seemed to be pulled from her in pain. I began to have a cold feeling of dread about it. I stepped across quickly and seized her hands, the better to command her attention. Perhaps the movement was too abrupt, for Dog stood up and growled at me, his hackles lifting. She looked at him and tried to speak – to reassure him, I suppose – and the tears spilled over.

'Let me go,' she gasped. The tears ran down her face and into her mouth. 'You must let me go.'

'I want you to stay,' I said, anxious that there should be no doubt. 'I want you to marry me, and stay with me always. I love you, and I believe you love me.'

'I *can't*,' she cried in anguish, and broke from me and ran. She slammed the door behind her, just in time to stop the dog following her. He pawed at the door a moment, but when I reached it and tried to open it he turned on me, growling again, confused, I think, by the emotions he must have been sensing in the air. It took a moment or two to calm him and make him let me near. When his hackles were down and he ducked his head under my hand in apology, I opened the door and he bustled through, running downstairs and straight to the front door. She had gone, then.

I grabbed Dog's lead from the coat hook and clipped it on; shrugged on my coat and opened the door. 'Find her, then.'

Without the lead he would have dashed off and lost me; as it was he strained at the collar, his feet scrabbling for hold, almost pulling me over down the steps. He knew where to go, turning unhesitatingly right. She was nowhere in sight. She must have run, and I knew she was fast.

The rain was falling steadily, splattering in my face with the gusts of wind. I eased the pull on Dog's lead and ran with him. It was hard to see ahead with the rain in my eyes; the pavements were slick with it, the roads empty with a wet Sunday's lack of traffic. We crossed the road, turned left, then right at another junction. I had a moment's doubt whether the Dog really was following a scent, for the route made no sense. But he pulled eagerly: she must have been running blind.

And then I saw her. Dog saw her too, and barked. I saw her face, a white flash, as it turned an instant to look back; then she went on. I saw her stumble slightly, catching her foot against an uneven flag. We were gaining. She looked back, and then turned sharp right and out of sight.

It was an alley between two high buildings with shops on the ground floor, and led nowhere but into a yard behind them, the access to a workshop. By the time Dog and I reached the opening, she had realised it, and was standing facing me, the rain streaming over her, shivering. I dropped the leash and Dog raced to her, leaping up, trying to lick her face, and she fended him off with feeble hands.

I reached her, and she looked up at me in agony. 'Whatever it is,' I said, 'it isn't worth all this grief.'

'You don't know,' she said. It was hard to understand her, because her teeth were chattering with cold. 'You don't know about me.'

'I do. For ten years—'

She shook her head. 'Long ago. Before I met you. Something that happened – something terrible – in Africa.'

The shock hit me like a jolt of electricity. I felt cold to my stomach. 'Africa?' I said out of the numbness of it. Did she really mean—?

'In Kenya. I can't tell you about it. I must never tell anyone.'

'I know about it,' I said, and my voice

sounded remote to me, as if it were someone else's.

Her head went up, a movement of fear. 'You don't.'

'I know what happened in Kenya. Rob told me.'

'Rob told you?'

'Years ago. After your father died. But he said you had no memory of it. He wanted someone who cared about you to know, because it might come back to you some time. But he told me you didn't remember anything about it.'

She shook her head, a blank, inward look to her eyes as she took in the new situation. 'I didn't. I didn't remember. My mother told me.'

I was appalled. 'She *told* you?'

Her eyes closed, her mouth bowed downwards with agony. I pulled off my coat and stepped close, put it round her. I don't think she even noticed it. Rain ran down her face so that I could not tell if she was crying or not.

'She told me everything. When we got back to England. Told me what they did, why I'd been in hospital, why we came back. She said after that I was soiled goods.'

'Oh Jo. Oh God.'

'Bad, dirty. No use to anyone. That's why I can't be with you.'

I took her in my arms, and she did not

resist, though her body was rigid, not bending into mine. 'How can you think that's true?' I said, seeking desperately for words that came near my anguish and pity. 'How can you think it could make any difference to me – something you couldn't help?'

She shook her head again. 'She took me to see a doctor one day, took me to one in London so no-one would know. He said – when that thing happened, I was damaged inside. Never be any good again. Mother said – no use to anyone. Soiled goods. Never let anyone know. Then, the next day, she killed herself.'

'Oh God, Jo.'

'I should have too. But I was just a child. And there was Daddy. I was all right with Daddy. But he sent me away. And then he died. I didn't know Rob knew. He shouldn't have told you.'

She was shivering so violently I could hardly understand her. I pressed her closer, rigid and shaking, in my arms. 'But he *did* tell me. Don't you see? I've known for years. It didn't make any difference – only to make me love you more.'

'You can't.'

'I *can*. I *do*. For God's sake, Jo, why do you think I'm not married? For ten years I've loved you and waited for you, hoping one day you would want to stay with me, settle down.'

She put her hands against my chest so that she could look up at me. She *was* crying, I saw now. 'I'm damaged inside. I can't have children. I'm no use to you.'

The words hurt me, like a barb in my flesh being tugged. 'You're all I want. The only woman I want. I've loved you since the first moment I saw you, riding Mistral that day out on the downs. If I never saw you again, I would never stop loving you.'

She whispered, 'I wanted to stay, so often. But I couldn't. I didn't dare let myself feel too much. I had to keep moving on.'

'If only I'd known,' I said. 'I thought you didn't know, and I was afraid of making you remember.'

She had known all along. Why hadn't I guessed? Fool, fool! I thought of her carrying that burden all those years, alone with it, sickened by it; thinking herself unworthy of affection, tainted, worthless. So much now made sense to me, and it was bitter knowledge. A murderous rage against her mother burned in me. But she had paid already, with her life; and what must she have been suffering, to make her do what she did to her own child?

'Jo, your mother was mad, don't you know that? She was mad at the end, poor lady, not responsible. What she said wasn't true, wasn't true. It was the words of a poor mad woman and you mustn't believe any of it.'

395

She shook her head, wanting to believe but not daring. 'Can you really love me, knowing that?'

'I do. I always have.' I pressed her close again, kissed the top of her wet head, at a loss for words.

Now she held on to me, some of the rigidity going out of her. I became aware all of a sudden how wet we both were. I must get her home.

She said, 'Then – there's no need to go.'

'There never was.' I wasn't sure if it really was a question.

'Oh God, I can't believe... It's too much to take in.'

The thought that she might still leave me made me shiver. I held her tighter. 'I want you to stay. Darling, please stay. Don't ever go away again.'

She rested against my chest a long time in the silence only interrupted by the pattering rain. Then she said, muffled a little, 'It will be hard at first – to give in. To stay put. I'm used to...' She stopped again.

It was the hardest thing I had ever done, to say, 'If you get restless – I won't try to stop you. As long as you come back. As long as—'

I felt her shake her head. 'You deserve better than that, George.' She lifted her face from my chest to look at me clearly, steadily, in her old, soldierly way. 'Daddy always said, if you surrender, you have to stop fighting. I want to stay. If it's really all right. Is it all right?'

'Everything's all right,' I said.

'Oh George, I do love you.' She pressed closer.

It was not the moment to move. We stood together in the rain, and my heart sang with triumph, and ached with grief for her, for all she had carried with her all these years, and with regret for the lost time. But perhaps there was a pattern to things that had to be worked out. Perhaps what had happened could not have happened earlier. It began with my decision when she left in April that things could not go on as they had; but it had not been until she came to me in her need that we could move to this conclusion. Her action, not my wish: in everything she had always had the power, however fragile she was underneath it. Well, now I could start to put things right. She had re-entered the real world.

The wind had stopped gusting, and the rain was falling straight and steadily. Over her shoulder I saw Dog, sitting patiently, his coat slick with it, raindrops beading on his eyebrows and whiskers. He waited for us, in our human wisdom, to decide to move, enduring without complaint.

'We should go home,' I said at last. 'That poor dog...'

'He's used to being wet,' she said. 'Come to that, so am I. But let's go home.' She smiled suddenly, a pale and watery smile, but a beginning. 'It's nice to be able to say that.'